# *Dealing* DOUBLE

# Dealing DOUBLE

*A Heartbreaker Novel*

## TAMRA BAUMANN

Montlake
Romance

Published by Montlake Romance, Seattle

www.apub.com

Amazon, the Amazon logo, and Montlake Romance are trademarks of Amazon.com, Inc., or its affiliates.

ISBN-13: 9781503954199
ISBN-10: 1503954196

Cover design by Tammy Seidick

Printed in the United States of America

*This book is dedicated to my brother, Gary, so he'll stop asking me why I never dedicate books to him. This one's for you, big bro.*

# Chapter One

Sophia Moretti was pretty darned impressed with her usually reserved self. While on the run, and in just under thirty hours, she'd evaded trained assassins, driven without a bodyguard for the first time, and had managed to make it from DC to New Mexico without stopping, except for the essentials. A new record according to her burner cell phone. Her main cell, the one tracked by her mobster father, was probably still riding around under the back seat of the cab, where she'd purposely left it, in DC.

To buy herself some time.

Her journey, which was thankfully almost over, was especially impressive for a dead person. Sophia Moretti had "died" in a car accident when she was just sixteen, as far as the rest of the world knew. Faking her death had been the only way to keep herself safe from the people who had killed her mother and brother twelve years earlier.

Her father had a lot of enemies.

Before her faked death, getting shipped off to Europe at ten years old with a new name had kept her safe. But the charade had left her mostly alone and with an empty heart.

Since then, she'd dyed her brown hair red, finished college with advanced archaeology degrees, and was now Gabby Knight. Keeper of artifacts in the underbelly of a DC museum, living a quiet life. That is, until her father broke his promise to clean up his act and stole the statue she'd been working on, right out from under her.

She glanced in her rearview mirror as she approached her destination and reminded herself she was done being that meek person. She was going to conjure up some of her family's famous Italian tempers and show her father that he'd finally crossed the one person who wasn't afraid of him.

She needed to start living the life she'd been spared twelve years ago.

As she pulled up to a secluded cabin in the woods, one with a property line that backed up to the land she needed to search, her eyes felt as dry as the desert she'd just driven through for hours.

New Mexico was like landing on the moon, compared with DC. It was an odd combination of sandy deserts; looming red-, orange-, and purple-layered cliffs; and mountain passes with pine trees and aspens reminiscent of Colorado.

Despite the beauty that was almost too much to take in, all she wanted was a soft bed. Even a hard one would do. Then, in the morning, she'd search for the Son statue purportedly buried on sacred land. The matching Father statue usually stood under guarded glass at a national museum. Until a few days ago. When her father decided to make it his own, forcing her to find the Son statue before he or his hired hands did.

She'd resorted to using Google Earth to locate the best cabin for her temporary stay. She couldn't use her credit card to rent one or check into a hotel, which would expose her whereabouts. The nearest hotel to the dig site had said she could pay in cash, but she'd still need to show ID. Her father's men, who wouldn't hesitate to pull a gun for information, would find her in a heartbeat.

She'd reluctantly have to break into an empty cabin. Especially because a snowstorm was predicted to hit later, and she'd need shelter against the February cold. Hopefully, it wouldn't snow too much so she could hike across the sacred Indian land to the site where the matching statue was buried.

Evidently, burying things—and dead people—in the New Mexico desert wasn't so unusual. There were massive areas of undeveloped land due to the Indian reservations and old family land grants, so it happened more often than one would think.

Fascinating, really.

So, she'd hide out in a cabin, like Goldilocks, and hope no bears showed up later. But unlike Goldilocks, she'd leave money for the repairs after she broke a window to get in, and for any resources she used. She wasn't a thief. Or so she'd told herself every half hour of the last twenty-four—she was *not* like her father.

She pulled up slowly to her first choice of hideouts. Looked like she was in luck. No cars out front, nearest neighbor pretty far away, and dark inside—all looked promising. After maneuvering her Jeep around a few stumps and foliage, she parked the car behind the little cabin and killed the engine. She hopped out, sucked in a deep breath of cold, pine-scented air, and then tiptoed to a window. It was dusky out, with just enough light to see inside the pretty wooden home with its green metal roof. It was a cozy-looking place, warm and inviting. And it surely had a bed to lay her tired head on.

She ran back to her Jeep; grabbed the gloves, duct tape, and all the rest of the items she'd picked up to repair the damage; and broke the window. After climbing through and falling hands- and headfirst onto the wooden floor with a thump, she dusted herself off. Then she found the kitchen to test if the utilities were on.

She slowly lifted the handle on the faucet in the sink just as she noted a light was on in the hallway. Warm water poured out of the spigot. So, the utilities were on, and the owners could appear at any moment. She glanced around the warm cabin and spotted a calendar on the wall, *X*s marked on certain weeks. Was it a vacation schedule for the cabin? She flipped backward and forward through the months. Sometimes it noted two female names, or simply said "kids." Like the children didn't always come. But the best part was that the calendar was clear for weeks. Yes! It'd be safe to stay.

The grumble of her stomach joined the chorus in her head, begging her to get on with things and settle in for the night. But not before she fixed the window. It was too cold to leave a gaping opening in the wall. After that, she'd sleep like the dead before she set out on her artifact-retrieving quest.

In a foul mood, Detective Jake Morris tossed enough groceries for two weeks into his shopping cart. Suspended from duty for shooting an asshat? The guy had been hell-bent on killing a woman and her child. Some reward for being a good cop. Then confiscating his gun to investigate the shooting and putting him on administrative leave? That was the pretty term for it, but it felt like punishment for doing his damn job.

Next came the meeting in the lieutenant's office. Ordered to take a month's vacation because Jake hadn't had one in five years. Insulting. Like crime ever took a vacation.

He'd been a little busy being the guy who closed more cases than any other detective in his squad. Sure, since his ex-wife, Dani, had cut back on sharing her woo-woo visions with him to help him nab bad guys, he hadn't closed as many cases, but still, he was a damn good cop. Wasn't he?

It was just a slump. That's all. Nothing to do with his divorce, as his boss had suggested. Dani was still his friend despite now being engaged to a stuffy lawyer. He and his ex got along great. Always would.

His other choice had entailed spilling his guts to the department shrink in lieu of the extended vacation. He didn't want to talk about his crappy childhood again or explain why he didn't like to be touched unless he was making love to a woman. Or how he'd been forced as a teen to work on a ranch run by a cruel foreman because he had nowhere else to go, or that his marriage had failed because he put his job first. He knew all of that. And he hated to be told he had to change his ways. He was fine.

When he found the right woman, that's when he'd put the lessons he'd learned into play. He'd work less, settle down, and have a family. A nice family, dammit. With parents who'd never leave their kids to fend for themselves.

He threw his favorite chocolate cereal into the cart a bit too hard, earning a sideways glance from the one other patron in the store.

Maybe having a family had been a pipe dream, too. Hard to think straight when he was still seeing red after being told he'd be fired if he was caught using any police resources for the next thirty days. They'd taken his badge to be sure he complied. That had been beyond humiliating. His badge represented his heart, all that he believed in, the one thing he was proud of in his life.

Where was a punching bag when he needed one?

He got to the liquor section of the small country store and grabbed plenty of fuel for his pity party. Chips, dips, pretzels, and beer by the case? Check. Might as well get some hard stuff, too, for the lonely, cold nights and days ahead he'd need to fill. Doing what?

Maybe he'd do some fly-fishing in the river. He'd been meaning to do that for a long time. Or read books on his e-reader. Thank God he had Internet in the woods. He'd go nuts otherwise. He didn't know what to do with himself when he'd had a few free hours at home, much less a month in the secluded cabin. The thought was depressing.

His demanding schedule meant Dani used the cabin more than he had. And she'd been nice enough to tell him to use it whenever he wanted, even though she'd gotten it in the divorce.

The times he'd joined Dani for the weekend, he'd never been bored. They had usually spent the whole time in bed. That part had never been a problem in their marriage—just everything else, because of him.

After topping off his cart to overflowing with junk food and frozen dinners, he made his way to the front to pay. He was starving and couldn't get to the cabin quick enough. He'd been so busy trying to tie up loose ends before he'd left the station he'd forgotten to eat lunch. It was almost four in the afternoon, so a PowerBar at checkout was going to have to do until he could make it up the snowy hill the rest of the way to Dani's cabin.

"Nice to see you again, Detective. Find everything okay?" said the daughter of the store's owner. Shelly was a pretty blonde, too young, and completely off-limits, no matter how hard she flirted with him.

"It's just Jake to you, kiddo. How's that boyfriend of yours? Wes, wasn't it?"

"Yeah." Shelly nodded as she bagged up his food. "He's fine and belongs to some other lovesick fool now. So if you ever change your mind, and need someone to keep you warm up there in that fancy cabin, I'm always here." She handed Jake the bags to pile into his cart.

"You'd be better off with someone your own age." Being thirty-two had never felt more ancient.

She leaned forward and ran her scanner gun across the cases of beer he'd stowed on the bottom of the cart. She whispered, "I'm legal now, Jake. And eager to know what it'd be like to be with a real man. Like you."

He made a note to himself: No more flirting. For the rest of his life. "I'm damaged merchandise, kid. Not nearly good enough for someone as sweet as you."

"I'll have to settle with having you only in my dreams, then, I guess." She smiled coyly while he put his card into the reader to pay.

Probably best to ignore that comment. When the machine indicated he could, he removed his card. "Say hi to your folks. See ya." He turned and pushed the cart out and into the snow as fast as the ice would allow.

Once he was all loaded up, he slowly hit the highway and navigated the slick asphalt to the cabin. He took the turn off onto a dirt road covered in fresh powder. Looked like none of the neighbors had been down their street to leave tire tracks, so he forged down the middle and christened the pristine, glistening snow.

Pulling up in front of the cabin, he maneuvered the truck as close as he could to the front door and then shut things down. Once he'd hauled all the groceries in, he'd grab some wood from the back and make himself a cozy fire. He loved when it snowed at the cabin. Something about trudging through it to get inside, sitting in the warm living room with the blinds open, and watching the animals leave tracks in their wake made his heart grow lighter. Maybe his time in the woods would do him some good after all. Maybe he did need to recharge and relax and learn to stand his own company for more than ten minutes. And just maybe he'd finally read that self-help book his buddy had given him to learn to relax.

He stomped the snow off his boots and then reached for the key in his coat pocket. But it wasn't there. Had it fallen out in the truck?

He walked back to his 4x4 and put the groceries down as he searched the passenger side and then under the back seats in the extended cab for the lost key.

Dammit. It was probably an omen. Had coming to the cabin been a bad idea after all?

After sleeping for sixteen hours straight, Gabby, still feeling guilty for breaking into the cabin, sipped good coffee and enjoyed the light snowfall as she peered out the kitchen window, watching for her father's men. The little crisscross prints the flitting birds left in the snow made her smile.

She'd woken up in the early afternoon, taken a peek outside, and realized that her plans for trooping miles to the dig site were instantly thwarted. Maybe the sun would come out the next day so she'd be able to continue her mission in the morning. Until the snow melted, no one else could effectively dig at the site, either, so she probably hadn't lost any time there in her race to be first.

She turned and smiled at the coziness of the cabin. It had all the amenities of a five-star hotel, including central heat, so she was still padding around in her socks and pj's at four thirty in the afternoon.

She crossed to the living room and ran her hand over the back of the rich-leather furniture while admiring the fine wood of the shelves that held homey knickknacks and books. She danced her fingers along the spines, searching for a fun story. She spotted a framed picture of two little girls and a handsome dark-haired man. She picked it up, studying it. They all looked happy. And the girls were so cute it melted her heart.

If she kept on living the way she had been, always under heavy guard, she'd probably never have a husband or kids, because no decent man would ever marry her when he found out the truth about her father.

She was two years shy of thirty. The clock wasn't just ticking—it was clanging.

She'd always dreamed of having kids. To have people to love who were good and sweet, like her mom had been. A child to nurture and love with all her heart, the way her mom had loved her. She'd been essentially alone the last twelve years, hiding out, keeping her head down. Her love tank was practically overflowing with the need to share it with a handsome husband and their happy children. Like in the picture.

The slamming of a car door quickly ended her little daydream, and she hopped into action. She peeked out the peephole in the front door. A truck had parked in the driveway. Crap. Had they found her already? She could make out only the back of a man, bent over, gathering something out of the vehicle. Only one man instead of the usual pair who guarded her. Maybe her father had hired a new guard to retrieve her?

Her heart pounded as her mind raced for a solution. She could go out through the same window she'd come in from, but then a car chase for an inexperienced driver in the snow could be fatal.

She ran to the kitchen to look for something heavy. No way she'd use her gun or a knife. Threatening her father's men with weapons wouldn't work. They knew she'd never use those. It sucked those guys knew she was so wimpy.

She'd have to hit the guy.

She hated to do it, but she was trapped. And it wasn't like she'd be hitting someone nice. Her father's men were bad people. She'd hit the guy just hard enough for a chance to get away. But how hard was that? She'd never hit another person in her entire life.

She dug through cabinets and drawers, picking up a meat tenderizer to test its weight in her hand. Not nearly heavy enough.

Where was a baseball bat when a girl needed it?

Then she saw it. A cast-iron skillet. That'd do the trick.

She'd wait behind the door. When the man got close enough, she'd swing. And hope for the best. She'd been a pretty decent cricket player at her boarding school in England. How different could swinging a pan be?

It was the only plan she had, so she took her place in the hallway and tried to draw enough air into her lungs so she wouldn't pass out.

She waited, but then the footsteps retreated, and the car door opened and closed again. Was the guy leaving? Maybe it wasn't one of her father's men after all. A neighbor perhaps? Checking on the place? Her heart rate had just settled when the footsteps came back.

Then the knob slowly turned.

She had to do it. No choice. She couldn't let her dad's thugs catch her and drag her back to DC. Not yet, anyway. She lifted the heavy pan above her head and sucked in a breath for courage. She could do it.

When the tall, blond man passed by her, she swung. The sick thud of the pan hitting something solid, and the way the bags of groceries sailed out in front of him, indicated she'd gotten in a good lick.

The man landed facedown and went completely still. Dead still. She dropped the pan as if it were on fire. What if she'd killed him?

She'd be no better than her father.

What had she just done?

# Chapter Two

Jake tried to open his eyes, to defend himself against the next blow, but couldn't find the strength. Flowery perfume filled his senses as something cold and lumpy landed on the aching side of his head. Like frozen veggies? What the hell had just hit him and why?

A voice whispered, "Please don't die. Please don't die. I'm so sorry I hit you. Please don't die." She lifted his head and then laid it back down on something soft.

He opened his mouth, to ask who she was. "Whaaaa?" But it came out garbled.

"Oh, good. You're waking up. But you can't tell my father you found me. I can't let you do that. So I'm sorry I have to use this duct tape on your hands. And for smashing your phone."

*Your father? Duct tape? What the hell? Is it Shelly from the store? No, she'd never have been able to get to the cabin first. And what about my phone? God, my head hurts.*

His hands were lifted and then wrapped together in duct tape at his wrists. He really needed to snap out of it and put an end to things. But instead, everything went black again.

The next time he heard her voice, she was whispering, "Oh God. Please wake up. Please don't have brain damage." Then tapping sounded. "Hurry, WebMD, tell me what to do for this poor man I hurt." She huffed out an exasperated breath. "Here it is. Pupils enlarged. Slurred words. Fuzzy vision. Needs ER. Got it."

Soft fingers lightly brushed his forehead. "I'm so sorry I hit you. What can I ever do to make it up to you? I was just trying to hide from some bad people, not become one. But you'll probably never believe me when you wake up."

The woman was hiding from bad people?

Pressure on his left eye and then a blinding light brought him fully back to his senses.

He blinked both eyes open. Focus wasn't the best, but he could see well enough to make out a pretty redhead, with her hair in a thick French braid, kneeling by his side, shining her cell phone light at him. She wore a thin, white tank top without a bra.

Was he in heaven? He'd always had a thing for built redheads, and, boy, this one was just his type.

She leaned closer and whispered, "Hi. Are you okay?"

"Urgh" was all he could manage.

"Oh jeez. You do have brain damage. And it's all my fault. I thought you were someone else, and then when I calmed down, I realized you had bags of groceries. Who'd bring bags of groceries to capture me? No one, that's who. You probably live here, and now I've gone and damaged your brain. I'm so sorry."

He might've laughed if his head didn't feel like it'd been run over by a garbage truck. He cleared his throat and tried again. "I'm okay," he managed to croak out.

He tried to sit up, but with his hands bound in front of him, he gave up and lay back down on the pillow under his head. A pillow? She couldn't be too sinister if she'd placed a pillow under his head.

"Thank God." She slipped her long arms underneath him and tugged him up and into a sitting position. She was amazingly strong. "Let me help you to the couch. You can't be comfortable on that hard floor."

He cringed at the thought of her touching him, but he needed her help to sit up. Then his brain took a spin around his skull. "Hang on. Give me a second here." He closed his eyes and waited for the cabin to stop spinning. "What's your name, Pippi?"

She sighed. "I know. Red hair. And I'm tall and gangly like Pippi Longstocking, too. It's why I never leave the house with a braid. But it makes it easier to comb my hair out in the mornings. Oh, and I'm Gabby. What's your name?"

"It's not morning." He opened his eyes again to be sure. Luckily, things had stopped spinning. "And it's Jake."

"Well, it's good you know the time of day, Jake. Maybe you don't have brain damage after all. Ready now?"

She insisted on helping him stand, but his head hurt too much to argue. When they were both fully erect, he was surprised they stood eye to eye. She was just about six feet tall, and he loved that. He'd always had a thing for tall women. "Why is your father after you?"

Her eyes widened before she turned away and avoided his gaze. "I don't know what you're talking about." She wrapped an arm around his waist and pulled him toward the living room.

"You said you thought I was someone else. Who came to capture you, but then you saw I had groceries. You were hiding from bad people but didn't want to be a bad person. I heard you."

"No, you didn't." She shook her head. "You have brain damage, remember?" With his hands still bound, she helped him to the couch and laid a pillow down for him before she gently guided him onto the cushions. Then she made a peace sign. "How many fingers?"

"Six?" he said just to be annoying. His already bad mood had just gotten worse.

"Seriously, Jake. I might need to take you to the ER. Now, how many?"

"How are you going to take me to the ER and not blow whatever your plan is here?" He'd obviously surprised her.

Tamra Baumann

"Well, um." Her brow furrowed as she thought about it. "I know. I'll drop you off and then drive away. So answer the question please." She lifted her hand again.

"That seems kinda rude, considering it's like twenty-five degrees out."

"Please?"

She'd asked nicely, so he said, "Two. And no need for the ER. I've had a concussion before, and this isn't one." He lifted his bound hands. "Can we take care of this?"

"No." She sank to the coffee table and placed a bag of frozen peas over his temple. "I'm sorry, I really am, but I can't have you calling the police. Not until I find what I'm looking for, anyway. I won't hurt you, I promise."

"You've already done that." But he appreciated the cold peas.

Tears formed in her deep-brown eyes. "I know, and I really am—"

"Sorry. Yeah, I got that." He was about to tell her how many laws she'd just broken when something told him he might want to play along for a bit. Find out who was chasing her and why.

She'd been trying to make him comfortable and even been willing to take him to the ER. And binding his hands in front instead of behind had been an amateur move. She wasn't dangerous. But he had a knife in his boot and his backup piece if he needed them.

Pippi was in some sort of trouble, and he'd never been able to resist a damsel in distress.

Besides, he had nothing better to do while on administrative leave, so why not help her out? "If you're not going to let me go, then will you please go out to my truck and bring in the rest of the groceries? I'm hungry, and I really need a beer."

She blinked at him, and then a smile lit her face. "I saw some lasagna in the freezer. Shall I heat that up? It looked really delicious, but I didn't want to eat it without permission."

Dani had made that, and it made his mouth water to think about it. She was an amazing cook. "You think stealing my lasagna would be the worst thing you did today?" She was a piece of work. But a pretty one.

"No. I know this is wrong, but I mean well. You have to believe me." She shook her head as she slipped into her shoes and coat. "Things weren't supposed to get so complicated. I'll get the groceries and your things. Be right back."

He called out, "Put the lasagna in the microwave first, okay? I really am starving here."

"Sure." She stopped and turned around. "Did you bring any fixings to make a salad? I make a pretty mean salad." She headed for the freezer and unwrapped the lasagna.

"Nope. Just junk food. I don't eat anything resembling vegetables when I'm on vacation. It's a rule I have." And since he hadn't had a vacation in five years, he'd planned to take full advantage.

"How long were you planning to stay?" She quickly looked away and then programmed the microwave.

"You mean, how long before someone comes looking for me?" The woman was completely transparent. It was kind of cute. "Maybe the better question is, how long do you plan to keep me as your hostage? Or maybe your gigolo? I could totally clear my schedule for that."

"I'd never . . ." She threw her hands up, all flustered. "A few days is all. I hope. I'll go get your things."

When she'd blushed, it'd made his bitter, damaged heart go pitter-pat. His detective Spidey sense told him she was a sweet woman. Just a nice person in a bad spot. And the more he teased her, the more information he was bound to get out of her. She flustered easily. "But wait, how old are you? I wouldn't want to break any laws."

"Now who's being rude?" She placed her hands on her narrow hips. "I met so many men like you in college, all handsome and . . . flirty. That stuff doesn't work on me, Jake. I'm a *serious* scientist."

*A seriously adorable scientist.*

"And I have a *serious* headache. Could you grab me something for the pain from that cabinet over there, darlin'?"

She frowned at the mention of pain—or maybe it was the "darlin'" comment he'd used to fluster a professional woman like her—and quickly jogged to the cabinet. When she returned with a glass of water and the bottle of pills, she held them out.

"My hands are a little restrained at the moment. If you still won't let me go, then you'll have to open that bottle."

"I'll unbind your hands as soon as I get what I came for." She sat on the coffee table again and tapped out the pills into her palm. "You won't bite me if I lay these on your tongue, will you?" She opened her mouth, to indicate he should do the same.

"When I get a chance to bite you, it won't be your fingers I'll be after." He opened up for her.

Her forehead crumpled. "Are you ever serious?"

"Rarely."

"Hmmm." She leaned closer and stared intently into his eyes as if searching for something.

It made him squirm.

What if she saw all the damage in there? He never let anyone see that. "What?" he asked, and then let his jaw go lax again.

"Nothing. I just had to be sure." She smiled, then softly laid two pills on his tongue. "Your eyes are the same shade of blue as the Mediterranean Sea. It's my favorite part of the world. Have you ever been?" She tilted the glass to his lips.

"Nope," he mumbled around the pills and then swallowed. "What were you looking to be sure of?"

"To see if you're kind. And you are. Believe me, I've seen the opposite. I can always tell if people are good or bad by the look in their eyes."

"If that were true, there'd be no serial killers. Or sociopaths." He needed to stop before she figured out he was a cop.

She shrugged and then rose to go outside. "Maybe those types can fool a normal person, but I've never been wrong. Ever."

*Normal person?*

He pondered that as she went out to the truck to get his groceries. Gabby intrigued him. There was a quiet sadness about her. Maybe because she was afraid of her father, or the people trying to take her back to him? And she claimed to have seen evil in someone's eyes before.

What had she been through to make her break into a cabin in the middle of winter? And make her hit someone, when he'd bet she hated to kill even a spider?

Looked like he had a day or two to figure that out while she found what she was looking for. And like the good detective he still was, no matter what the LT had insinuated about him, he'd get to the bottom of Gabby's story. All he'd have to do is find the right buttons to push, and she'd crack like an egg.

Gabby hauled in the rest of the groceries and enough liquor to stock a restaurant bar. Then she slipped out of her coat. When she looked down, she let out a quiet gasp. She'd never gotten dressed. And she wasn't wearing a bra. No wonder he'd been staring at her chest like that earlier. She called out from the kitchen, "Be right back."

"Hold up. I think I deserve one of those beers after you bashed my head in, don't you? Help yourself to one, if you'd like."

She still felt so guilty for hitting an innocent man that she'd do anything to try to make it up to him. Every time she glanced at his bruised face, her stomach hurt. "Coming right up." She opened the fridge, now overflowing with beer, and grabbed two. She could really use a drink, too.

She opened his and then hers. "Can you manage the can?"

"Let's give it a try. Although it wouldn't be a hardship to enlist the help of a gorgeous woman." He swung his feet to the floor and sat up. His gaze zeroed in on her chest again. "By that little noise you made, I'm guessing you just figured out the no-bra thing there, didn't you?"

*Does the man flirt 24–7? And notice everything?* She placed the beer between his fingers. "Yes. I plan to rectify that right now."

"Don't go to any trouble on my account. Cheers?" He held his can out toward hers and smiled so sweetly it made it hard to refuse. Jake was blond haired, blue eyed, lean but muscled, handsome, and too charming for his own good. She needed to remember that he was also the one who could ruin all her plans.

She still wanted to crawl under a rock about the bra thing, but instead, she'd play it cool like the brave new woman she'd just become and tap his can back. "Here's to your hard head, Jake."

"That was a good one, Red." He smiled as he clumsily managed to raise the can to his lips. When he tilted his head back, only a few drops landed on his shirt. After a very long drink, he said, "Wait! You're trying to do that Stockholm syndrome thing on me, right? To make me like you. By making me laugh, serving me beer, and prancing around without a bra. The bra thing was a nice touch. My favorite one actually. Or maybe the lack of bra confirms the gigolo theory?"

Mortified, she just shook her head. "I don't know how to deal with a comment like that, Jake. I'll be right back." She stood and headed for the bedroom. She'd rather crawl under the covers in that big, soft bed and pull them over her head. But she had a guest she had to feed and keep an eye on. How had things gone so terribly wrong? Her plans had been so perfect. Then Jake had come strolling through the front door and messed everything up.

He called out from the couch, "What does that mean? Don't you want to be my friend?"

She yelled back, "No. Not especially." That was a lie. She could use a nice person in her life right now. And Jake had a pair of the kindest eyes she'd ever seen. If only his smart mouth would stop trying to cover up whatever pain he was hiding.

In her experience, people who acted like him always had baggage. And having her own unfortunate past, she was always drawn to those types. She had a feeling she and Jake were kindred souls in the pain department, although a guy like him would probably never admit it. He reminded her of Brian, the only man she'd ever loved, who'd broken her heart back in college. And her best friend at school, Charlie, who'd grown up rich and unloved. Both had mouths on them like Jake.

She yanked her shirt off and found her bra hanging on the bathroom doorknob where she'd left it the night before. After she'd put it on, she didn't see any reason to get all the way dressed when they were going to go to sleep again in a few hours anyway, so she slipped her tank back over her head.

He'd already seen her with no makeup and in her pj's, so who cared? It wasn't like she needed to impress him. Or make herself more attractive to him, that was for sure. He already seemed attracted enough to her, oddly. Maybe that was part of his shtick, too. He probably flirted with anything female, that one.

She walked back into the living room and sat beside him on the couch as they waited for their dinner to heat up. She hated that she had to keep his hands bound. But he'd surely be able to escape and call the police if she let him wander around freely.

Picking up the remote, she asked, "Do you want to watch some TV?"

He finished off his beer. "I'd rather talk about you."

"No thanks." He had cable, so she quickly found the sports channel for him. After enduring scores and news about people she'd never heard of, she said, "I'm going to check my e-mail. Want another beer?"

"Yes, please." Jake grinned at her. "You're a pretty accommodating kidnapper. I appreciate it."

She went to get his beer, and when she returned, she said, "Please don't call me a kidnapper. You don't understand."

"I'm all ears here." He held out his hands for the can.

"Really? From what I can tell, you're all mouth." She placed the cold beer in his hands and walked to the bedroom to retrieve her laptop.

"Ouch! Now I'm not so sure you're very nice," he called out from behind her.

She dropped to the side of the bed as a wave of guilt rushed through her again. She *wasn't* being very nice at the moment. "Under normal circumstances, I'm a very nice person, Jake. Wi-Fi password, please?"

"If you come back out here and keep me company, I'll give it to you."

She grabbed her laptop and huffed out a breath. "Fine." It was his cabin, after all. She was the one who had broken in and hurt him.

Just as she walked back into the living room, Jake tossed his empty beer can over his shoulder with both hands in an attempt to hit the trash basket. It hit the rim, and then popped out and onto the floor. "Denied!"

It reminded her of how some of the pig guards in her house often behaved, throwing beer cans and leaving them for the housekeeper to clean up. Worse, while doing that, they often sat around bragging about the people they'd killed.

It flipped a very big switch inside her.

"If you think I'm picking up after you, then think again. Just because you're a hostage is no excuse to forget your manners." Her clipped tone surprised her. What was she doing? He'd just missed his shot, that's all. She needed to take a deep breath and regroup. She wasn't home, where she felt like the prisoner. Jake was the one being held against his will.

She was obviously tired and cranky. She'd had a rough few days. Or maybe it was Jake. It was hard to tell. The man was confusing and sexy at the same time.

"No need to get all testy." He slowly stood. "You might have been raised in a proper English boarding school, but I went to public, so my manners aren't as nice as yours."

"What makes you think I went to school in England?" Fear shot up her spine as she whirled around and faced him. Was he one of her father's men after all? Just pretending to be the owner of the cabin?

"Just a guess." The corner of his mouth lifted. "You have the slightest English accent when you panic. Or you're mad. It's sort of cute. I'm guessing that had to come from living overseas a long time ago?"

Sort of cute? Who in his right mind flirted with his kidnapper nonstop? Maybe he had a little brain damage after all. "Well, you're right, I did go to school in England. I'm very big on manners because of it, I suppose."

"A kidnapper with manners? That's probably an oxymoron, wouldn't you say?"

"I'm not a kidnapper, Jake. You were just in the wrong place at the wrong time."

"Clearly. So, is what they say about redheads true, then? That they all have tempers like snarling bears?"

"That sounds about right to me." But she wasn't really a redhead, so she didn't have any idea if that were true.

The microwave beeped, thankfully, so she went to the kitchen and searched the drawers for hot pads.

Jake bent to pick up the can. After three attempts, he finally grabbed it and threw it away. Then he moved behind her and slipped his bound hands over her head and laid them on her chest. Just above her now-bra-restrained breasts. His thumbs slowly caressed her collarbone. "The rest of that saying involves something about redheads being wildcats in bed. That sound like you, too?" His mouth was so close that his warm breath tickled her ear. It made her shiver with fear that he could break her neck if he wanted to.

She whispered, "That's none of your business. Please go sit down at the table." She used her best stern schoolteacher voice that only worked on her dog. None of the thugs at home ever took her seriously.

"No denial? Must be true, then. The pot holders are in the drawer right beside the oven." He lifted his hands over her head and backed away. "FYI. The next time you kidnap someone who isn't me, you should tie their hands behind their back. I could've taken you out just now."

"And yet you didn't." She turned around and sent him her cockiest grin while she tried to pull herself together. She needed to keep her guard up better than that. She'd had a ton of self-defense classes. She needed to remember to use what she'd learned.

Jake chuckled but sat at the table after he managed to get them their beers from the coffee table. It was incredible what a man with bound hands could accomplish when there was beer involved. And how would he have known where the hot pads were unless he lived here? It made her shoulders relax again.

After another long drink from his can, he placed it on the table. "Can I ask you a question?"

"If I said no, I doubt that'd stop you from asking." She dished up two plates of lasagna, one heaping and one regular portioned, and slid the fuller plate in front of him before she sat down. "You talk a lot for a man."

"I'm the curious sort. That's all." He struggled with his fork but finally managed to get a bite to his lips. After he swallowed, he said, "Just wondering about the overall plan here. What's to stop me from walking out of here tonight after you fall asleep?"

*Yeah, what was to stop him?*

She took a long drink from her beer to stall for time to figure that out. Then she took a big bite because the answer hadn't materialized quite yet. By the time she'd swallowed, the answer had come to her. "I'd planned to duct-tape your ankles together tonight. And I took your keys while you were passed out. Along with a gun, and the knife in your boot. Why do you carry a gun and a knife?"

He frowned at her. For the first time, he seemed truly angry. But still not enough to hurt her. "When my head stopped banging some, I noticed you stole those from me." Then his face softened, and he leaned closer. "You had your hands in my pants, and I wasn't even awake to enjoy it? You play dirty, Red. But I like that. A lot."

She shook her head as she scooped up more food. "You flirt even when you're mad? Or did you do that so you wouldn't have to answer my question?" She stuffed a bite of some of the best lasagna she'd ever eaten into her mouth. Different from her aunt Suzy's, but still delicious. The melty cheese and garlicky red sauce nearly made her moan.

Good manners would question the size of that bite, but she hadn't had a proper meal in days, so she'd give herself a break. She practically inhaled her food.

"You want to know why I carry a gun and a knife?" He shot her a panty-melting grin as he lifted up his foot. "I'm a cowboy. Hence the boots. I sometimes need the knife to free animals caught up in things. And the gun is for the wild animals that sometimes like to creep up behind a guy while out on the range."

"What kind of wild animals?" She'd read there were bears in New Mexico. It worried her about her long hike to the ruins.

When he shrugged, his whole bite of lasagna dropped from his fork and back to his plate, so he stabbed it again. "Coyotes, bobcats, bears, that kind."

So, there *were* bears, darn it.

She studied him as she chewed. Her normally reliable gut told her he was telling the truth about being a cowboy and yet lying at the same time. "Coyotes are dangerous to people?"

"Only when they're hungry and in packs. Mostly, I just shoot off the gun. That's usually all it takes for critters to get the hint. Too bad people don't work that way." He frowned deeply as he concentrated on getting the food into his mouth.

"Here. Let me help you." She was full, so she pushed her almost-empty plate away and scooted closer to him.

"I'd appreciate it." He opened his mouth wide and tilted his head back, like a baby bird waiting for a worm. It made her smile.

After she had shoved in a big bite, she said, "Why'd you get upset after the 'too bad people don't work that way' comment just now?"

Jake's brows drew together as he chewed. "What makes you think you know what people are thinking and feeling?"

"Ah. You admit I'm right." She shoved in more food. The man was like a human trash compactor and must've been as hungry as she'd been.

He nodded as he chewed. "You're right, but I don't want to talk about it." He opened for another bite. After she had complied, he said, "In case you hadn't noticed, there's only one bed in this place. That couch is too short for me, and I have a major headache. I intend to sleep in my own bed, duct-taped or not."

She fed him another heaping forkful. The look in his eyes as he watched was filled with desire. It was downright sexual. And it probably wasn't all for the lasagna, even as good as it was. "If that couch is too short for you, then it'll be too short for me, too."

"Yeah. But you're the criminal here, not me. You should take the couch. Or, you'd be welcome to join me. How much trouble could a man with taped-up hands and legs get into?" He waggled his blond brows.

She shoved the last bite into his mouth and then grabbed their dishes from the table. "I doubt a little tape would ever stop a guy like you from getting into a woman's panties, Jake."

"Look who's talking. You've already been in mine. Turnabout is fair play. Don't you think?"

"You are seriously tempting me to use my duct tape on that cocky mouth of yours." Why hadn't she met Jake under different circumstances? When she might enjoy all his playful flirting. He had probably talked more women into bed than Casanova himself. And she would have been one of them. Just for a night or two, anyway. That's all the time she dared spend with a man. They asked too many questions after that. Hard to hide the fact for too long that she had bodyguards and drivers.

Jake suddenly appeared beside her, his face inches from hers. "Don't ever duct-tape someone's mouth, Red. I'm serious. People can asphyxiate and accidentally die that way. *Comprende?*"

"Asphyxiate?" She laughed as she rinsed their plates in the sink. "That's a pretty big word for a cowboy."

"Are you saying cowboys are dumb? Couldn't possibly be as smart as a serious scientist?"

"No. I was just . . ." She turned and stared into his earnest eyes. He was being serious for a change. Had she hurt his feelings?

She whispered, "I'm sorry, Jake. I was just teasing. I'd never actually tape your mouth closed because I don't mind all of your chatter. I normally live a pretty solitary life, and you're sort of like my dog. He's good company without saying anything."

"Now I'm as dumb as your dog?"

She hadn't meant it like that. Jeez, what had set him off? Must have something to do with that personal thing he didn't want to discuss. "For your information, I have a border collie. And his name is Einstein because he's so smart."

"Oh well, then that makes all the difference." He walked to the fridge and grabbed himself another beer while muttering something about damn dogs.

He laid it on the counter and popped the top. "You know what, Red? You act pretty high and mighty for a common criminal."

"I'm *not* a common criminal. I'm an archaeologist searching for a statue that belongs in a museum so the whole world can appreciate its beauty. Not some rich collector's home. Someone who'll go to great and illegal lengths to get it. I have to find it before some very bad people find me and make me stop."

Jake's right brow lifted. "Then why not call the police?"

"Because I happen to love the bad person trying to stop me." Crap, crap, crap. She needed to shut up, immediately. "Look, if you can have off-limits stuff, then I can, too. And go easy on the beers. You'll have a hard time going to the bathroom later with your legs bound."

"Speaking of that, can you help me with my jeans? Nature's calling right now." His lips tilted into a very naughty grin. No one did a naughty grin as well as Jake.

She didn't want to touch him there. Well, that wasn't entirely true. She sort of did want to touch him there, but it'd be totally inappropriate under the circumstances.

"Fine." She moved closer and released the top button first. Because that was fairly safe. As she stood and stared, trying to figure out how to lower his zipper without becoming intimately acquainted with him, the situation became worse. Evidently, staring at his crotch aroused him.

He whispered, "Quick might be better."

She reached for his zipper. Quick *was* probably better.

Just as her fingers grasped the little tab, a woman's voice called out, "What's going on here?"

Gabby hadn't even heard anyone come through the front door. She was in trouble now.

Gabby moved her hand back to her side as she turned around. A beautiful woman with long, curly light-brown hair and a figure like a twenties pinup girl pointed a twenty-two at them.

Jake called out, "Hey, Dani. Gabby here was just getting into my pants."

She blew out a long breath. Looked like the jig was up. Gabby Knight *was* a common criminal and going to jail.

Worse, she'd failed all archaeologists worldwide.

# Chapter Three

Jake didn't need to be rescued by his ex-wife. He'd just flustered Gabby enough by flirting with her incessantly and pressing her buttons to make her confess some useful information. Another hour and he'd have solved the mystery that was Gabby on his own.

He held out his hands toward his bumbling captor. "Now that you're busted, will you please get rid of this tape? I really have to go to the little boys' room. Oh, and Dani Botelli, meet Gabby with no last name."

Gabby said, "It's Knight. Gabby Knight."

Dani nodded. "Nice to meet you, Gabby Knight."

Jake glanced at Dani, who was trying not to laugh. By the amused expression on her face, Dani must've known Gabby wasn't a criminal, either. She'd had a dream or a hunch, or she wouldn't have shown up. His ex had random prophetic dreams and hunches that were right 98 percent of the time, and he'd used them to help solve crimes in the past. Her famous movie-star mother, Annalisa Botelli, had them, too, but they both kept their abilities on the lowdown to protect Dani's mother's ticket sales.

"Lovely to meet you, too, Dani." Gabby's English accent was back, so she had to be nervous. Then she added, "I saw some scissors in the drawer over there. I'm sorry that it'll hurt when we rip it off, Jake."

He hadn't thought about that. He'd probably have bald forearms for a bit. "That's okay. Just hurry, please."

Gabby returned with the scissors. While she lowered her red head and concentrated on freeing his hands, he said to Dani, "Keep an eye on this one while I'm gone. She likes to bonk people over the head with frying pans."

"I can see that." Dani smirked. "But that was your mistake, Gabby. Jake is the most hardheaded man I know."

Gabby whispered, "I didn't enjoy hitting you, Jake. I regret hurting you more than I can say. And I won't be any more trouble. I promise."

The sadness in her voice pierced his heart. She probably thought she'd go to jail. But he didn't care about what she'd done so far, just about keeping her out of any more trouble in the future. "I'm going to help you, Gabby. Just as soon as I get back, we can sit down, and you can tell me what's really going on."

She slowly shook her head as she laid the scissors down. "Thanks for the offer. But I can handle it on my own from here." Then she ripped off the tape.

All the air whooshed from his lungs, and he saw stars for a good five seconds until he could breathe normally again. That hurt almost as badly as the frying pan had. He was proud of himself for not crying out like a baby.

Dani put her gun in her purse. "Gabby, why don't you have a seat on the couch for a minute while I talk to Jake. And don't go anywhere, okay? The roads are like an ice-skating rink out there."

Dani grabbed his arm and yanked him toward the bedroom. He glanced over his shoulder to be sure Gabby had complied with Dani's instructions. Gabby sat on the couch with her eyes cast downward and her shoulders slumped in defeat.

Because he really did have to go, he went into the bathroom but left the door open a crack. If Dani looked, she wouldn't see anything she hadn't seen before. He called out, "Thanks for the save, but I had it under control."

"Sure looked like it when I walked in, you all taped up like that." Dani flopped on the edge of the bed. "You're calling her Gabby, but the person in my vision was Sophia Moretti. I googled her while I was driving here."

*Why did she change her name?* "You googled while driving? We've talked about that, Dani."

"For argument's sake, let's pretend I was at a red light. Anyway, she supposedly died years ago. And she's the daughter of Luca Moretti. That name ring any of your cop bells?"

*The mobster? How could a sweet woman like Gabby be his daughter?*

Jake washed his hands. "Is she for sure the same person? Was there a picture?"

Dani appeared by his side with her phone tilted in his direction. "What do *you* think?"

He dried his hands and then scooped up the phone from Dani. It was of a little kid. "Yeah. That's her. Not that I would've necessarily seen the connection if I wasn't looking for it, though. I'm disappointed she's not really a redhead, but those adorable dimples are the same." Seemed Gabby was dealing with some dangerous people. She might need help if she wanted to outwit her father.

Dani grinned. "You like her, don't you?"

It felt weird to discuss another woman with his ex-wife. Especially because he'd always love Dani, even if they weren't ever meant to be married.

He said, "She's in over her head, that's all. But don't mention I'm a cop until I figure it all out."

Dani's right brow spiked. "I didn't have just one dream, Jake. I saw—"

"Stop!" He held up a hand. "Don't tell me. I *hate* when you ruin endings for me. I'm going to do this, so don't try to talk me out of it."

He'd prove to his boss and to himself that he could be a good detective without his ex-wife's help. "And were you telling the truth about the roads? Is it safe for you to drive home?"

Dani rolled her eyes. "Typical. First you tell me what your stubborn ass is going to do despite what I think, and then you act all concerned about me."

He smiled. She still had his number. "You should stay. It'll just be a side benefit that it'll drive Michael crazy thinking about us together in this cabin all night."

"I've already talked to him about how dangerous the roads are. And at another of those imaginary red lights, he said he'd rather I not drive home tonight, either. He trusts me."

"Uh-huh." He walked back into the living room with Dani on his heels. "You guys had a fight about it, didn't you?"

"Yes. So you have to sleep on the couch. Gabby and I will share."

Dammit. He had a major headache and didn't want to sleep on the couch. "We can talk about that in a minute. We reheated some lasagna. Help yourself."

"Help myself? To my own lasagna? I made that for the next time Michael and I come up, thank you very much. Now I'll have to make more." She headed for the kitchen.

He planted himself on the coffee table in front of Gabby. "Okay, Red. What's the real deal?"

Gabby blinked at him. "Is Dani Annalisa Botelli's daughter? Annalisa is one of my favorite actresses."

"Yep." He nodded. "Dani is my ex-wife. This is her cabin, and she gets pissy when I eat the food she makes for her fiancé for when they come here for their romantic getaways. Now we're all acquainted. Start talking."

"Wow. You were married to *her*?" Gabby glanced over her shoulder and watched Dani move about the kitchen while making herself a plate. "She's *gorgeous*."

He was starting to get a little offended. "What? Dumb cowboys can't have pretty wives whose mothers are major movie stars?"

"No." She reached out and gave his tender forearm a squeeze. "I don't think you're a dumb cowboy, Jake. Please stop saying that. And although I'm pretty sure you're lying to me about being a cowboy, I don't care. Not after the way I treated you."

That took him aback. Not many people could read him that well. "Enough about me. Tell me what's really going on. So far, I know your father has men he sends after you. That's why you hit me over the head. You thought I was one of them. And you want to get some artifact before a bad guy does. That about right?" Now that he knew who her father was, it made more sense.

"Yes. But the bad guys won't hurt me. *You*, I can't guarantee the same for. I should just go. I've done enough damage here—that I'm paying you back for, by the way." She pointed to the bedroom. "You can have as much money as you think you'll need to make any repairs. Help yourself. I have plenty. It's in the blue bag beside the bed."

He ran a hand down his face, searching for patience. "Gabby. You don't know me. The last thing you should tell a stranger is that you have a bag of money and to help themselves! How have you gotten along this far in life and not known that?" Jeez, the poor woman would get robbed or worse left on her own.

"I know that, Jake. I'm just trying to make up for hitting you over the head." She shrugged. "But the truth is I don't deal with money often. I usually have drivers and bodyguards who pay for everything. It's pretty annoying, actually."

Dani sat beside him on the coffee table with her plate in her hands. "I had them, too, growing up. You're right. They're *so* annoying."

Jake shook his head. "Your sheltered life tells me you can't be trusted on your own. You could be in real danger, Red. You either let me help you, or I'll call the police, and you can do jail time for assault, kidnapping, and B and E for starters. Do we have a deal?"

Gabby looked at him, then at Dani, who was nodding her head up and down as she ate, and then back to him. "Can I please sleep on it tonight? It's a very big decision. Bigger than you could ever guess, actually."

She was buying herself time. "Sure. But you're going to be sleeping with me tonight while you ponder. In the nice, soft bed, because Dani's fiancé wants her to sleep on the couch. As far away from me as possible." He wasn't going to let Gabby slip out during the night. Who knew what kind of people could be out to hurt her? He might have been relieved of his duties for a month, but any decent person would help her out.

"Wait a minute." Dani lifted a finger. "This is my house, remember? I get to—"

"Be reasonable, Dani. You on the couch makes the most sense. You're the shortest one here. Gabs or I won't fit."

"I'm shorter by, what, three inches?" Dani laid her plate down beside her. "Gabby, could you move please so I can make a point to stubborn, bossy Jake here?"

Gabby slowly stood and stepped aside, then Dani lay on the couch.

He smiled. She and the couch were the exact same length. "So who was stubborn and *right*, Botelli?"

Dani sat up and frowned. "Oh, all right. I'll sleep here, then."

Gabby's eyes widened. "No. I can't sleep with him." She threw a thumb his way. "He's the flirtiest man I've ever met."

He plastered on his best smile. "Why, thank you. Now, where are my gun and knife please?"

She reached into a pocket in her flannel pants and pulled out his keys. "I put them in your glove box when I was bringing in the groceries." She tossed his keys to him. "But we're not sleeping in the same bed. Right, Dani? You know how he is."

Jake shook his head and walked toward the front door. Gabby wasn't going anywhere, and she was going to sleep with him even if he had to duct-tape her to the bed. Luca Moretti's men were dangerous. He still had a duty to protect her. Badge or not.

～

Gabby panicked as Jake walked out the door. "Dani, seriously. I can't sleep with him."

"Who are you afraid is going to misbehave? You or Jake?" Dani smiled and then finished her lasagna.

Gabby's cheeks were suddenly on fire. How could Dani know? "Jake, of course."

"Hmmmm." Dani stood and took her plate to the kitchen sink.

"Okay, I'll admit I'm a little attracted to him." She followed behind Dani. "You were, too, at one time, so you must know how impossible it is not to want to kiss him. Just to shut him up sometimes, if nothing else."

Dani laughed as she loaded her plate in the dishwasher. "I like you, Gabby." She turned and leaned back against the counter. "Here's a little truth about Jake that he'd kill me for sharing. Something happened when he was a kid, so he doesn't like to be touched."

"Ever? Like not even a hug?"

"He likes to do the touching just fine when he's in bed with a woman he's going to sleep with, but that's the only time." Dani held up a finger. "Oh, and only he can initiate the touching. He doesn't like to hold hands, cuddle, or engage in any displays of affection. At least he didn't with me at first."

"I don't understand. Why are you telling me this?"

Dani sighed. "I used to get so hurt by what I thought was his lack of affection until he finally confessed after we'd been together for almost a year. I'm only telling you this because I think it'll make it easier for you to understand him. All you have to do is ask him not to touch you, and he'll respect that because it's what he'll ask of you."

Her heart ached for the little boy who'd been Jake. "Who hurt him?"

Dani shook her head. "That's a story for only him to tell. But I'll make him sleep on the couch if you're still worried."

Gabby didn't know what to do. But now she felt really sorry for Jake. "He'd be more comfortable in the bed, especially with his head injury. And I am a little worried about him. It'd probably be good if someone were with him in case his injury gets worse in the night. Brains can sometimes swell hours later."

Dani nodded. "Yes, there's that. And you'd be doing me a huge favor, actually. My fiancé and Jake don't care for each other. Michael would feel better knowing I'm on the couch and you're with Jake to keep an eye on him."

"Okay." She hoped she wouldn't regret that decision. But she'd still leave at first light, before Jake and Dani awoke.

Jake came through the door along with a rush of cool air. "Gabby, you forgot to check the bed of my truck, under the lid. There was more liquor. I make a mean Moscow mule, if you ladies would like one. Oh, and I disabled your Jeep and my truck, so you can forget running away without me."

*Crap! Now what am I going to do?*

Jake chuckled. "Gabby, your escape plan in the night was written all over your face. You need to work on that."

She did. She was terrible at lying. She just wanted to get her statue and go home.

Dani whispered, "Just let him help you, Sophia. We'll keep your secret so you can get your statue guy before Luca can. You'll need Jake's help to do it."

*Sophia? And my father? How could you possibly know?*

"My name is Gabby. I can show you my license." Her knees went weak. No one could know her true identity. Her life depended on staying hidden from her father's enemies. If anyone found out, she'd have to move in the middle of the night and have no interactions with anyone except her father's men. "And who's Luca?" She backed away from Dani and ran into Jake's chest. She spun around. "Don't believe her, Jake."

He laid his boxes on the counter and then held up his hands in a "calm down" gesture. "Look. We both know she's not lying, but I get why you need to tell me she is. You have to trust us here, Red."

"You're the one who just said I shouldn't trust strangers. Who else knows?" Tears slipped down her cheeks as overbearing sadness crept into her heart. "Now I'm going to have to disappear for good. And my father won't ever let me have a real job. I'll be a prisoner in my own home."

Dani wrapped her arms around Gabby. "Stop. We aren't going to tell anyone. We promise. But you need some help. You'll never outrun your father without Jake's help. Believe me, I know."

She shook her head. "But if you figured it out, then so can someone else. My father was so careful. And we're never in public together. I don't understand how you could possibly know."

Jake took her by the upper arms and placed his face in front of hers. "You said you were never wrong about people, so look into my eyes while I promise you that I'll never reveal your secret."

She blinked at him through her tears. Then she shook her head. "I can't trust myself anymore. I meet so few new people—"

"Okay. Wait." Dani took her arm and pulled her to the couch. Then she sat beside her and held her hand. "Do you know who I am?"

She nodded. "You're Annalisa's daughter. You were kidnapped as a kid. And I saw the gambling thing in Vegas on the Internet recently. You were being chased by a man out for revenge and were almost killed in front of the casino. It was all over the news."

"Right. So if I told you a secret about myself, will you promise me you'll keep it in return for me keeping yours? Then we'll both have a secret on the other. Deal?"

Gabby could barely think straight with all the fear about being discovered running through her veins, but she nodded. "Okay." She wanted to trust Dani so badly. Dani had kind eyes. Just as nice as Jake's. Gabby had never been wrong in the past. She was usually surrounded by horrible people who worked for her father. She'd always known how to gauge the bad side in people. But now, she wasn't so sure.

Dani leaned closer. "If no one has figured out your secret in all these years, then you're safe. The only reason I know is that I have these prophetic dreams and sometimes just know things. And I saw your statue. Go ahead. Ask me something about it. Anything."

What? Dani wasn't making any sense. "Your dreams told you who I am?"

She nodded. "And that Jake was going to be taped up. That's why I came. I thought he was hurt."

Jake added, "You broke my cell, Gabby, if you'll remember. I had no way to call her. Here. Drink this." He handed her and Dani Moscow mules in copper cups.

Dani whispered, "You need to let Jake help you get what you want. *Everything* you want, Gabby."

It was all too much to take in.

She took a deep drink. The combination of ginger and lime was really good. She'd never had a Moscow mule before. "Okay, wait. If your dreams or whatever are real, then what is the artifact made of?"

Dani took a sip and then put her cup down. "It's a guy who might be a king or something and is made of gold. It's about yea big." She held her hands about ten inches apart. "And it has this cool pattern on the tunic that I can't describe. But maybe I could draw it for you." Dani rose and found some paper and a pen.

Gabby took another drink as she tried to wrap her head around what Dani was telling her. She could've seen the statue's match, the Emperor Father, on TV. It had been on the news when it had been stolen. But if that were true, she'd draw it wrong, because the Father and his Son had different patterns on their tunics.

Her scientific brain wanted to fight what Dani was saying about the visions, but there was real research on the subject that proved some people were more sensitive than others. It didn't sit well with her, though. She needed proof.

Dani finished and held up the paper. "It looks like this, right?"

Holy crap! She'd done a fairly decent job that not many could have, outside the archaeology world. "Yes. That's right. But why would you help me? It makes no sense." She had her proof but wasn't still all the way convinced about Dani's and Jake's motives. Her father always said you have to understand people's motives to figure out how to get what you want from them. He was probably talking about stealing stuff, but still.

Dani patted Gabby's leg. "Jake won't let me tell you guys what my other dreams were about. He hates when I ruin the ending of any story for him. But I can tell you this much. While I can't comment about him"—she pointed to Jake, who was sitting in an armchair and drinking a beer—"I saw that you and I would be friends long into the future, Gabby. And I recently found out my dad has a bit of a checkered past, too. That's why I want to help you."

*Friends?*

She hadn't been able to have real friends since her boarding school days. Just online ones. She'd like very much to have one again. Especially one who knew her secret and might understand. One who'd trust Gabby with her own huge secret. Turnabout was fair play. "Thank you, Dani. But, Jake, what are your motives to help me?"

Jake shot her a mischievous grin. "I love redheads. What can I say?"

That made all the spit in her mouth dry up. She wasn't a flirt. Jake threw her off-kilter like no one else. "You want to help me because I have red hair?"

*Seriously? This guy is more than I can handle.*

Luckily, Dani saved her when she threw a pillow at his head. "Ignore him, Gabby. He's just messing with you because he hates to let people think he has a heart. He wants to help you because there's a very good man hidden under all that BS."

She'd kind of figured that out on her own. And he'd been married to Dani, so he couldn't be all bad.

She was going to do it. Go with her gut. Tell them the whole truth and hope she was doing the right thing. She'd just change her name and disappear if they turned out to be lying. "Okay. Thank you both for helping me. And I won't run, so you can put the cars back in order, Jake."

Her father would probably lock her up and throw away the key just to keep her safe anyway after the stunt she'd just pulled. Better to accept the help she needed, quickly find the statue, and then let the museum figure out how to keep it safe. Letting Dani and Jake help her might be the only way she'd have a fighting chance to get the Son statue before her father did.

# Chapter Four

Jake studied Gabby as she drained her Moscow mule. Apparently, she'd found her new favorite drink. Strangely, it made him happy that he'd been the one to introduce her to it. He'd bet she had a lot of things in life yet undiscovered. Gabby had a sweet wonder about her he'd never seen before in a grown woman. Especially for the daughter of a mobster. It didn't add up. Now that she'd agreed to let him help her, her story should be an interesting one to untangle. "Still waiting for that explanation about the statue and how your father is involved, Gabs."

Dani laid her cup down and slid to the edge of her seat. "Yeah, I'm curious about these statues now, too."

Gabby took a deep breath and then said, "Okay. So a few months ago, a historian found some old letter and a map in a run-down estate in Europe that told the history of the statue I'm looking for. He's a good friend of the man I work for at the museum in DC. He told my boss the Son statue had been buried on sacred tribal land here in New Mexico during World War Two to protect it from the Nazis. But apparently the owner died, and the statue is still buried here. There's supposedly a curse if the two matching statues, the Father and Son, are ever reunited, but we think that's all a bunch a hooey."

Dani raised a finger. "It's not, actually. I got a creepy vibe when I saw the two pieces side by side. But go on."

Jake said, "Wait. How many people know about this buried statue and the letter?"

"That's the tricky part. The historian knew how valuable the pieces would be together to an art collector, but that was never going to happen because we had the Father statue in a museum here in the US. He asked around to gauge the interest of some museums in Europe to set a price for us to buy the Son statue, too. So other people know about this so-called find. But the catch is we have the map. He brought us the original to show the Indian Tribal Council so they could see for themselves that it's real. We've already presented the council with a formal request to dig, and in the meantime, we need funding to do the dig right and disturb as little as possible in deference to the sacred land."

Jake took another drink while he mulled all that over. "Could others have already beat you to it, while you were following all the rules?"

"Maybe, but because the map was timeworn, we had to enlist an expert's help to pinpoint where the statue is. That took weeks. And we have the top expert in the world working for us at the museum. He was sworn to secrecy." Gabby held out her cup. "Could I please have another one?"

"Sure." He stood and grabbed both Gabby's and Dani's cups and went into the kitchen. "But be careful how much you drink. The altitude here makes these go down easy and hit hard. You might lose all inhibitions and then get some big ideas about getting in my pants again tonight. But go on, I'm still listening."

"That's absolutely not going to happen." Gabby's cheeks were still red when she said, "Anyway, we were having trouble getting the funding, so I thought I'd ask my dad for the money and just tell my boss I found an anonymous private donor. So I told my father all of the details. After asking a lot of questions about how valuable these pieces were, he finally gave me the money, but then said he was 'going dark' for a bit, which isn't all that uncommon. Then a few days ago the Father statue from the museum went missing, along with all the copies of the map."

Dani said, "You think your dad figured out how valuable the statues were as a matched set and decided to steal them both?"

"Looks that way. And my boss, Dean, went on emergency leave right before our statue of the Emperor Father went missing from DC, so I worry my dad has Dean and is going to try to get him to find the Son statue for him before I do. I need to find both statues and return them to the museum in DC where they belong."

Jake called out from the kitchen, "What if your boss took the statue and the map, and your father had nothing to do with it?"

"Dean loves to preserve history. I don't think he would do anything like that." Gabby blinked like a baby owl for a few moments. "But now that you mention it, I guess it could've happened that way. I might have jumped to an incorrect conclusion about my father."

Jake returned to the living room and held out Gabby's cup. "Either way, how long before your father sends someone to find you? He must know you'd come here."

"Thanks." She smiled at him when she accepted the drink.

Gabby had a sweet smile that made the cutest dimples appear.

After she had taken a long drink, she said, "If all went well, they won't know I'm gone until tomorrow. I was just going to e-mail my aunt to see what's going on. She lives in the other house on the gated property where I live. She helped me escape."

He sat in the armchair again. "Could e-mailing your aunt alert your father to where you are?"

"No." Gabby laid her cup on the coffee table. "We both use the same free e-mail account and write notes to each other but keep them in draft form. If you don't send an e-mail, it can never be traced."

Dani's face lit with surprise. "Really? I had no idea you could do that."

Gabby nodded. "It's how my father and I communicate, too. Technically on the grid, but not."

So that's how they stayed in touch. And how she'd never been seen with her father but remained a part of his life. But she'd just admitted she might have made an assumption about her dad. Maybe he wasn't the one who stole the statue. It could be her boss who was behind the theft and was planning to sell both pieces to a private investor himself. He could've already beaten them to the dig site. Either way, Gabby might be in danger if she showed up at the site alone. "What happens when your father's men come looking for you? What will they do if they find you?"

"They *will* find me eventually, I suppose. Then they'll force me to go home." Gabby sighed. "These few days of freedom without guards have been amazing."

The forlorn expression on her face killed him. "We'll go first thing in the morning. How far is the hike?"

"About three miles. The GPS on my phone should take us to the exact location. But I don't have snow gear, so I might have to risk going into town to get some before we go. My father's men, if they already know I'm gone, will be staking out the town for sure, so it's risky. But I need to get to the statue first."

Dani said, "I have boots and snow pants in the closet. You're welcome to use anything you find." Then she finished her drink. "But I'm beat, so you two need to take it into the other room now so I can go to sleep."

He wasn't looking forward to sharing the bed with a beautiful woman he couldn't make love to, but at least he'd know if she tried to sneak out. He was a light sleeper. "Sounds good. Ready to hit the hay, Red?"

"Okay. But no touching, Jake. I mean it." Gabby finished off her drink and then took all the cups to the kitchen.

While Gabby loaded the dishwasher, Dani whispered, "She's so sweet, Jake. And she trusts you. What will you do about her father if you cross paths? He's a dangerous, wanted man."

He nodded. "Gabby's problems are more urgent to me than her father's at this point. The Feds haven't been able to catch her father for years. He's wanted for money laundering and racketeering. But if I come in contact with Moretti, I have to detain him. It's my job to throw criminals with outstanding warrants in jail. You know that." He stood and went to the bedroom to get ready and tried not to think about Gabby's innocent Bambi eyes or her pretty smile. He didn't want to hurt her, either. He hoped Gabby's father kept his distance. That way he wouldn't have to make that decision.

The door to the bedroom stood open, so Gabby took that as an all-clear sign for her to enter. She didn't want to catch Jake undressing or anything. Well, she wouldn't mind just an innocent peek—he was a handsome man, after all. Built like a soccer player, with muscular legs and a strong chest.

Jake was lying on his back in bed with an ice pack over his forehead. His bare chest proved just how nicely developed it was, from what she could see above the blankets. Hopefully, he didn't sleep in the nude. That'd be too much temptation to bear.

After she got done in the bathroom, she circled to the empty side of the bed and quietly crawled under the covers. She propped herself against the headboard with her laptop and sat beside Jake. He smelled like toothpaste and temptation.

She needed to think about something else.

She logged in to the e-mail account she shared with her aunt Suzy and read the note her aunt had left for her.

Still quiet here. You okay?

Gabby replied:

> Yes. Going to look for the statue in the morning.
> No word from dad?

She switched over to her father's e-mail to see if he'd left any notes. The one drawback to communicating in draft e-mails was if the other person wasn't online, the communication went slowly. Although her aunt Suzy always checked the mail before she went to bed, so Gabby was hopeful she'd log in and wait up a bit to hear from her.

Her father hadn't written anything, so he must not know yet she was missing.

She switched back to her aunt's account. Suzy had left her a note. Now they could talk live. Gabby smiled as she read her beloved Italian aunt's broken English.

> No a peep from your father. But tomorrow be interesting when they figure out what you done.

Gabby typed:

> I know. Crossing fingers they won't find me at the site. Hopefully, I'll get the statue and can get right back to the museum with it.

> What? For you papa to steal again? You need better plan.

> Good point. Better think on that. Sweet dreams.

> You too, amore. Be safe.

> Will do.

Jake said, "You do need a better plan."

"Hey." She quickly slapped her laptop closed. "That's private."

"You're sitting right next to me. If you want privacy, go somewhere else. I told you I'm the curious sort."

"More like the bossy and nosy sort. How's the head?" She reached out and lifted the ice pack. "It's all kinds of icky colors. But the swelling doesn't look too bad now."

After she had replaced the ice pack, he said, "Thank you, Doctor. So how exactly did you slip away from all your bodyguards?"

She reached out and turned off the lamp beside her. Soft moonlight streaked in through the small openings in the blinds as she snuggled into her pillow and faced Jake. "Did you ever do that thing when you were a kid where you'd tell your mom you were spending the night at a friend's and then your friend would say she's spending the night at your house, and then you both stay out all night?" She hadn't been old enough to do that with her mom before she'd died, but she'd done similar things at boarding school.

Jake grunted. "I didn't have parents who gave a crap where I was at night, but I get the concept."

That tugged at her heart. "Why didn't they care?"

"They were out committing crimes themselves, most likely. Go on."

She hated the sadness in his eyes. "Well, my dad doesn't trust many people, but he trusts me. Maybe not so much after this, but then that's his own fault for stealing the statue. Anyway, he's terrible with computers. I often have to fix his for him."

"Wait." Jake held up a finger. "Earlier you said you and your father are never seen together."

"We aren't. My aunt and I are my father's only living relatives. To keep us both safe, we changed our names and live in a gated, guarded property that my dad owns through one of his corporations. He has a bunch of companies that look like other people own them. Anyway, his driver parks in the garage at my aunt's house when he comes to dinner on Sundays so no one ever sees my father. I sneak through our connecting backyards and join them for dinner."

"Really?" Jake's brows furrowed in confusion. "Every Sunday?"

"Yeah. If he's in town. Why does that surprise you? A lot of families do that."

"Huh. I just wouldn't think a guy like—"

"I know. My dad has a bad reputation, but he loves me. And I love him."

"Why?" Jake rolled over and faced her. "How can you love someone like that? Your mom and your brother died in retaliation for things he did, and you have to live with guards and a huge secret, and yet you can still love him?" Jake's voice had gotten louder by the second. "That makes no sense, Red!"

"Shhhh. You'll wake Dani." She laid a hand on his shoulder and rubbed it to calm him. "I understand how you feel. I had some of those same thoughts, too, of course. But as I got older, I came to terms with what my father is. He swears he's on the up-and-up now. And while I don't like what he used to do for a living—I know it was wrong—hating him isn't going to make anything better. Now, my mom, she was a good and kind person. I think that's why my father married her. He told me it was love at first sight for him. I think deep down he doesn't want to be like he is. But his grandfather and his father brought him into the business as a child, and by the time I was born he was in so deep, there was no turning back."

"But . . ."

She forged forward with her point. "Remember the Stockholm syndrome thing you mentioned earlier? It's probably not so different. My father treats me like a princess. He and my mom sent me to boarding school when I was young so I wouldn't be like my brother, who saw the money and decided it was easier to steal than go to college. My dad is so proud of me for earning my degrees and that I'll never be like him.

I think I represent the only thing that's good about him. Honest, Jake, I've never done anything like I did today, and I'll never do it again."

Jake blinked at her for a moment. "I can't decide if you're the most forgiving person I've ever met or the most naive, Gabby. I could never love a parent who committed crimes on a regular basis. That type deserves to be in jail, doing hard time, not given love."

"Are you talking about *your* parents now or my dad?" He was seriously upset. She was still rubbing his shoulder to soothe him. Interesting he hadn't seemed to mind, but she wasn't going to poke the angry bear any more than was necessary, so she slowly moved her hand and tucked it under her chin.

His jaw clenched. "My parents lost jobs, partied too much, and died when I was fourteen. During a bank robbery. They were too stupid to think about what would happen to my younger brother and me if they were both caught. Or killed. I'll never forgive them for abandoning us. I had to lie about my age and work on a ranch to support us."

So he *had been* a cowboy at one time anyway. Her gut had been right, there.

She scooted closer and whispered, "They were flawed people like my father is. And that's their problem, Jake. Not yours or mine. You can carry around hate for your imperfect parents that eats at you and makes you angry like this for the rest of your life, or you can decide they were just two losers who happened to be your parents. Your ultimate revenge is to be better than they could ever be. And look. We both are."

He ran a hand down his face. "I don't want to talk about this anymore. Finish your story. How'd you fool the guards?"

"You have a lot of things you don't want to talk about, don't you? Maybe if you talked about them more often, they wouldn't upset you so much."

"Thanks, Pollyanna. Still waiting."

"Fine. I don't know why my escaping fascinates you so much in the first place, but because I help my dad with his computers, I know all of his passwords. When he goes dark, he uses a particular e-mail account, so I just sent a message to the head of my security on his account, telling them that I was at his house in Florida. And that I'd be back Monday."

Jake's brow furrowed. "Where do you think your dad is right now?"

She shrugged. "No idea. But I'm sure he'll be screaming at me tomorrow loud enough to figure that out. He might even be here in New Mexico if he's the one who stole the statue." She flopped onto her back. "I hope he wasn't behind the theft and it was Dean, but that's not likely."

"It's tough to have to doubt your parents." Jake was quiet for a few minutes, then he whispered, "Are you afraid to have kids? Because of your father? Bad blood and all that? Worried they'd turn out like him?"

*He* clearly was. "No. I *really* want kids. I'd never let them turn out like my father. I'd also like a normal life. I'd give anything for it. Being free these past few days makes me want it even more. Maybe if I moved to a smaller town and changed my name again, I could pull it off. I'm seriously considering it."

"But your father would probably just find you again, right?"

"Probably. And dating to find a husband to have those kids with wouldn't be easy with bodyguards around. I couldn't even get loud in bed, or they'd come rushing in to make sure I'm not being strangled or something. So embarrassing."

Jake chuckled. "You're loud in bed as a rule, are you?"

"No. I just want the *option* to be loud." She turned in his direction again. His deep-blue eyes danced with amusement and lust. Talking about being loud in bed wasn't helping her stop thinking about his being half-naked beside her. "I haven't been with many guys since college because of my situation. How about you? Do you have a girlfriend?" If he said yes, it'd be so much easier to sleep beside him and keep her hands to herself. She'd never poach.

He shook his head. "Just ran the last one off a month ago. Evidently I'm not the best spouse or boyfriend."

"Maybe it's all that bottled-up anger? That and the flirting at every opportunity to cover it up." She'd bet it wasn't because he was lousy in the sack.

He rolled over and gave her his back. "Good night, Dr. Phil."

She laughed. "Good night, Jake. Sweet dreams."

"You don't say 'sweet dreams' to a full-grown man, Gabby." He mumbled, "Freakin' Pollyanna, I'm telling you."

"Fine. Happy nightmares."

She closed her eyes, puzzled that Jake hadn't flirted with her once since they'd been in bed. Dani had been right about Jake respecting her wishes, but Jake hadn't seemed to mind when she'd rubbed his shoulder. Or maybe he was so angry about his parents that he hadn't noticed.

Her first impression of Jake had been of someone fun, sexy, and flirty. But beneath all of that, despite being all those things, there was a pit of anger and pain. She'd always had a soft spot for wounded animals, and that's what Jake was.

He whispered, "Hey, Red? Since neither of us has had much sex lately, we could put the other out of their misery. You could be as loud as you want. Dani's a sound sleeper."

There it was. He couldn't go twenty minutes without flirting. "How sound?"

Jake turned over quickly, and it shook the whole bed. "Very. So was that a yes?"

"No." She moved closer, testing his boundaries. "I'm just asking because when I get really tired and have had a little too much to drink, I sometimes snore. And cuddle in my sleep."

Jake narrowed his eyes. "Dani told you about the touching thing, didn't she? That's how come you gave in so easily to sleeping with me. I knew something was up with that."

She moved a few inches closer and reached for his hand. "Yes. And I know you don't want to talk about it. So I won't ask." She gave his hand a squeeze and was just about to let it go when his grip tightened on hers.

"Maybe if I told you why I don't like to be touched, it'd make you understand why I can't love a criminal. And why you shouldn't, either." He sat up and laid her palm on the deep ridges and raised scars on his back.

In an eerily calm voice, he said, "Do you feel those? The guy my brother and I worked for after my parents died knew we weren't old enough to work. And he hated our father. He took advantage of our desperation by making me work harder and longer than anyone else. Luckily, Ben was much younger than me and mostly stayed out of the way by helping with the animals. I'd often have so much work I'd miss dinner and just land flat on my face into bed and fall sound asleep in the bunkhouse. But after my boss had his evening fifth of whiskey, sometimes he'd decide that maybe I hadn't worked hard enough, so he'd drag me out of my bunk, tie me to a pole, and whip me just because he was a sick bastard. I only put up with it because of my brother. I think that guy knew if he ever touched Ben, I'd kill him."

Tears stung her eyes. "Jake, I'm so sor—"

"Don't say you're sorry. It wasn't your fault. It was his. That's why to this day I don't sleep soundly, either. But my brother and I had nowhere else to go, Gabby. No one else would hire me in the small town I grew up in because I had despicable parents. It was assumed my brother and I must've been the same way, too. I saved all the money I could for a decent car and got my brother out of there the day I turned eighteen and could legally be his guardian. We moved to Albuquerque where no one knew us, and we started fresh. So, your little pep talk earlier about how carrying around hate for my parents will just eat at me doesn't help. They scarred me for life. And please stop crying. That just makes me feel like an even bigger shit for telling you this."

Tears dripped slowly down her cheeks. Jake had suffered from trauma like a soldier coming home from war. He'd had to fight to survive. She'd been given only the best in life. And had at least one good parent to emulate. Jake had figured out how to be good all on his own.

"I shouldn't have teased you. I'm sorry, Jake." She wiped her cheeks dry with the back of her hand. He needed her to man up.

"I don't know what made me tell you that. Maybe it's because you love your criminal dad, and I *hate* mine." He closed his eyes and pulled her against his chest. "I'd never upset you on purpose, Gabby."

He held her close as he settled them back under the covers. He gave her comfort when he was the one who deserved it the most.

She sucked up all her sad feelings for a good kid like Jake, who took care of his brother, and said, "I know you'd never upset me on purpose. It's in your eyes, remember? And I'm fine, Jake. Do you think that's the worst story I've ever heard? My guards are asses. They often brag about the horrible things they've done to people."

"Still. I know it's upsetting. We'll just agree to disagree on this one, okay?"

"Sure. But you don't have to hold me if it makes you uncomfortable."

"No. If you're going to snuggle in your sleep, I'd rather start out that way. Then I can fall asleep without anticipating it happening later."

"No thanks." She didn't want the temptation of being plastered against his hard body all night. She gave him a hug before she wiggled out of his embrace. "I was just teasing you about the snuggling. I've never spent the whole night with a man. It was never allowed."

Jake blinked at her. "But you've had sex before, right?"

"Of course. I'm just not supposed to get attached, because what's the point? Would you ever marry me knowing who my father is?"

"No." He tilted his head. "Would you ever marry a guy like me knowing what I just told you? I didn't tell Dani until after we were already married. I was afraid she wouldn't be with me if she knew the truth."

It was sad that Jake felt he had to hide his past. None of it was his fault.

She tapped fingers over her yawning lips. "How did you explain the scars on your back, then?"

"Motorcycle accident." He punched his pillow up and then laid his head down again.

"Yeah, that'd work, I guess." She got comfy on her side of the bed as she thought about his marriage question. "I can't say from a typical woman's perspective, but someone like *me* would be lucky to be able to marry a guy like you, Jake. I hope you meet the right girl soon. Night."

"Night."

Jake was quiet for a few minutes before he said, "If your father was in jail, getting his due, I might consider marrying a woman like you, Gabby."

She smiled. That was a kind thing to say to a person with a father like hers. "Happy nightmares, Jake."

"Sweet dreams, Polly."

She rolled away from him and sighed at the sadness that filled her for Jake. He'd had a childhood no one deserved. Hers had been a difficult one, but not even in the same realm as his. She loved her father, though, despite everything. And she wanted the chance to love a man the way her mother had loved her father, flaws and all. But she'd pick an honest man, never a criminal.

Maybe after she found the Son statue, she'd put her new identity plan into place. The odds it'd work were low, but she had to try. Even though it'd most likely mean never seeing her father or aunt again, it was time she had a life of her own.

# Chapter Five

A thump sounded, and Jake sat up straight in bed. He glanced beside him in the dimly moonlit room. Gabby was missing. He leaped out of bed and headed for the door, until a movement to his right made him change direction. Had Gabby's guards found her? He flung himself toward the person.

A feminine yelp sounded. Then something wet flew into his face. Gabby. They hit the plush carpeted floor with a muffled thud. Her tempting, hot body was plastered underneath him, while his face had landed between her full breasts. "You okay?" He wiped the water from his face.

"Yes." She blinked down at him in the stingy moonlight. "You scared me. What are you doing?"

"The better question is, what are *you* doing?" She was still braless. Not surprising since she was still in her pajamas. Not trying to escape.

"You were moaning in your sleep. I was getting you more pain pills. And for the record, I tried to wake you, but you just mumbled something and fell back to sleep."

What? He'd never slept that soundly. Must've been the head injury. "You sure you're okay?"

She nodded. "But you're kinda heavy."

She felt just right underneath him, but his pounding brain commanded him to roll off her. "Sorry. I thought your guards had found you. Then when I realized it was you, I assumed you were trying to make a run for it."

She stood and headed for the bathroom again. "I said I'd let you help me. I gave you my word I wouldn't run tonight. Jeez."

Yeah, if he had a dime for all the criminals who had lied . . . but Gabby wasn't like her father. "I know. I don't trust easily. Another of my bad traits."

She returned with another glass of water and the pills. "Here. Good night." She handed them over and then crawled over his side of the bed to hers.

He took the pills. "Are you mad?"

"Just tired." She had her back to him.

He'd probably upset her.

Was he actually feeling guilty for not trusting her? Why did he care what a woman who'd hit him over the head and had broken into Dani's cabin thought of him?

He placed the glass on the nightstand and then slipped into the bed beside her. Wrapping an arm around her waist, he pulled her closer. But not enough so that her back touched him. He might not wake again if she was mad enough to leave, so better to hang on to her. "I'm sorry, Gabby. I was sound asleep. I just reacted."

She grunted.

Yep. He'd annoyed her.

He leaned his mouth next to her ear. "Or, maybe I do have brain damage?"

"I'm starting to wonder if you had it before I hit you."

"Probably." He liked how she always had a quick comeback. "Thank you for the pills. That was nice of you."

She drew a deep breath, and then her shoulders slumped as if in resignation. "You're welcome. But I know your arm around me is just to be sure I won't slip out again. Therefore, I refuse to enjoy it."

She'd said she'd never spent the entire night with a man. He should make it nice for her. He moved a tad closer. "Is it okay if I enjoy it for both of us, then?"

"Please. Stop. Talking."

*God, I like her.*

"Shutting up now." He smiled and closed his eyes as he fell back into a deep slumber.

The next time he opened his eyes it was six thirty. The scents of coffee, eggs, and something cinnamon filled the air. He hoped Dani was making her famous rolls. They were the best. He glanced over his shoulder, and Red was gone again. What was up with how soundly he'd been sleeping?

Gabby's voice from the kitchen reassured him that his ward was still there, so he quickly showered and then dressed in warm clothes. When he joined the women in the kitchen, they were laughing and sipping coffee. "Good morning, ladies." He made his way to the cupboard for more pain meds. His head wasn't pounding, but the dull ache was annoying.

Both said, "Morning," in unison.

He glanced over Gabby's shoulder and read her computer screen. She was checking e-mail. "Busted yet?" he asked as he poured himself some coffee.

She nodded. "According to my father, I have two hours to tell him where I am, or he's coming after me personally."

He took a sip of some excellent coffee. "Did you ask him if he stole the statue? And kidnapped your boss?"

"No." Gabby glanced up at him. "I learned a long time ago not to ask my father about what he does. Less disappointment for me that way. Besides, he'd never tell me the truth if he had and make me an accessory to a crime."

Dani got up and fixed him a plate. When she handed it over, she poked him in the ribs. "You're an awful nosy *cowboy* this morning, Jake."

Code for back off or Gabby will figure out you're a cop. "I'm just a little worried about running into her father's men at the dig site. That's all."

Gabby slapped her laptop's lid shut. "That's why we need to hurry and get started. Thanks for breakfast, Dani. It was great. I'll just be a few minutes, Jake." She rose from the table and disappeared into the bedroom to get dressed.

He sat at the table and dug in. "Did she tell you anything I can use?"

Dani poured herself some more coffee and then slipped into a chair next to him. In a low voice, she said, "Her aunt had to come clean with the guards. They knew Gabby couldn't have done what she did on her own. They know she's in New Mexico and what car to look for. And Gabby checked with a colleague at work. Dean is still out on leave."

He nodded as he bit into a cinnamon roll. "So we still don't know if Dean is innocent in this."

"Or if he and her father are working together."

He finished the roll. "These are damn good, Dani."

"Thank you. They're Michael's favorite, too, so I keep the fixings here."

Of course, now they were *Michael's* favorites. Apparently, they had stopped being called *his* favorite after they'd divorced.

He lifted his fork to scoop up eggs but stopped. "Are Dean and her father working together? Do you know something?"

"I don't know if they're working together, just that Dean and her father are involved. Luca could've kidnapped Dean, but it's not clear. This was one of those annoying dreams where I only get pieces." She reached out and squeezed his hand. "You guys need to be careful, though, okay? Luca and his men aren't nice people. Luckily I know you can trust Gabby completely."

"I'm aware. Thank you." He was a cop, for God's sake. He knew whom he could trust and whom he couldn't. Red was as innocent and sweet as they came.

He swiped up some egg yolk with his toast. "Is my hunting rifle still on the top shelf in the closet?"

"Yep." Dani stood and started doing dishes. "And we have an ATV out in the shed you guys can use if you want."

"An ATV? When did you get that?"

"A few months ago." She opened a drawer and then tossed keys his way. "Michael's kids come occasionally. He bought it to entertain them, but I think he and I get just as much fun out of it. I love to take the girls on it. They squeal in fear while they beg to go faster."

Michael's kids adored Dani. She fit right in with them, making a complete happy family. It sent a pang of envy to his heart. He hated that. He wasn't the jealous type. "You're going to need a bigger cabin soon."

"We already have plans to add on two more bedrooms and a bath. They'll start next month if the weather holds. You're still welcome to use the cabin, but it could get noisy."

"Michael is really okay with me using this place?" Michael was a good guy, but they didn't enjoy each other's company on any level.

She turned and leaned against the counter. "He accepts that I'll always love you. As a brother. And I *think* he's finally recovered from the girls calling you Uncle Jake at Thanksgiving." She smirked.

Gabby came back all decked out and adorable in Dani's pink snow gear. Gabby must've overheard the conversation because she said, "You guys *are* really friendly for being divorced. It's nice to see that can actually happen."

He grunted. "That much pink isn't going to make it hard for your father's men to find you. Go change. We have an ATV now, so we'll only have to walk the last bit, most likely."

Dani said, "The pink is cuter, but I have some darker things, too."

Gabby looked down at herself. "Oh. Right. Didn't think about that. Be right back."

He shook his head. "Has she been living under a rock?"

"Essentially." Dani sat down at the table again. "She told me earlier how during college she wasn't allowed to live in the dorms. A guard, who she told people was her boyfriend, lived with her and walked her to all her classes. After she had graduated from college, her father would only let her work in the museum because it's guarded twenty-four seven, and if she agreed to drivers, and to live in one of his gated homes. She has a couple of work friends, but none outside the job. She had a few years while at boarding school to be like the other kids, but everything changed after her mom and brother were killed."

"That's on her father's head. But she loves him anyway. I don't get that." He stood and rinsed his plate off, then put it in the dishwasher. "Be careful on the drive home, okay?" He kissed her cheek. "And thanks for saving me, even though I didn't need it."

Dani's right brow arched. "You still need it." She patted his chest. "There's a big heart in there, if you'll just allow yourself to use it fully. Gabby needs you, Jake. And maybe it couldn't hurt to need her a little bit, too."

"I don't need anyone but myself." Besides, Gabby was going to hate him if he had to turn her father in. Rock. Hard place.

But he had a feeling Gabby might just be worth the trouble. She had good intentions. He liked that. And he liked *her*. So he'd focus on keeping her safe.

∾

Gabby hung on to Jake for dear life as he navigated the ATV over rocks and around low scrub and trees. The bright sun was out and melting what was left of the snow. Dani's black boots, knit hat, and gloves complemented by jeans and her own coat kept Gabby cozy and warm. And Jake was like a furnace plastered to her chest. It wasn't a hardship to feel his muscles shift as he drove them to the site, guided by her phone.

She needed to buy Jake a new phone because she'd smashed his to bits. His had been an older version, so she'd upgrade him to the latest and greatest. It was the least she could do for him. Especially because she was secretly relieved that he'd insisted on helping her get the statue. She wasn't sure she could outwit her father's men while searching for it alone. And the hunt for her had begun just a few hours ago.

Jake braked hard and then cut the engine.

He unstrapped his helmet and said, "We'd better walk the rest of the way. ATV noise is fairly common around here, but we don't want to get too close. If someone beat us to the site, we don't want to let them know we're here." He swung his leg off and hung his helmet on a nearby tree branch. Then he grabbed his rifle and his backpack.

She got off and shed her helmet, too. Then she reached for her bag that had what she'd need to dig. "If we accidentally run into my father's men, I know it will pain you to be quiet, but let me do the talking. Your life could depend on it."

Jake shook his head. "We aren't going to *accidentally* do anything. I was in the military and know how to sneak up on the enemy. You need to listen to me and do as I say. Or *your* life might depend on it."

"My father's men won't hurt me."

"What if it's Dean who's out there? And he's operating alone? I bet he'd shoot us in a heartbeat rather than go to jail for stealing the statue and map. Or, what if your father hired strangers who know what they're doing to dig that statue up and have no clue who you are? We don't know if we'll find dear old Dad or his minions, so you aren't safe, Red. Is that clear?"

"Perfectly." Interesting—Jake had been a cowboy and then went into the military. "But you don't have to be so bossy about it," she mumbled as she reached into her bag and pulled out her gun.

Jake's eyes grew wide. "Whoa, there, Red. What the hell is that? And do you actually know how to shoot it?"

"It's a nine-millimeter semiautomatic with a built-in silencer. It has a fifteen-round magazine. Pick a target."

"May I?" He held his hand out for the gun.

"Sure." She carefully handed it to him, the way she'd been taught.

"This looks like something out of a science fiction movie." He flipped the safety and aimed at a tree. "See that big knot on that trunk straight ahead?" He pulled the trigger, and a loud pop sounded. Jake didn't even flinch. Suppressors didn't really make guns silent like in the movies, and he hadn't been surprised by that. Which surprised her a bit.

He handed her the gun. "Can you hit that, too?"

She lifted it and aimed. "Above or below your shot?"

"Getting cocky, huh? Above."

She shot, flipped the safety, grabbed her things, and started walking toward the tree. Jake caught up and matched her long strides. As they got close, he said, "I'll be damned. You're good, Red. And that's some gun. Suppressors are illegal in some states. But then I guess your father knows all about that."

"Yeah. I grew up with guns lying around the house like knick-knacks. And was taught to shoot one as soon as I could handle the kick. How did *you* know about suppressors?" She tucked the gun into the waistband of her jeans at her back.

"Hello? Military?" He hitched up his backpack, pocketed the ATV's keys, and tucked his rifle in the crook of his arm, pointing down as a hunter would. "Let's roll."

She followed behind him. The sunshine was intense at the higher altitude, the light layer of snow just thick enough to cause resistance, and the air super thin. She huffed a little trying to keep up with him.

When he got too far ahead, he'd shorten his stride for her to catch up, but the man seemed to be in a bigger hurry than she was.

He finally slowed enough so that they could walk side by side. "Tell me about this statue we're after."

She sucked in enough air to talk and run-walk at the same time. "Are you familiar with the Inca of Peru?"

He sent her a smug look. "Ancient civilization wiped out by the Spaniards about four hundred years ago?"

"Yes." She smiled. It pleased her that he knew about the tribe that fascinated her. Maybe there was more to him than met the eye. "Then you might know that there were thirteen emperors according to most historians, the first seven the most important and well known. They were warriors, constantly attacking other nearby tribes. In the case of our statue, the son killed his own father for control of the tribe, stealing his father's statue, too. That's where the curse part comes in. Legend says the first time they were paired together, the Inca were invaded by the Spaniards shortly after that. The second time, World War One happened."

"Please. That's just a coincidence." Jake checked her phone to gauge their location. "Was our guy one of the important seven?"

"No. He was further down the road, right before their civilization was left in tatters by the coming of the Spaniards. The value of all that stolen booty was so great, it altered the whole European economic system. It caused a recession."

"Probably what they deserved for stealing all that in the first place."

She chuckled. "You're really big on right and wrong, aren't you?"

"Yes. You need to remember that, if we run into your father's men or Dean."

"What's that supposed to mean?" She lengthened her stride again to keep up.

"Nothing. I'm curious about something, Red. How did you manage to date in college if everyone thought you had a live-in boyfriend?"

Dani must've told him about that. "There's the nosy chatterbox I've come to expect. I thought I'd left him back at the cabin."

Jake abruptly stopped. "You did for the most part. This is serious stuff we're doing, Red. You're not from around here, but disturbing Native ancient burial grounds is not a laughing matter. We could go to jail if caught. But I have to admit, this is a clever place to hide the statue. No one would ever mess with it here." He started walking again.

She caught up. "I'm aware of the consequences. That's why I was trying to do things legally, until my father made it impossible to save the statue unless I went rogue. It's the only way the world will ever see that artifact in a museum again. Once in private hands, it'll be gone for good."

She tripped on a root, but he caught her before she fell flat on her face. He said, "It means that much to you? To risk so much for a statue?"

"Yes." She regained her footing, but he still held her arm. She'd have thought he'd let it go like it'd been on fire. "It's important for generations to learn from previous ones. And museums play an important role in that. I think it's sad that it's so hard to obtain funding for preservation of international treasures."

Jake nodded. "I see your point. Now, back to the dating question." He finally released his grip on her arm.

He was like a dog after a bone when he wanted to know something. "I'd meet guys at parties, and if they called, go out with them. I'd tell them that I'd just broken up with my boyfriend, but he hadn't moved out yet so we couldn't go to my place. If after some time I liked a guy, I'd sleep with him. If things got too serious, I'd tell him I'd reconciled with my ex. You'd be surprised how many guys just wanted to have sex and didn't care I had a boyfriend at home."

Jake laughed. "Men are dogs. Didn't any of your guards ever try to hit on you?"

"No. My father made sure all my guards knew I was off-limits. Why are you so interested in my sex life?"

He slowed his pace and checked the phone again. "Maybe I'm trying to figure out how dangerous it'd be to my health if you decided you wanted to have sex with me. We're almost there. Keep your voice down."

The only sound emitted from her mouth was "Ack." The man threw her off-balance like no one else. No men had ever told her they were weighing their options in case she decided to sleep with *them*.

She cleared her throat and tried again. "News flash. Not every woman instantly falls for your charm and good looks." Although *she* had, surely not *all* women would.

"Ouch. So that's a no to sex?" He crouched down behind some rocks and dug binoculars out of his bag.

She wouldn't mind having sex with him, but he was never serious about anything. He was probably just teasing her, as usual. Besides, sex with Jake would most likely be a bad idea.

She whispered, "You can be so annoying, Jake."

He smiled as he peered through the binoculars. As if it made him happy he'd flustered her. "But in a sexy way, right?"

"Stop." She shook her head in exasperation. "What do you see?"

"You said you missed the nosy chatterbox. I aim to please."

She leaned closer, trying to see what he was seeing. "I didn't say I missed it. Can I have those please?" She held her hand out for the binoculars.

"It was implied." He handed the glasses over. "Looks like we're not the first ones here. The snow's all beat up and muddy. Bet we're too late."

Dammit!

Had her father gotten the statue first?

# Chapter Six

As he peered through high-powered field glasses, Jake asked, "Why do you want to go out there, Red? Judging by all the footprints, surely the statue is gone." After spotting disturbed snow at the dig site, he checked the perimeter again to see if they were alone.

He'd asked Gabby about her escape from home and her sex life to see how closely her father guarded her. Looked like she'd been locked down tight. Her guards could be lurking nearby, so they'd have to stay on their toes. He couldn't let the thugs get her back before she got her statue.

Gabby picked up her phone from the rock where he'd laid it. "I need to see if whoever was snooping around here dug in the right place."

It was a risk, but she was right. They didn't know who the footprints belonged to. It could've even been someone from the tribal police patrolling the area now that they'd seen the request to dig. "Okay. Follow me and stay close."

He scanned the trees that surrounded the clearing one more time and then slowly set out across the lightly snow-covered ground.

Gabby laid her hand on his back as she followed behind. It bugged him a little. But she'd been nervously chewing on her bottom lip a moment ago, so he'd let it pass. She usually had bodyguards who protected her 24–7. And she worked in a dusty, guarded museum all day, so she was clearly out of her element. Like a lamb facing a lion. Of course, she was afraid.

He glanced over his shoulder to check behind them, and Gabby held her gun at the ready. "Put that away before you accidentally shoot me."

"But"—she stopped walking—"what if I need to use it?"

When he stared her down, she reluctantly tucked her gun back where it was before.

"Thank you." He started walking again. "Do you think you could shoot someone with that if you have to?"

"No. I was just planning to shoot *near* someone. I'd never be able to actually shoot a person."

He dug deep for patience. She'd violated the first rule of gun ownership. "What are the chances your guards know that about you?"

She caught up, and her hand returned to the same spot on his back, right between his shoulder blades. "About a hundred percent. Are there bears out here, too?"

"Probably still hibernating. Don't take that gun out unless you're prepared to shoot someone. Or a bear. Promise me, Red."

"Okay. I think I could shoot a bear. Maybe."

They approached the dig site. It didn't look like anything as special as ancient burial grounds to him. Just a bunch of muddy snow and an empty hole in the ground. "Looks like we're too late."

Gabby grabbed her phone from her pocket and checked the GPS location. "This is the spot, but seriously, how accurate could someone have been back then? It was buried during World War Two. They didn't have the technology we do now."

He continued to scan the trees and cliffs while she got down on her hands and knees and pulled out her shovel. He asked, "Did the map say how deep it was buried?"

"Yes, thankfully, but the blowing winds here and the sandy soil could affect that." She glanced at the empty hole beside her. "That's about the right depth according to what we'd guessed, darn it. But the man who buried it had used the length of his footsteps from that big rock over there to measure, so it could still be here. That's not an accurate way to mark the spot."

He examined the lone hole. "If someone hadn't found it, wouldn't they be doing exactly what you're doing? Digging more holes?"

Gabby stopped her frantic digging and glanced up at him. "You're right." She tossed her shovel aside and stood. "Crap!"

He continued to watch for signs of movement while she stomped around the site, muttering to herself. She grew quiet midmutter and crouched to the ground.

"Jake, look at this. It makes no sense."

He took one last look around and then knelt beside her. She had a piece of broken pottery in her hand. "What? This place is supposed to be full of artifacts, right?"

She shook her head. "Not from this tribe. This shard is from a tribe in the Dakotas. See this distinctive pattern? We have a ton of pieces like this back in the lab right now."

Back in the lab? Where she and Dean both worked? "Gabby, if someone kidnapped you and told you to find the statue, what would you do when you got here?"

She frowned. "It depends on my motivation. If I wanted the statue, I'd dig it up. If I didn't want to find it, I'd dig in the wrong place and say the information must be wrong. We had strong theories about two other burial grounds before the cartographer told us it was here."

He nodded. "What if you didn't want to find the statue but knew someone with some archaeology knowledge was going to be right behind you? Someone who could save it?"

Her eyes went wide. "Dean must've left this here for me to find." She scanned the distance between the hole and where she'd found the pottery. "I wonder if the placement of the shard is another clue." She laid the chunk of pottery down and ran to her bag. She pulled out some string, a metal spike, and a pen. "Could you hold this right here, please?"

He leaned down and held the string while she unraveled it. She lined up the spike with the big rock and then ran it into the ground. She marked the string with the pen and then wrapped it around the spike. Then she stood back to take a picture with her cell. "He might be telling me it's right here, while he leads his kidnappers on a wild-goose chase." She leaned down and started digging.

She dug hard and fast. He wanted to help, but her guards knew she'd visit the site, so he needed to stay alert. The shortest distance to cover if anyone started shooting was a good fifty-yard run across open terrain. It made him itchy.

"Gabby, I imagine your dad owns a plane or two, right?"

She nodded. "One for domestic and one for overseas. Why?" She continued to dig at a breakneck pace. The anticipation on her face was amusing. Like a kid opening a present at Christmastime.

"How early this morning do you think your aunt confessed?"

"She said they woke her up. And she's a pretty early riser usually, so I'd guess it was before six thirty." Gabby flipped to the other side of the hole she was working on and widened it.

"How long does it take to reach the airport where your dad keeps his planes from your house?"

She stopped and laid her hands on her knees. "Oh, you're calculating how soon they could be here. I already did that this morning. They're two hours ahead, which doesn't help, but I figure my guards couldn't be here before twelve thirty or one o'clock."

"That soon." He glanced toward the trees again. All clear. "Maybe you should dye your hair a different color. Red is too easy to spot."

"Good idea." She looked up and smiled. "I've had red hair long enough. Maybe I'll go blonde."

"Blonde or red haired, you'll always be pretty."

She shook her head and started digging again. "Making myself more attractive to you isn't the point, Jake. Brown or black hair is more common and would probably blend better."

He smiled. *Now* she was thinking more like a cop.

He laid a hand over his heart. "No matter what color you choose, it'd be impossible for me to be any more attracted to you than I already am." He wasn't joking about that. Gabby was pretty inside and out.

"I've timed it, and you are evidently incapable of being serious for more than twenty minutes. Did you know that?"

"I think it's more like nineteen minutes." He shrugged. "Because that last thing I said was stone-cold true. Hurry please."

Her head whipped up, and she stared at him with those big brown eyes for a few seconds, before she blushed and went back to her digging.

Why had he confessed that? He was an idiot, that's why. If and when she found out he was a cop, she'd probably run as fast as she could the opposite way. But he wanted to know more about Gabby. And to help her find her statues that she so vehemently wanted to protect. He admired her determination.

Something about her hit him square in the heart.

Gabby dug for another half hour before she gave in and stopped. Disappointed, and with burning muscles, she looked up at Jake, who had been keeping watch. "I don't think it's here. But the pottery being here means Dean most likely has been. I need to figure out why Dean left this shard for me to find."

Jake glanced her way. "By the number of footprints and variance in sizes, I think it's safe to say one or two big men and a smaller one were here. Or it could be a woman's footprints. How big a guy is Dean?"

She packed her things. "He's short, skinny, and a perv. Dean comes up to about here on me." She held her hand just below her collarbone.

"He says the best thing about working with me is the view. He's very dedicated to archaeology, and the ongoing study of my chest." She hated that about her boss. It was creepy. *He* was creepy.

Jake's right brow spiked. "Want me to smack him around some if we find him? Explain what workplace sexual harassment is all about?"

"No. My workplace choices are limited by my father. I hate Dean's behavior but put up with it only because I want to have a job." She laughed. "Besides, I'm used to being around annoying men at work *and* home. Hence my ability to put up with you." She flung her bag over her shoulder. "Let's go back to the cabin and look at my notes. I need to figure out this clue."

As they jogged for tree cover, Jake said, "So on a scale of one to ten, Dean being a ten, how much do I annoy you?"

"See? That you'd even ask that question shows your inability to take anything seriously. And ten, by the way. But not always in a bad way."

Once they were a few feet into the woods, and out of sight from the dig site, they slowed their pace. Jake asked, "Tell me how I annoy you in good ways, and I'll try to keep that up." His mischievous smile made it hard to actually be annoyed with him sometimes.

"You can't help the good ways because you were born with them." She shifted the heavy bag to her other shoulder. "It's science really. People are attracted to certain attributes and tend to have 'types.' You happen to be my type on many levels. I once read a study that showed people are naturally attracted to specific features in others that we secretly desire for ourselves. But attraction is simply physical desire and can be controlled."

"You're just my type, too, Red. And we're both single. Why would we want to control our desire for each other?" Jake's forehead crumpled in question. "I've been thinking about how much I want to kiss you since yesterday."

"Because we can't always have what we want. It's best to accept that and not dwell." She glanced his way again, and her heart sighed. She wanted to kiss him, too. She hadn't ever been so confusingly attracted to a man. But it'd be a mistake to get too involved with Jake, because she feared he was the kind of man she could fall in love with. He'd said flat out he could never marry a woman like her if her father weren't in jail. And that wasn't a trade she'd ever make—love for her father's freedom.

He was quiet for all of fifteen seconds while he pondered her words. "What about living in the moment and enjoying the pleasure while we can?"

She shook her head. "Have you ever gone to the freezer, just dying for your favorite ice cream, but when you open the container there's only one bite left? You have to decide if you'd be satisfied with just that one bite or if it's better not to have taken that small taste and be left yearning for more the rest of the evening."

Jake's fingers slipped around her arm to stop her. "Who only has one flavor of ice cream in their freezer? I'd just eat that bite and then open the other container sitting right beside it."

Was he talking about actual ice cream, or was that supposed to be a metaphor? "Is that what you do with women? Move on to the next flavor rather than committing to your favorite?"

"What? No." After a quick look around, he shook off his backpack and gently laid down his gun. "I was talking about the ice cream in my freezer, not hypothetical women. I take my ice cream pretty damned seriously, Red."

Oh, so he really did have more than one flavor of ice cream in his freezer at a time? She always finished the container before she bought more. Maybe that had been a bad example.

She dropped her bag at her feet. "So I've finally found the one thing you take seriously?" She crossed her arms.

"I take a lot of things seriously." He leaned closer and whispered, "Especially sexy scientists." His mouth was less than an inch from hers. "Can I stop controlling my desire now and kiss you?"

She stared into his turquoise-tinted eyes, debating if she should let him. Warning bells sounded in her head, reminding her it might be like that ice cream and leave her wanting more. "Fine, you weak man."

His smiling lips met hers and silenced the annoying thoughts screaming at her. She wanted to know what it'd be like, because she took first kisses seriously. If it were bad, it'd make it easier to ignore her attraction to him.

He used just enough pressure to show how much he wanted her, but with enough restraint to keep it on a G-rated level. For a sweet kiss, it packed a punch. It made her want to feel what the R-rated version would be like.

She slipped her arms around his neck and pressed her whole body against his. Forget her ice-cream analogy. What could one little taste hurt?

When his whole body stiffened, it reminded her that he needed to be the aggressor of touch, so she released him and abruptly ended the kiss just when it'd been getting good. She took a step back. "I'm sorry. I forgot about the touching thing."

"No worries." He reached out and pulled her against him again. "It sometimes takes me aback for a moment, that's all. Now, where were we?" He leaned down and pressed his mouth to hers, this time just the way she wanted. Lots of heat, tongue, and lust. It sent a shot of tingling thrill up her spine, and her stomach into a swooping free fall.

She snuggled closer and ran her hands through his thick hair as he changed the angle of the kiss. He turned up the intensity and shot her to the next level, making every part of her body feel alive. Heat spiraled through her veins, burning her up, filling her with need, sending her heart rate into overdrive.

His hand slipped down her side, cupped her breast, and gently kneaded, making her back arch into his hand for more. Dammit. He wasn't just a good kisser. Jake was an *extraordinarily* good one.

He slowly ended the kiss and then whispered, "See? Living in the moment isn't so bad." He tapped her butt playfully and then picked up all their things and started walking back to the ATV.

What? He'd laid a kiss like that on her and then just walked away? Hadn't it meant anything to him?

She stood with her hands on her hips, confused. What was her next move? Tell him that had been a mistake that'd never happen again, or, just like that last bite of ice cream, now she wanted more.

She jogged to catch up. Maybe he wasn't as impressed with the kiss as she had been. Maybe he kissed women all the time and then walked away. It was probably all a game to him.

She finally caught up and matched his long strides, still huffing a bit from the altitude. "Can I ask you a question, Jake?"

"Yep." He turned and met her gaze. "Why do you look so upset?"

"Because." She gulped in another deep breath. "I'm not like you. I don't have one-night stands and then walk away whistling. I have to have some feelings for someone before I sleep with them. Or kiss them."

"You're making incorrect assumptions." He swung his free arm around her shoulder and pulled her close. "I don't do one-night stands, either. I've always wanted the whole deal, kids, and a minivan. Dani didn't."

That made her heart do a little backflip before she remembered he'd never want to be with her. "Do you still love Dani?"

He nodded. "I'll always love her on some level. Maybe that's why I'm not boyfriend material, like the last woman I dated declared so loudly."

Love her on some level? So not actively in love with her? "Or, maybe it's because you lack kissing manners and walk away like it never happened?" Especially a hot kiss like they'd just shared. She wasn't asking for a ring, for goodness' sake—just some common respect.

"Kissing manners?" He laughed. "It's cold out here, and the woods could be full of your father's men. No time to linger for safety purposes.

I didn't just walk away proud of myself for stealing a kiss, and I certainly wasn't whistling. But if you'd rather I didn't kiss you again, just say the word."

She glanced at his face to see if he was serious for a change. "I didn't say that. I was just . . ." What? Did she want him to kiss her again? "Clarifying. That's all." He hadn't removed his arm from her shoulder, and that surprised her.

"Then I'll clarify." He gave her a quick squeeze. "I'm attracted to you because of the kindness in your heart, all the amazing things that lurk in that exceptional brain, and because you're beautiful inside and out. But you're going back to DC soon. I have a life here. If we slept together, I think we'd both enjoy it. But it can't be anything more than that. So, I'll leave that decision up to you."

"I'll have to think about it." She'd never had a man talk to her about having sex like it'd be a business deal. But, he was right, and she respected his honesty. "How long does your vacation last? Before you have to go back to work, whatever that is?"

He sighed. "I'm off for the rest of the month. If you wanted to keep me company, no matter what you decide about the sex, I'd like that very much. I'm not good at being alone."

That tugged at her heart. "I'm an expert at being alone. Maybe I can teach you a thing or two about it in return for your help with the statue?"

"That's a deal." His grin wasn't his usual naughty one. It seemed . . . sincere for a change.

They'd arrived at the ATV, so he let his arm fall away from her shoulder, to strap on their things. It left her feeling cold again.

She picked up Dani's helmet from the seat and put it on. She'd find the statue first, assuming someone else hadn't, and then decide what to do. Maybe lying low and spending a month with Jake was just what she needed to help her decide the plan for the rest of her life.

But should she sleep with Jake? Her hormones voted yes, but her brain was pulling the emergency brake. Spouting off little reminders of how they'd never be together long term. And that it'd only be sex. Reiterating that the goal was to find a nice guy to settle down with. That she could get hurt. Best to stay friends.

There was something special about Jake she couldn't quite put her finger on. Would it be worth the risks her brain was warning her of to find out what that was?

Jake fired up the engine, so she wrapped her arms around his waist and snuggled close to stay warm. His sexy, hard muscles plastered against her chest made it difficult for the logical side of her brain to think. Only feel. And it felt just right to be with Jake.

# Chapter Seven

Jake paced back and forth in the cabin as time seemed to crawl by. He was going nuts, wanting to jump in and help Gabby figure out her clue, but she'd used that slightly snooty British accent to politely decline his offer.

Maybe he should come clean with her and explain that he could help because solving clues was what he did for a living. She was bound to figure out he was a cop sooner or later. Especially if she googled Dani or Annalisa. But then what if she bolted? Nope, better to maintain cover as long as he could.

So, rather than sitting around, he'd help her with her disguise. Gabby's bodyguards should be arriving soon according to her calculations, and they'd be bound to stop at the grocery store to ask about her. There weren't that many businesses in town.

He called out to Gabby, who was at the kitchen table, frowning at her computer screen. "I'm going to run to the store for that hair dye. What color did you decide on?" While there, he'd ask if anyone had seen any bodybuilding-size strangers.

Maybe he'd get a big box of condoms, too. His blood had already been humming for Gabby, but after that kiss, it roared in his ears. He hoped to God she decided to sleep with him. If not, then maybe she'd consider hanging out with him as just friends. He genuinely liked her.

She glanced up from the screen and blinked. "Um. Light brown, I guess. Two boxes for my long hair. And could you pick up some tea? I'm not a coffee drinker."

Not surprising, being raised in England. "Sure. Anything else?" He shrugged into his coat.

"No, thanks." She shook her head and went back to studying copies of maps, searching for clues about the shard they'd found. And what its placement could mean. She'd been at it for over an hour and didn't appear to be making any progress deciphering Dean's hidden message.

"Oh, wait." Gabby jumped up and disappeared into the bedroom. A moment later she came back with a fistful of cash. "Please buy yourself a new phone. Is this enough for the best one they have?"

She'd handed him eighteen hundred bucks. He handed most of it back. "Plenty. Thanks. Don't leave the cabin without me, Red." He was going to have to stop calling her Red after she dyed her hair. He'd miss that.

She lifted a hand in absent acknowledgment and then got back to work.

He shook his head in wonder at her determination over a hunk of gold that purportedly could start wars. What a load of BS. But to each their own.

He climbed into his truck and drove down the lane to the highway. The bright sun had taken care of most of the remaining snow, leaving slick mud behind. After he had hit the pavement, he headed for the store. It'd be the first place he'd stop if he were looking for someone in the small town, or possibly the gas station. He'd ask around there next.

When he arrived at the edge of the tiny town, the aroma of roasting green chile wafting from his favorite little burger place cemented his plans for the way home. He'd pick up a couple of green-chile cheeseburgers for lunch. Red needed to experience one of the best things New Mexico was known for—its kick-ass chile.

He parked and then made his way into the store, hoping it was Shelly's day off. He wasn't in the mood to spar with the kid.

A quick glance showed he was the only customer, and Shelly's father was manning the register for a change. Maybe it was his lucky day.

George lifted a hand. "Hey, Detective. Heard you were in town. Can I help you find anything? Like an ice pack for your face? What happened?"

Jake joined the owner at the counter. "It's nothing. ATV accident. The tree looks worse than me. What I really need is a new phone." He scanned the display behind George. There were only four, so he picked the newest version of what he had before. "That one will do."

"Betcha. You want the same number?"

"Yep." Jake left George to do the setup and download all his contacts from the cloud.

Weaving through the aisles, he grabbed tea for Gabby, and then he looked for women's hair stuff. He finally found the small display. There were three shades of brown. Which one should he choose?

"I doubt the tree looks worse than your face. Thinking of dying that pretty blond hair of yours, Detective?" Shelly said from behind him.

He couldn't say it wasn't for him and possibly blow Gabby's whereabouts. Shelly couldn't be trusted if Gabby's guards asked questions. What the hell else would someone do with hair dye? Stain something? His brain quickly ran through possibilities.

"Nope. Not for me. This is for . . . the carpet. I spilled something in the bedroom. Dani is a freak about stains, so I hope this fixes it." He really had stained her carpet the last time he'd been there.

Shelly frowned. "We have carpet cleaner over there by the rental machines. You should try that first." Her face softened, and she leaned closer. "I could come up and show you how it all works if you'd like." Her hand landed on his forearm, and she gave a squeeze. It made him cringe. "I'm good at using machines in bedrooms. You might enjoy watching."

*Seriously?*

He slowly moved her hand off his arm and whispered, "Talking to men like that could get you in a world of trouble you aren't ready for, kid."

"Whatever." Shelly shrugged and stepped back, out of his personal space. "But you should use the stain remover first. That dye might make an even bigger mess."

"Dani already tried to get the stain out. This is the last resort before I have to buy her a new carpet." He grabbed two boxes of the lightest of the brown dyes. How was he going to buy condoms with Shelly dogging him?

Shelly said, "Oh. I saw Dani drive through town yesterday. Did she and Michael have a fight? You two getting back together?"

"You never know." He couldn't help his grin. There was his excuse to buy condoms. Dani would kill him if she knew he'd implied that, but he'd take his chances.

"Either way, I think Michael is hot, too. Dani has good taste in men." Shelly popped her gum.

"That's debatable." He walked down the next aisle toward the condoms. Maybe if she thought he and Dani were getting back together, Shelly would give up on him and go back to work. "I should probably be prepared in case Dani changes her mind about taking me back, right?"

He knelt and picked up the largest box of condoms they had so he wouldn't have to endure any more of Shelly's torture for the rest of the month.

She leaned over his shoulder. "If you want to please a woman, those aren't the best we've got."

*Dammit! You're the last person I want to have a condom discussion with.*

Dropping everything and driving a hundred miles to the next town for the condoms tempted him. But then, he wanted to give Gabby all the pleasure he could, if she decided to let him do that. "Which would you suggest?" He refused to think about how barely legal Shelly had gained her condom knowledge.

"Those." She pointed with a bubble-gum-pink-tipped fingernail. "The ridges can make a lousy lover into an amazing one. Well, along with massive amounts of alcohol. Wes—"

"Stop. Fine. Sold." He grabbed three of the little boxes and jogged to the front counter, hoping Shelly wouldn't continue her lesson about amazing lovers in front of her father.

He laid all the boxes on the counter and pulled out his wallet. "How's the phone coming?"

George, tall and thin as a scarecrow, beamed a big smile as he handed it over. "All set. Wait. Let me get the box for it, too." He turned around and stuffed instructions back into a cardboard cell phone box.

The first thing Jake planned to do with his new cell was to set up a tracking app on Gabby's phone to keep an extra eye on her. "Anything interesting going on in town? I want to stave off boredom for the next few weeks."

Shelly whispered, "You wouldn't be bored with me and those condoms."

He gave her the side eye and then smiled at George, waiting to hear the local gossip. If Gabby's guards had been in, the owner would spill. The people in the small resort town lived for gossip, drama, and interesting strangers.

George shook his head as he finished ringing up Jake's purchases. "February's our slow time. Most are waiting for the weather to warm a bit. We'll have another rush come spring break for the kids."

So Gabby's men probably hadn't arrived yet. "Well, I'm here for the rest of the month. And you have my number now, so if you decide you'd like to show me the secret to fly-fishing, I'd be grateful."

Shelly piped up, "I can show you anytime you'd—"

"Go finish stocking those shelves, Shelly. Now!" George barked. He shook his head as she walked away. "Kids. Tough to get a full day's work out of 'em. All they want to do is mess with their phones, texting their friends, right?"

Probably hooking up with guys. But it wasn't Jake's place to tell. "Yep. See you around."

"I'll give you a holler next week if I can squeeze out some fishing time. Say hi to Dani for me."

"Will do." The bell above the glass doors tinkled, and two guys the size of linebackers walked in. They were dressed in jeans and leather jackets and had matching scowls.

Gabby's guards? If so, Gabby had been spot-on in her travel-time calculations. She had the oddest combination of smarts and naivety he'd ever seen.

Maybe he'd linger over the magazines for just a bit.

The men approached George. After he greeted them with his usual smile, they pulled out a picture. The bigger one asked, "Have you seen this woman? She's driving a Jeep."

Of course, that got Shelly's attention, and she ran to the front counter, not to be left out of the action.

George took the picture, studied it, and then shook his head. "Nope. Haven't seen her."

Shelly snatched the photo from her father. "Red hair. Yeah. I saw a woman in a Wrangler drive by a few days ago. It could've been her." She looked up at Brute Number One. "Why? What's she done?"

Brute Number Two took the picture back. "Nothing. We're her brothers, and we're worried about her. Which way was she headed?"

Shelly pointed. "Up the mountain. Hey, Jake. Your cabin is that way. Have you seen this woman?"

*Shelly and her big freakin' mouth.*

He strolled over with his bag of tea, hair dye, and condoms, and accepted the picture of Gabby. He pretended to study it closely. "Nope.

Not out my way. The only tracks in the snow I've seen have been mine and Dani's." He handed the picture back while studying the goons. Both brown on brown, early thirties, one six-two, the other just under six feet, the shorter one two twenty, the other two fifty. Both all muscle, the short one had a scar above his eyebrow. "But I think I saw a Jeep with a redhead heading south just a few minutes ago. I was behind it at the stop light." He pointed out the window. There was only one stop light, and it was right outside. The highway ran through the middle of town, so no one could drive through without passing in front of the store.

The men nodded their thanks and hurried out the door.

Were they the same men who'd been at the dig site? Why send out a new contingent if Gabby's father already had people in New Mexico? Or was Dean working on his own? But then, why leave Gabby a clue? It didn't make sense.

He'd have to ask Gabby how her security worked.

George and Shelly stood beside Jake at the plate glass window, watching the SUV pull out of the parking lot. Shelly said, "Those guys gave me the creeps."

George nodded. "Yep. Up to no good, those two. Good riddance. What do you think, Detective?"

"If they come back, be sure to text me. But don't call me 'Detective' in front of them, okay? Better if they don't know I'm a cop." He plastered on a smile. "Have a good day."

He hurried out to his truck and tossed the bag onto the passenger seat beside him. The men were headed for the next town a hundred miles away, it was after one o'clock, and he still needed that burger.

∽

The sound of boots stomping on the front porch made Gabby glance up from her laptop. Her hand slipped closer to her gun, just in case.

But she doubted her father's men would take the time to clean off their boots. They never had at home.

The key scraped in the lock, and then the door swung open to reveal a grinning Jake. He looked like a kid with a big secret he couldn't wait to tell. It made her smile. "Hey there."

"Hey back. I have some news, but not until you taste this." Jake tossed a plastic grocery bag onto the counter, then laid a white paper sack in front of her with the words "Burger Barn" and lots of small grease stains. It wafted the lovely aroma of cheeseburger, fries, and something fruity yet smoky.

"You brought us lunch?"

"Not just lunch, Red. I brought you an unforgettable culinary experience. According to the banner on the wall inside the Burger Barn, women have claimed these green-chile cheeseburgers are better than sex. Not any women I've slept with, mind you."

"Of course not." She dug into the bag and pulled out two wrapped burgers and a large bag of fries. "I imagine you think you rank up there with chocolate truffles and soufflés, right?"

He placed two glasses of water and the bottle of ketchup on the table before he sat down. "No food can compare with the way I make love to a woman. Now, there are a few dessert foods I like to use on occasion to give my partner an optimal experience—"

"Stop." She unwrapped her burger and then squirted ketchup onto the paper. "I'd like to get through my entrée before I think about dessert."

"You should always have dessert in mind. The anticipation is half the fun." He hitched his brows before he took a big bite and moaned as he chewed.

She'd been contemplating having sex with him ever since he'd kissed her. But she hadn't made up her mind, so she'd keep their conversation food related.

After a big bite, a slow-growing heat filled her mouth. The burger was juicy, the cheese melty, but the chile had a sweet, smoky, and hot flavor that made the taste buds on her tongue stand up and dance. It was the best burger she'd ever had.

Gabby opened her bun to investigate where the awesome combination of flavors had come from. "Wow! Avocados, too? This actually *might* be better than sex."

Jake grinned as he swiped his fry through her ketchup. "Gives me a goal to beat, now doesn't it." He locked gazes with her as he slowly stuck the fry into his mouth.

She had to look away. Other parts of her were beginning to dance, too. "Seriously, Jake? You can't even eat a burger without making it about sex?"

"I didn't start it. The banner did." He paused for a long drink of water. "I saw your bodyguards in town."

"Way to save the important stuff for last. What did they look like?" Her stomach cramped as she laid her burger down.

Jake rattled off features. With each new fact, her stomach grew tighter. When he mentioned the scar, that did it. "Was it jagged and right here?" She pointed to her forehead, right above her brow.

He nodded as he continued to eat, seemingly unaffected. Most people were scared of her bodyguards. Why wasn't Jake?

"That's most likely Sal and Louie." As great as the burger was, she wasn't sure she could continue eating with her stomach tied up in knots. "The one with the scar, Louie, usually drives me to work."

Jake wiped his chin, then asked, "How many people usually guard you?"

"Eight. Always in sets of two. They work different shifts." And they couldn't possibly know she was in this particular cabin, so she picked up her burger again and forced herself to eat. She needed to eat when she could in case they had to make a sudden run for it.

"What does Louie do all day while you work?" He swiped more fries through the last of her ketchup.

She grabbed the bottle and squirted out more ketchup for him on his paper wrapper and then replaced what he'd stolen from hers. "I have no idea what he does, but he's never far away. I text him when I need a ride, and he's always there by the time I get out to the steps. Can you imagine how bored those guys must get?"

"I bet." Jake nodded as he chewed. "So what are the chances they were already here? And are the ones who left the prints at the dig site?"

"None." Shaking her head, she grabbed some more fries before Jake could eat them all. "My security detail only guards me and my aunt. Have forever. They never get transferred to other duties like my father's other security teams, so fewer people know about our existence."

"They told the people in the store they were your brothers, and they were worried about you."

"Most of my guards have been with me since college and aren't much older than me, so that makes sense. I've only had to ask my dad to replace one of them over the years because he was too mean. My father does most anything I ask of him."

"Except let you have a life." Jake finished off his burger and then the rest of the fries.

He was right about that. What was the point of living if it had to always be like a caged animal? It made her even more determined to make a permanent change. After she found the statue.

She quickly finished off her lunch so she could get back to the hunt. "That was the best burger I've ever had. Thank you. Did you get the hair dye?"

"Yep. It's in the bag over there." He pointed to the sack on the counter.

She threw their lunch paper away and then opened the bag. Just as her hand dived inside, Jake called out, "Wait. Some of that is . . ."

Too late. Her hand drew out a box of ribbed condoms. She peeked inside the bag and found two other boxes, along with a cell phone box, tea, and her boxes of dye. She studied the condom box, intrigued by the claims it made to satisfy women. She hadn't agreed to sleep with him. Maybe Jake planned to satisfy all the single women in town. He certainly had enough condoms for the job.

Before she could comment, Jake was beside her, tugging the box and bag from her hands. "Clearly, I'm an optimistic man." He dug out the dye and handed it over. "Why don't you go transform yourself? Then after, maybe you could fill me in on what you've figured out about the clue? I have a few ideas . . ."

Jake dragged her toward the bedroom while babbling about the shard. It made her smile. He was trying to change the subject because he was embarrassed. She didn't think Jake got embarrassed about anything. "I didn't get to finish reading about how those fancy condoms will give me orgasms at a whole new height of pleasure. But wait! Are you actually a gigolo like you suggested yesterday? Are those for your clients? Maybe that's why you haven't mentioned what you do for a living now?"

"I'm not a gigolo." He stopped in his tracks and ran a hand down his face. "What I am is someone on a mandatory leave from a very stressful job, and I don't want to talk about it because it's embarrassing, okay?"

The sudden sadness in his eyes was real. He seemed to be telling the truth about that much, at least.

She placed her hand on his stubbly cheek, and he flinched only a little. "Bottling up all these things inside isn't good for you, Jake. Talking about them might help." She leaned closer and gave him a quick kiss. "Thanks for the fancy condoms. They might make the decision to sleep with you an easier one. If only for experimentation and curiosity's sake." She gave his cheek a quick tap and then headed for the bathroom with her dye, eager to see anything close to her natural hair color for the first time in twelve years. But if they had to go back out to the site, or other places, would the new color be enough to buy her the time she needed now that her bodyguards were close on her tail?

After she'd combed the dye through her hair and wrapped her head in the plastic bag for heat retention, she waited twenty minutes like the box instructed. When the time was up, she stepped into the steamy shower, eager to see the transformation.

After a few minutes, the water finally ran clear instead of a murky brown, so she turned off the tap and wrapped herself in two fluffy white towels. She stepped out of the shower, still worked up about finding the statue before her bodyguards found her, and the price she'd pay because of it.

She wiped a circle in the foggy bathroom mirror with her hand. Then she freed her hair from its towel and rubbed most of the moisture away. When she was done, she blinked at her reflection.

A younger version of her mother stared back at her. Emotion clogged her throat as she studied her image. All the love for her mother came rushing back. It was like being hit in the gut with a wrecking ball. She looked so different, and yet the same. Older, maybe, but in a good way.

Would Jake think so?

She shook her head. Who cared what Jake thought? She was probably just a convenient female, one who would scratch his itch before he moved on and went back to whatever job he'd been banned from. Speaking of that, in all the confusion she hadn't thought to google him. Feeling like an idiot, she lifted her phone and started to type in his name but then stopped. She called out, "Jake? What's your last name?" He'd never mentioned it. But he was once married to Dani Botelli, so it shouldn't be too hard to figure out. It'd be interesting to see if he would lie to her about his name or tell her the truth.

He appeared in the bathroom doorway, and his jaw dropped. "Damn, Red. You look amazing."

Well, that answered the question of whether he thought she still looked good, at least. She shouldn't enjoy the little burst of relief the hungry expression on his face brought her, but she was a little hungry for him, too. But back to business. "I can't sleep with a guy if I don't know his last name. I need to google you." She lifted her chin, trying to look indignant while standing before Jake in just a towel. Maybe she should have rethought the outfit choice.

He stepped closer and tucked stray locks of hair behind her ear. The light brush of his fingertips made her shiver. "It's Morris. And if you do that, you'll see I'm a cop. A detective, actually. But I was stripped of my badge and gun the other day, so I'm without a job at the moment."

A cop?

Her knees buckled so hard her hand flew to the counter to hold herself up.

Holy crap. She'd told him things about her father she'd never told anyone. She'd trusted Jake enough to do that.

But he'd just been playing her.

# Chapter Eight

Gabby suddenly paled and then swayed. Jake feared she'd pass out, so he grasped her by the arms to keep her from falling.

"Listen to me, Gabby. I just want to help you. I don't have a badge. I can't use police resources. So I'm as much a private citizen as you are right now."

"You lied to me, Jake." She shook her head and struggled to slip from his hold on her. "Does my Jeep work?"

"No. But I can fix it." Her color had come back, along with the anger filling her eyes, so he let her go. Sick to his stomach she might pack up and leave. "I never lied to you."

She spat out, "Holding back the truth is the same as lying!"

Not when he had a duty to be sure what her role was in the theft of the statue, but she wouldn't want to hear that. He stepped back and let her slip around him as she gathered up her things. "Where will you go?"

"As far away from *you* as I can."

"Your father's men are here. Dani said Dean is involved, but she wasn't sure to what level. How are you going to do this alone?"

"I'll figure it out." The tears forming in her eyes killed him.

She jogged to the kitchen and grabbed her laptop, then came back into the bedroom and stuffed it into her duffel bag. She pointed to the door. "Can I have some privacy please?"

She was still dressed in that towel, looking sexier than hell. "Fine. But I hope you'll reconsider. I just want to keep you safe and out of harm's way." He slowly walked out to the living room and sat on the couch.

He couldn't let her go. She was an innocent. She had no idea how much danger she could be in. What if Dean had bad intentions? She didn't like the guy, but she trusted him because he'd left her the shard. Maybe the shard had been a trap of some sort. He called out, "Don't trust Dean. Okay?"

Gabby reappeared, dressed in jeans and all packed up. Her new hair color looked even better now that it'd dried some. She'd gone from beautiful to stunning.

"I can take care of myself, Jake."

He wished that were true. "You're welcome to any food you'll need. But if your plan is to break into another cabin, I'd advise against that. We all pay an off-duty deputy to check them out once a week. You just got lucky with your timing here."

She huffed out a breath and grabbed her shard from the kitchen table. "I'll just have to think of something else, then, I guess." She jammed the pottery into a side pocket of her bag.

Like what? She was out of options with her father's men on her heels. He didn't want her to be caught and dragged back to her former restrictive life. Especially without the statues she cared about so much. "Take my truck. At least it'll give you a fighting chance. Those guys asked about your Jeep earlier."

She stopped stuffing bags of potato chips into her duffel and blinked at him. "You'd let me take your truck?"

He shrugged. "I trust you to get it back to me. Dani trusts you, too. We can load the ATV in the back if you'd like. But leave me your keys. In case I have to go to town for something."

She crossed her arms. "What's to stop you from calling your police buddies and telling them I stole your truck?"

"What's been stopping me from calling my buddies and telling them that you broke into Dani's cabin, hit me over the head, and held me hostage?" He didn't want to have to worry about her out there on her own. But he didn't want to make good on his earlier threat, when he'd told her he'd either help her or he'd turn her in. He'd never turn her in, so why upset her even more?

She sank into a chair at the table. "I need to think this through for a minute."

Gabby needed more than a minute, and he'd let her have it. He rose to grab a beer while she decided whether to walk out on him, like all the other women in his life had.

Where had that thought come from? She wasn't walking out on him. She was going after a damn statue. "I'd rather you let me help you. But if you're still determined to forge out on your own, I could call a friend who rents out his cabin from time to time. It's just up the road from here." He didn't want her sleeping in a vehicle. That could be dangerous for a woman alone in the boonies.

She dropped her head into her hands and moaned. "If I were going to do that, I might as well stay here. All you'd have to do is tell the sheriff where to arrest me."

He took a long swig from his beer. "If you still don't trust me, then your best bet is to shoot me with that fancy gun of yours. I'd be out of the way, and no one would be the wiser for weeks."

She lifted her head. "You know I'd never shoot you. But it's tempting to hit you. Just once."

"I already gave you one free lick, Red." He pointed to his bruised face. "You said I had kind eyes, remember? And that you trusted Dani and me. Listen to your gut. It hasn't been wrong yet as far as I can tell."

She studied her clenched hands, as her shoulders slumped. "Being a cop, don't you have to turn me in for what I've done?"

"If you'd hit someone else, maybe. You're lucky it was just me you clobbered on the head. I won't call the police unless I think your life is in danger. Don't make me do that." He got up from the couch and then knelt at her feet. "Look at me, please."

When she lifted her gaze, it was filled with fury and defeat. "What?"

He took her hands in his. She had long, graceful fingers and soft palms. "I honestly care about what happens to you, Gabby. Let me help you with the clue. I'm a detective. It's what I do."

Before she could answer, his cell chimed in his pocket. He reluctantly let go of her warm hands and swiped the screen as he sat in the chair beside her.

Gabby glanced at the screen, and then her eyes grew wide. "Why would a Sheriff Martinez be calling you if you're banned from duty?"

"He's local." Dammit. This wasn't going to help her trust him again.

Panic and adrenaline made her hands shake so hard she clenched them together to still them. Had he lied about not calling the police, too? It was one thing to make her own mistakes, but when they could compromise her father's freedom, that took Jake being a cop to a whole new level.

Sure, she'd lied to the world about her identity, but her life span depended on a lie. Jake's lie was a deliberate cover-up. He asked numerous questions about her father, surely digging for ways to arrest him. Every cop knew her father was on the most-wanted lists for money laundering and racketeering charges. Trumped-up charges according to her father. He'd avoided arrest for years.

Would it do her any good to run? She'd probably either run right into Sal's and Louie's arms or be arrested. Both felt like the same thing—a prison sentence.

Jake poked the "Speaker" button and laid the phone on the table between them. "This is Morris."

The cop said, "Hey, buddy. Heard you'll be here for a few weeks?"

Jake's forehead creased in annoyance. "Yeah. Taking a little break."

Not a break he'd wanted, clearly. Jake seemed to be telling the truth about that part. He'd said to trust her gut, but she was so hurt that he'd lied to her she couldn't find it in her to forgive Jake. She'd trusted *him*, dammit.

The sheriff said, "George is worried about a couple of guys you all saw earlier. They're at the diner now. But you know how he can be."

"Yeah." Jake beamed a relieved smile her way. "But this time I think he's right. They might be worth watching. If I see them around, I'll give you a shout."

"Appreciate it. Let's grab a beer this weekend. Catch up."

"Sounds like a plan. I'll call you. See ya round, Rich."

"Yep." The call disconnected.

Jake met her steady stare. "See? I didn't turn you in."

Relief cooled her temper a bit, but what would she do? What could she do? It was cold enough at night that she needed some place warm to stay. Staying a few cabins away could work, but only if she trusted him not to call the cops.

He was right. He'd had plenty of chances to turn her in if he'd wanted to. Was he helping her because he was bored? Or had he been trying to get information about her father?

Rather, how much had he tricked her into telling him after he and Dani confessed to knowing her father's true identity? Was the story about his parents even true, or had he made it up to gain her sympathy? To make her explain why she loved her criminal father? Maybe those scars had really come from a motorcycle accident. But then, he wasn't faking the part about not wanting to be touched. That was real.

What exactly had she told Jake about her father? Nothing specific. Just that her dad had many homes, owned businesses under different names—all things the cops probably already knew or suspected. That he had planes, but those had been owned under different corporate names for years, too.

Dammit. There was one thing she shouldn't have said. The weekly Sunday dinner revelation was something the cops couldn't have known. If they could figure out which house was hers, it'd be too easy to catch him with that information. Those dinners would have to end. A wave of sadness squeezed her heart. She loved the little bit of time she had with her father.

Worse, Jake and Dani knew who she was. If they told anyone, her father's enemies would find her and kill her, just like her mom and brother. It probably meant getting a new degree in something and starting over in a new town. Or sticking with her father and living like her aunt, with nothing to do all day but shop online and watch television. What kind of life was that? She loved archaeology. It was the only reason she got out of bed every day.

Everything was a mess. If she still wanted to find the statue, she could use a borrowed cabin, but what was the point of that? She'd be able to hide easier with Jake if that deputy guard came knocking at the door to check on things. Her only choices were to call it quits and go home without the statue, or let Jake help her. It pissed her off.

He said, "I can see those wheels turning inside, Gabby. What are you thinking? Are you going to let me help you or not?"

It was hard to look at him because she was so . . . disappointed in him. That's what it was. She had actually seen herself with him. At least for the month he'd invited her to stay. She'd never felt more comfortable yet at the same time more challenged by a man before. Jake pushed just the right buttons, or at times annoyed her enough to become the bolder person she'd envisioned being.

Just one more kick in the teeth, like the rest of life. But before she threw in the towel and started over, whether on her own or with her father's help, she was damn well going to find those statues. It was probably the last thing she'd ever be able to do for the archaeology world. She didn't have anything left to lose. Why not go all in? She could probably do it without that traitor's help. "Any chance I could convince you to let me find the statues alone but stay here at night until I do?"

"Nope." He shook his head. "You heard what Dani said. You're going to need my help. She'd seen something that indicated you're going to be in danger."

"Then I'm thinking I have no choice but to let you help me. But I have one condition, Jake, that I won't compromise on."

His right brow quirked. "What's that?"

"No more questions about my past life, or my father. Is that clear? Once I decide to talk to him, I'm going to tell him I'm with a cop so he stays away. And I'm sleeping on the couch from here on out."

Jake's jaw clenched, but he nodded. "Fair enough. But no worries if you ever change your mind about the couch . . ."

She studied his eyes, looking past the man flirting with her as usual, and searched for the truth in them. "So, you still want to help me?" She certainly wasn't getting anywhere on her own. She had no idea why Dean would've left that shard for her. She'd looked at it from every angle and was out of ideas.

"Yep. Let's get busy with the clue Dean left. Let me get you a cup of tea." He stood and filled the teapot with water.

That he'd still help her, even knowing her father was off-limits, made her feel a little better about working with him. And the sooner they found the statue, if they weren't too late, the sooner she'd be able to decide what to do with the rest of her life. Besides, because he knew who she was, it was safer to work with him, keep him close, until she had to disappear forever.

She grabbed her laptop and the notes she'd brought along from the backpack at her feet. Then she checked her e-mail while Jake's back was to her. She wanted to see how mad her father was.

She quickly scanned the messages that he'd left in the draft mailbox, each angrier than the next, proving her father was losing patience with her. And he was worried for her safety. She hated for him to worry about her.

I'm safe. Extra so, because I'm with a cop. So please don't come after me yourself as promised. I'll be home in a few days if all goes as planned.

She held her breath and waited for her father's response. Maybe she'd be lucky and he wouldn't be online.

What the hell do you mean you're with a cop? I know you're in New Mexico looking for that damn statue. Your aunt told us the whole story. Are you in trouble?

She couldn't catch a break.

No trouble. Just enjoying the company of a handsome man. Be back in a few days. Sooner, if you'd call off my guards and let me find the statue in peace.

A lead ball formed in her stomach again as she waited for his reply.

Not happening. Dean's reneging on our deal. Other people might be involved now. He's on a flight to London this morning, probably to sell your precious statue. To thieves, Gabby, who will kill to get what they want. Don't get in the middle of my war, sweetheart. Call me so we can talk.

That was the last thing she wanted to do. Let him talk her out of doing what she needed to do.

Can't right now. I'll write tomorrow. XOXOXO

She quickly logged off.

Crap. That confirmed Dean was involved for sure. But by choice or by force? Dean didn't know who he was dealing with. Messing with her dad could be a big mistake. Or, maybe Dean wasn't cooperating with her dad to save the statue from ending up in the wrong hands. That might make sense, too. Either way, Jake might be right. Dean could be dangerous now.

Jake rumbled around the kitchen while she waited for her computer to load her cataloging software. "So was that story about your parents and brother true, Jake? Or was that just to get me to spill intimate details about my father?"

Jake slid a steaming cup of tea in front of her. "All true. My brother joined the military right out of high school instead of going to college as I wanted him to. I did my time, got out, and became a cop. He keeps re-upping for combat duty because he hasn't got anyone or anything else to come home to."

"Except you. Doesn't that count?"

Jake grunted, then grabbed milk and sugar. He placed them in front of her. "I was strict with him when he was a kid. Even sent him to military school while I served in the army. Didn't want him to turn out like our parents. I've asked him to come home. He's done more than his share for our country. But he still thinks I'm just a bossy SOB and keeps his distance."

Despite her anger, the pain in Jake's eyes made her heart ache for him again. His brother was the only family he had. "You *are* a bossy SOB. Maybe you should try a different tactic. With him . . . and me."

He smiled and sat beside her. "Maybe I get a little overprotective of people and ideals I care about." He laid his hand over hers and gave it a quick squeeze.

She moved her hand away from his and laid it on her keyboard. "Big words for a man who withheld pertinent information. And has me backed into a corner, and who won't let me out."

"You make it sound like I'm holding you hostage instead of protecting you. And I've never told you a lie, Gabby. I swear. Sometimes being a cop means I hold the truth close to my vest until I get the lay of the land. You could've been stealing the statue for yourself. I had to get to the bottom of it before I let on who I was. I knew you'd figure that out soon enough. So, can we call a truce please?"

Sipping her tea, she pondered his words. His defense made a little sense. Dani said he was trustworthy. And he'd been a perfect gentleman in bed the night before. He'd even asked her permission before he'd kissed her. She appreciated that in a man. And he was a cop, for goodness' sake—someone who took upholding the law seriously. For everyone. It totally explained his strict right-and-wrong attitude.

She still felt a little silly for not thinking to google him sooner. But a million things had happened in the last twenty-four hours, and googling Jake had been the least of her worries. Until she'd seriously considered sleeping with him, which was totally off the table now. "Fine. But only if you promise you'll never lie or keep the truth from me again, Jake."

He closed his eyes and finished off the rest of his beer. When he opened them, he said, "Deal. But Gabby, please understand that it's my duty to uphold the law. That includes arresting people with outstanding warrants."

She couldn't bear the idea of her dad living the rest of his life behind bars. "I told my father about you. So, that isn't going to happen, but something interesting has. My father said that Dean left for London this morning, most likely to sell the statue, and disregarded a deal they had. Dean might be dealing with dangerous thieves now. And that I needed to stay out of their war. I think the stakes just got higher." Now she was glad to have someone trained like Jake on her team. She was a match for her father, not real criminals who'd actually hurt her.

But that didn't mean she'd fall for his charm again. No way.

She was tougher than that—she hoped.

# Chapter Nine

Jake focused on pictures of Native pots on Gabby's computer screen as he and Gabby sat at the kitchen table in the cabin, relieved she'd seemed to have softened toward him a fraction.

She held up the shard. "The pattern on this piece and the type of clay tell all. New Mexico's dirt has a different texture and hue. Even if I mistook the pattern, because it's broken, the composition proves it'd never be found here. Dean had to have left it for me to find. Or, it could have fallen out of his bag when he grabbed for a tool, I suppose."

He said, "Let's go over the possibilities. Dean left the piece there to let you know he'd been there. But what good would that do? Could it be a clue for where they went? Possibly to reunite the statues if they have them both? Your father said he and Dean had a deal. What kind would they make?"

She shook her head. "I don't know. I've tried to think of all the angles, but nothing is making sense." Gabby turned and finally looked into his eyes. She'd been avoiding his gaze ever since he revealed he was a cop. Maybe it was progress.

He studied the rows of numbers and the diagrams on the screen again. "Then let's start from the beginning. Where did these shards in your office come from? Did someone on your team find them? If so, was there something significant that happened at that particular dig?"

"No. Dean's brother, Will, acquired them from a private collection. Will is wealthy and likes to dabble. He'd bought them and then donated them to our museum."

Jake stood to pace. "Would Will be interested in the two statues for himself?"

"I don't think so." Gabby's forehead crumpled. "The last time we had a date we went to dinner. Over dessert, he told me how much he hates that so many treasures are lost to the world in private collections."

*You have a boyfriend? Then why did you let that amazing kiss in the woods happen?*

"How often do you see Will? And what happened after this dinner filled with sexy archaeology talk?"

"We've dated a few times in the past six months. And after the last one, I went home, and he went back to his hotel." Her gaze quickly snapped from his to her computer screen. "Is that relevant, or are you just being nosy again?"

"Both." Her cheeks were turning red. He loved how easy it was to make her blush. But that she'd dated the guy who was responsible for the shard had some possibilities. "Why did he stay at a hotel instead of his brother's house? And did Will take you somewhere nice?"

*I want to be the guy taking you to nice dinners.*

"Yes. Will asked the concierge for the name of the nicest restaurant in Georgetown. Because he's considerate that way." She busied herself scrolling through pictures of pots. "And Will stayed at a hotel because he was attending a medical conference there. Dean was away in New York for business."

He leaned his face in front of hers and whispered, "Will had to have known his brother was going to be out of town. I bet Will picked that conference as an excuse to have a fancy dinner with *you*. He even paid the huge bill, didn't he?"

"I didn't say he paid. That's pure conjecture on your part."

He stared deeply into her doe eyes. "Oh, he paid. And you like him. It's written all over your face. Why didn't you sleep with him?"

*Please say because you like him only as a friend.*

She rolled her eyes. "I told you. I'm not a one-night-stand kind of woman. And Will attended the conference because his hospital in Denver was thinking of getting a new piece of equipment the sponsors were selling. Any other questions, Detective?"

"More of an observation." He leaned closer, so close her breath played across his lips. He wanted to kiss her, to wipe away any thoughts of Will, but she was still angry with him. "I think you want Will, but you're going to make him court you, like a gentleman."

*Please say I'm wrong.*

"A gentleman is something you're clearly not." She placed her hand on his cheek and slowly moved his face away from hers. "Don't you need another beer or something?"

"Good idea." He plastered on a fake smile as he headed for the fridge, a little hurt by her comment. He flirted a lot, but he was a gentleman, dammit. Maybe he should've just told her he'd like a chance to take her to nice dinners, too.

Then something rang a bell. "Did you say Lover Boy is from Denver?"

"He's not—yes. Why?"

"Colorado is only a few hour's drive away, that's why." Jake raced back to take his seat beside Gabby. "What if Dean told his brother where the statue was? Will could've driven here and dug it up before anyone else could get here. Maybe Will left the shard to clue you in that he had it? Maybe he didn't like what his brother was up to, if he really believed what he told you at dinner."

"Maybe. He and his brother are all the family either has. I get the impression Will loves Dean but doesn't like him very much sometimes."

Jake's gut told him they were finally on the right track. "You said Dean took emergency leave a few days before the Father statue went missing from the museum. So, let's make the assumption that Dean had agreed to steal the Father statue from your museum for your dad. Or helped your father steal it. Then Dean changed alliances for the Son statue buried here. What if the new buyer flew with Dean out here to look for the Son statue? Did you have more than one dig site in mind if the first wasn't the right one?"

"Yes. Because Dean wasn't convinced the cartographer could be that accurate and had lined out a few other possibilities. If we didn't find the statue at the expected site, we needed to be ready with more funding to search multiple sites while we had permission to dig." She tapped some keys on her laptop. "I have them all mapped out in red." She pointed to three places, all within a five-mile radius.

"Your father said Dean only got on the flight to London this morning. If his brother has the statue, what have Dean and his bad buddies been doing the past few days?"

She shook her head. "I don't know, because surely Dean would dig in the most likely spot first."

Jake held up a finger. "If he wanted to find it. Maybe he's buying time for something. Like making a better deal now if he has both statues. What if Dean and whoever was with him found the hole empty, just like we did, because Will got to it first? Meanwhile, Dean's shopping for the highest bidder, while keeping the people he's with on the fence until he figures it all out. Dean switched alliances once with your father. He'd surely do it again. If he's a greedy bastard."

"This is starting to finally make sense, Jake." Anticipation and joy shone in her eyes, replacing the anger at him they'd held before.

But then her face fell. "Wait. What if all of this is true? What if they found the empty hole and decided they don't need Dean anymore?"

That had crossed his mind as soon as she'd mentioned the deal going south with her dad.

He rubbed the back of his neck as he ran everything around in his head. Dean was playing a dangerous game.

Gabby said, "Wait. Maybe Will isn't involved. What if Dean dug up the statue but left the shard so I'd help him. Because he's figured out he's in over his head? And if that's true, it'd be my fault if I don't help him and he's killed, Jake."

"Hang on." He held up a hand. "We're just throwing around possibilities here. We still don't know what we're dealing with yet. What we do know is that your father told you to stay out of his war, so that would imply it's ongoing. Dean might have one or both statues. Otherwise, what war would there be?"

~

Gabby's stomach ached as she sat at the kitchen table, still pondering all the angles. Jake went to the fridge and grabbed a soda. Evidently, he was done playing the laid-back beer-drinking guy on vacation and decided to take things seriously for a change. He said, "Any way I look at this, Dean's probably in trouble. You should e-mail your dad. Get more information."

Even though she didn't care for Dean, she had to do the decent thing by him. He could die if he crossed the wrong people. "Okay. I'll talk to my father."

Jake sat beside her again. "Will he tell you the truth?"

"Hopefully." She picked up her laptop and moved to the living room so Jake wouldn't see her log-in password. She'd agreed to trust him but not to make it easy for him to arrest her father.

> Hey, Dad. I need you to promise me you'll do all you can to be sure Dean doesn't get hurt, okay?

While she waited for his reply, she glanced over the lid of her laptop and found Jake studying her intently. Where had the fun, flirty Jake suddenly gone? The one who'd made her knees weak when he'd kissed her. She met his gaze and asked, "Was our kiss in the woods real? Or was that a cop doing his job, to see what my motives were?"

He blinked at her for a moment, as if taken aback. "Of course it was real. No one could fake something that great."

*Yeah, it'd been a whopper of a kiss.*

Her father finally replied.

> The only way I'd agree to that is if you get your butt home!

Would he keep his word if she returned home?

> Do you know how Dean is involved?

Gabby chewed her bottom lip as she waited for her father's reply.

> Dean's big mouth got the attention of the wrong people. That's why I don't want you in the middle of this, sweetheart.

"Jake. Come see this, please." When he flopped beside her, she turned the screen so he could see it. "What should I write back?"

As Jake recited, she typed.

> Dean left me a clue so I'd help him.

Her father quickly replied.

> What kind of clue?

Jake said, "Tell him it's something you recognized from the lab. Then ask who your father had planned to sell the statue to in London."

She sent him a sideways glare. "So you can have someone there to arrest him? Not happening." But she typed in the first part about the clue.

Jake gave her shoulder a soft bump with his. "A guy has to try, right?" His usual smile was back. It made her stomach do that annoying flip.

Her father wrote back:

> You're in no position to help him now. He's dug his own grave by dealing out of both sides of his mouth. Let me handle this my own way.

His own way? That didn't sound like it could be anything good. She hated to pull out the guilt card, but she had to protect Dean. She'd never forgive herself if he got hurt because of his dealings with her father.

> You promised me you were done with this lifestyle after we lost Mom and Bobby. And that you'd never lie to me again. I trusted you. So please do the right thing now. Don't let Dean get hurt. And return the Father statue to my desk, please. Love and miss you.

She quickly slapped her laptop closed.

Jake, whose shoulder was still warming hers, whispered, "You really *do* love him, don't you? Even though you think he stole the thing closest to your heart?"

"Can't help it." Standing, because sitting so close to him was stirring things up that had no business being stirred, she went back to the kitchen table and sat down. "What do we do now?"

He joined her at the table. "Call Dean's brother. Lie. Scare the crap out of him. Do whatever it takes to get him to reveal Dean's plan."

Studying her nails—badly in need of a manicure—so she wouldn't have to look into Jake's bluer than blue eyes, she said, "I like Will. He's nothing like his brother. And I don't want to lie and scare the crap out of him."

Jake's large hand gave hers a soft squeeze. "If he loves his brother like you do your father, and he knows anything, then he'll spill to be sure Dean is safe. Or he'll want to know if his brother is in danger. If it came down to it, your father would keep you safe at any cost, right?"

She sighed. "Yes." Her father *had* done everything in his power to keep her safe. And he'd kept his word about giving up his old lifestyle, until the other day, as far as she'd known. She'd been so disheartened since the statue disappeared. It made it hard for her to believe a hundred percent that her dad would keep Dean safe. She hated doubting her father, but what choice did she have? "Okay. But maybe there won't have to be any lying involved."

Jake tilted her chin up with his index finger. Then his lips morphed into his signature naughty but cute smile again. "People's lives might depend on a lie. And why I'd kept the part about me being a cop to myself until I knew everyone's motives."

While she stared into his earnest eyes, she nodded. He was right. As much as she hated to lie about anything, Dean's life might depend on it. And, technically, Jake hadn't been wrong to withhold his identity from her until he knew the truth about her situation. But in her rule book, once he'd found out who her father was, he should've come clean.

She dialed Will's number and hit "Send." It rang eight times before she got voice mail. "Hey, Will. It's Gabby. Can you call me please at this new number? It's important. Bye." She hung up. "Hopefully, he'll call back soon. Let me see if I can book a private plane to London tonight under your name."

"Book a plane? Wait a minute." Jake's face scrunched into a frown.

"Don't worry about the cost. I've never had to spend a dime of my paychecks, so it's on me. I can't go commercial, or my father will find out."

"It's not the plane. What do you propose we could do in London that a mobster with bad-guy friends can't?"

"Haven't figured it all out yet." When he kept staring at her, as if waiting for something logical to come out of her mouth, she shrugged. "I have a rich former schoolmate there who loves Incan artifacts. He might be able to help us." She wasn't going to tell Jake about the idea she'd been toying with ever since her father had uttered the word "London." She could disappear for good in Europe. It might be easier than trying to hide in the States. She'd lived in London for years and loved it.

"So we're doing this purely for Dean's safety?" He crossed his arms, his belief obviously wavering.

Damn him for being a suspicious cop.

"Please, Jake? It's better than waiting for my bodyguards to find me and drag me back to DC. I just want to do this one last thing—find those statues and put them back where they belong—before I have to go back to my jail cell at home." If her escape plan didn't work and she had to go back home, that is.

He closed his eyes and ran a hand down his face. "Okay. But if I'm getting my ass on a plane for that long, then I'm calling Dani to see if we can borrow her mother's plane. Because it's really big. At least I know I can pace around on that one if I have to."

Pace off nerves? "Are you afraid to fly?"

He shook his head. "Claustrophobic. I was under fire. Had to hide in a tiny cave for days until my buddies saved me. Don't want to talk about it."

Another off-topic subject. How many more did Jake have? "Okay, using Annalisa's plane would be awesome. Let me send an e-mail to my friend, Charlie. Have him do some snooping to see if there's any buzz about selling the statues." She wouldn't tell Jake that Charlie was a dealer in illegal artifacts, as well as legitimate ones. She hated that he did that, but they'd been best friends at university and were still e-mail buddies, so she'd told him to never discuss that part of his business with her.

She opened up her laptop, and another message in the draft box appeared on her screen. She hadn't logged off the e-mail account, just closed her lid. Her father must've responded, so she tapped the box and the message appeared.

> I didn't steal anything. I saw on the news that the Father statue we'd just been discussing turned up missing from your museum, so I had one of my men ask around. Dean told my man he had two statues to sell, but you had just told me there was one still buried in New Mexico. My guy made an offer to buy them to force Dean's hand. Then I sent a guy to check out the burial site. Word is, the matching Son statue wasn't in the hole when Dean got there. Something else was buried there instead.

> What did they find?

> A box with a letter and a map of London showing where the Son statue is now. And who are the two most knowledgeable people when it comes to those damn statues? You and Dean. That's why I got involved. It's unclear if Dean has been kidnapped or just working with some dangerous black-market dealers. But you have knowledge they might want. Dean has dragged you into this mess, so if the dealers don't kill him, I will if anything happens to you. Nobody hurts my daughter and lives to tell.

Her heart leaped in happiness as she reread the message, to be sure it said what she thought it did. "My dad didn't steal the Father statue, Jake!"

He slid his chair closer and read the screen. "That's good if he's telling the truth. And he has a point about you being careful. But I don't like that last part. Especially if it was Dean who organized the theft. We need to get those statues back and stop Dean from whatever plan he's cooked up."

# Chapter Ten

Curiosity filled Gabby as they pulled up to Jake's one-story pueblo-style home in Albuquerque to get his passport. She was eager to see how Jake lived. At home, would he be a slob, a neat freak, or something in between? He'd been almost obsessive about keeping the cabin tidy, but maybe that was because it didn't belong to him.

She gathered her things in the front seat as the garage door rumbled and closed behind them. Just as she reached for the handle, Jake opened the passenger door for her. "Thank you." She hopped down from his 4x4.

He nodded and closed the door behind her. "Excuse any mess. Maid's year off."

Uh-oh. She braced for what was to come. Probably a typical bachelor pad with dirty dishes in the sink and stray clothes scattered about. "How long have you lived here?"

He held a door open that led into a tidy little laundry room. "About five years, I guess."

Then they crossed into the kitchen. It had shiny stainless-steel appliances and granite countertops. Not a dirty dish in sight. Nothing out of place. A plug-in air freshener made the kitchen smell like baking cookies. "This is nice, Jake."

"We renovated the place a few years ago. Want something to drink?"

"No. I'm fine. Thank you." The "we" he referred to probably meant him and Dani.

She wandered through the dining room with its tall table and four chairs, like those in bars, and then into the living room. There were pictures of beautiful Southwestern landscapes on the walls. He had a big leather sectional that looked comfy for watching his huge TV. No dirty glasses on the coffee tables or magazines anywhere. Two remotes lay perfectly aligned on a side table. It was as if no one lived here. Like it was staged for an open house. "You are a tidy one, Jake."

"More like I'm not home much."

"But when you are . . ." She turned and raised a brow, waiting for his answer.

He shrugged. "I like order. Maybe too much. The department shrink said it's my way of making up for my disorderly childhood. If you believe in all that headshrinking stuff."

"That makes sense to me." It still hurt to think of his past. "And I know that wasn't easy for you to share. So, thank you."

He jammed his hands in his pockets. "You don't judge my past. I like that about you."

"If I refuse to judge my father, then I have no right to judge anyone else." She continued her perusal. A bookcase stood on a far wall, with only a few comic books in plastic sleeves, like collectibles. And not a knickknack in sight. "Give away all of your books?"

He moved beside her and stood so close that his spicy aftershave lit up her senses. And other body parts.

"Dani used to read. A lot. I don't have the time. Well, until recently, I guess. Want to see the rest?"

She turned and met his eager gaze. "As in *your bedroom*?"

He nodded. "That's where my passport is."

She did want to see his private lair. "Okay, but keep your hands to yourself, please."

"Understood." He turned and started walking down a long hall. He glanced over his shoulder and grinned. "But if you change your mind after you see my sexy bathroom, just say the word."

That piqued her curiosity. "What makes a bathroom sexy?"

"You'll see." He kept walking down the hall toward his bedroom.

She probably shouldn't be following a guy like Jake into his bedroom, but she trusted him. He was a big flirt but, at the same time, respectful. He wasn't one of those handsy guys always trying to cop a feel. He was a gentleman. It might be one of the things she liked the most about him. Well, that and his sexy smile. And his butt. Her gaze dropped to that particular part of his body covered in jeans that fit just right as he walked in front of her. Yeah, that made for a nice view.

Jake stopped at his door and held out a hand for her to go first. "After you, Ms. Knight."

She stepped inside and scanned the room. There was a king-size bed with just two pillows—nothing fancy—a cherry wood dresser, and some photographs on one wall. The other walls were bare.

She crossed to the pictures and studied them. All were of his brother dressed in his army uniform in various posts, based on the backgrounds. Ben and Jake looked amazingly alike. But Jake was still handsomer.

Only one of the pictures had the two brothers together. Jake looked to be in his midtwenties. His brother had a military school uniform on. They both had ice-cream cones in their hands and mile-wide grins. "This is a nice picture."

"Yeah." Jake stood beside her, beaming a proud smile. "Ben's graduation day."

Jake obviously loved his brother. It was sweet to see it in his expression.

"Is he a minimalist? Like you?" She swept her hand out to include the rest of the room.

He glanced around, as if noticing for the first time how bare the walls were. "I suppose I *should* hang something else up. I had lots of pictures of Dani and me, but my last girlfriend pointed out that it was tacky to make love to her with my ex watching. So I took them down."

"I bet you didn't throw them out, though, did you? Just hid them so the girlfriend wouldn't see them?" He still cared for Dani, even though they hadn't worked out. Gabby liked how they got along. It said a lot for his character.

"Funny you should say that. The day she found them in the spare room was the day she broke up with me." He turned and headed for the big walk-in closet. "How'd you guess?"

"You're not the big mystery you like to think you are, Jake. I've got you pegged. Ask me a question about you. Bet I'll get it right." She followed him, curious to see if his closet was as neat as the rest of the house.

He had lots of jeans. And button-down shirts. And five pairs of cowboy boots. Along with some tennis shoes and a few pairs of dress shoes. Nothing gross, like stinky socks on the floor. Points for him there.

"You think you have me all figured out?" He pushed some shirts aside and tapped in numbers on a safe's keypad. "Okay. Then, after a long day at work, what's my favorite thing to do?"

He didn't read, and he couldn't stand his own company. He liked beer, so maybe he'd go to happy hour? But maybe not with his work crowd. Cops talking about their day probably wasn't so relaxing. It'd most likely be something he could do alone. "Go to the movies?"

His jaw dropped. "How did—" He crossed his arms. "What kind of movies?"

She smiled at her victory. "Not romantic comedies, that's for sure. Action movies?"

"That's a safe bet for most guys." He turned his attention back to his safe. "What kind of action movies?"

She had seen his collectible comic books earlier. "Animated. Superhero stuff, most likely. Bet you like those mutant ones the most."

"Everyone likes those." His lips thinned as he dug through his safe. "What's my favorite color?"

She glanced at his shirts. Most were a variation of the same color. "Blue. Seriously, Jake. I've got your number."

He followed her gaze to his shirts and smiled as he slid his passport out of the safe. Then he reached up and grabbed a duffel bag off the top shelf. "Okay, cheater. What kind of music do I like?" He sat on a bench and tugged off his cowboy boots.

She thought back to their conversation in his truck earlier for any clues. They'd talked all the way from the cabin to Albuquerque, never turning on the radio. He'd told her about being a cop, and she'd shared about her work. The three hours had flown by. Jake was deeper and more serious than he let on. He really cared about justice being served.

"Not country music, even though you wear cowboy boots. You'd hate all the emotion in those songs. Feelings make you itchy." She tilted her head and studied him. "Classic rock."

"Yep." He narrowed his eyes. "You like happy pop music, right?"

"What can I say? I hate depressing songs." She leaned against the doorframe. "What do you prefer, cats or dogs?"

"You mentioned your border collie named Einstein. So dogs would be my guess for you." He passed by her and crossed to his dresser. She was impressed he'd remembered her dog's name.

"Yes, but I was asking about you. I think a cat. Less commitment. They can take care of themselves a little more." She studied his shoulders. Besides being wide and sexy, they were rigid. His jaw was set as he dug through a drawer. "Am I making you uncomfortable? Seeing inside your chamber of deep, dark secrets?"

"No. That you care to guess so much about me means you're interested in my life. That's a good start to a relationship."

"Agreed." So did he want a *real* relationship? "I'm still trying to decide what I want from you, Jake. And I'm a little mad at you still. For not telling me you're a cop and at myself for telling you so much about my father." But she hated how attracted to him she was despite his making her angry. She only gave passes for bad behavior like that to the people she cared for. It scared her. "So, why are you all tense right now?"

"Because I have a beautiful woman in my bedroom and I can't touch her." He locked gazes with her while he unbuttoned his shirt. "I need to change. I wouldn't mind if you watched, but you'd probably rather go check out my bathroom."

No, she'd rather watch. But she made her feet move toward the bath anyway. "Take your time." She walked into the bathroom and the lights came on all by themselves. "Oh. My. God!"

Jake called out, "Told you."

Her bathroom at home was nice. Had all the best amenities, but Jake's bathroom was like walking into a spa combined with what she'd guess a makeup room on a movie set was like. The lighted area had a beautiful chair like she'd seen in expensive hair salons, and enough counter space to host a makeup party for an entire cast of a Broadway play. The mirror had settings for all different types of lighting. Evening, daytime, harsh office. Amazing.

Behind her was a sauna, a steam shower, and a tub big enough for ten. A couple of naked people could find lots to do in there. But then she spotted the shower. It had vertical bars with tiny holes and jets on the sides, along with four shower heads above. A remote showed more than fifty settings for fun times.

Jake's warm breath tickled her ear when he whispered, "Bet you can't guess which setting is my favorite."

She pressed buttons until she found one that shot pulsing jets of water from the sides and a waterfall setting from all four heads on top. "This one's nice." Visions of him inside, naked, filled her head.

"Amazing. You guessed right."

"See? I'm good." She turned off the alluring water show. It made her want to rip Jake out of the sweats and T-shirt he'd changed into.

She wandered over to a mirrored sliding door. Inside was a huge closet with jewelry cases, shelves for purses and shoes, gown racks, and a big center island with drawers. "Wow. This is impressive."

"Annalisa gave this whole setup to Dani for her birthday one year. They knocked out a bedroom and a study to make it."

"And yet it's empty." She turned to see his reaction.

Jake frowned. "My last girlfriend said that I didn't use it because I wasn't over Dani. Like the closet is sacred or something."

"I'd guess you don't use it because it'd feel weird to put your stuff in here. It's clearly meant for a woman."

"Thank you!" He lifted his hands in victory. "I told her I had plenty of room in my closet, but she insisted on making a big deal out of it." He leaned close and whispered, "Maybe you do have me all figured out. I can't decide if that's good or bad."

She wasn't sure, either. She'd guessed at a few things based on his house, but deep inside, it was as though she'd known him all her life. She'd never had that kind of connection with a man before. "It's definitely bad for you and good for me." She turned and walked toward his living room. His bathroom was too sexy and dangerous. Her resolve was slipping.

He grabbed a bag off his bed and caught up. "Why is it bad for me?"

"Because you don't want people to see what's behind the cocky, cowboy boot–wearing cop facade." She shrugged. "But I like the real Jake just fine."

He leaned closer. "I'll have to work on upgrading 'just fine' to 'a lot.'"

She started walking toward the garage again. "You've got some work to do there. Ready to go?"

"I'm always ready, Gabby."

She smiled. "No doubt about that."

Jake found a radio station for Gabby that played her happy pop songs as they drove to Annalisa's house. When she started singing along, so out of tune it had to be on purpose, he laughed. "If you're doing that to be annoying, it's working."

"I was." Gabby hit one of the preset stations, and screaming guitars filled the cab of his truck. "Do you realize you were cringing, even before I started singing?"

He hadn't. "It's just not my kind of music. Like, what does that 'funk you up' song really mean?"

When she smiled, her dimples showed. "It means, well, you know. Like you're having a night out dancing in the big city, showing off what you got." Gabby's shoulders moved to the beat in a way he'd never seen her move before. It was sexy. "Like the song says, do everything right, and the 'girls hit your hallelujah.'"

"So sex. It's about getting laid."

She rolled her eyes. "Aren't most songs, at their core?" She held a hand out toward the radio. "You can use guitar riffs or a dance beat—it all leads to the same happy ending."

"Ah." He listened more closely to the sixties classic song playing. He'd never paid the words much attention before. "This *is* about sex. Who knew?"

She shook her head. "For a man who spends so much of his life talking women into bed, you've been missing a pretty powerful tool."

Gabby would probably be surprised how few women he'd slept with. He didn't do one-night stands, either. The "touching" thing with a stranger was too much to bear. "I don't need any extra tools. I have all the equipment necessary for a good time."

She barked out a laugh. "That was so lame. Just for that, I'm changing the music back to mine." Gabby leaned over and found a station she liked.

Some sugary song came on, and he forced his face to stay impassive. When they were almost to Annalisa's house, he said, "Is this dance beat making you want to funk *me* up?"

"No, it's making me want to buy you a better joke book."

He smiled. There was an easiness about being with Gabby he liked. Whether they talked or not, it never felt awkward or uncomfortable to be with her.

They pulled up to the front gates of Annalisa's estate, and he said, "Hand me some ID please, Gabby."

She dug through her satchel. "I have a driver's license. And my passport. Just give me a second."

"Whatever you find first will work."

Out came brushes, string, headphones, and a bag of trail mix.

After a few minutes, he sighed. Why women felt the need to carry everything they owned at all times was one mystery he'd never solved.

Next came tissues, a plastic bag of what looked like hair thingies, and then an e-reader.

"Got it." She opened her wallet and handed a license over.

"And now I'm a year older. Happy birthday to me. Are you planning to haul all forty pounds of that around Europe, too?"

"Ten bucks says you're going to be grateful for something in here before our trip is done."

"You're on." He poked the button on the speaker box and held up her ID and his passport. "Jake Morris and Gabby Knight to see Dani."

Gabby whispered, "You were married to Dani. Don't they know you?"

The massive iron gates perched between thick stone walls slowly parted in front of them. "Most do. But the security is tighter here than at the White House. No one gets in without ID."

"Oh." She was quiet for a moment. "Why are we here instead of the airport?"

"Because your father hasn't eluded the law this long by being stupid. He told you Dean was on his way to London, knowing full well you'd follow."

Gabby cringed. "You're right."

"Your guards are probably already at the hangars, waiting to grab you. They flew in on your dad's plane, right? So, they'll have full access to the private-plane tarmac." He'd get a subpoena for the flight records. That way they could track at least one of Gabby's father's planes. It'd be a great piece of intel for later.

"Right. So how are we going to slip past them?"

"Annalisa's security team is the best. Dani said they had it under control."

As they drove up the long, tree-lined drive, Annalisa's Mediterranean-style mansion came into view.

"Wow!" Gabby's face lit up, and she leaned closer to the windshield of his truck. "That's bigger than my whole boarding school. And just lovely. Do you think I can meet Annalisa?"

"Maybe." He smiled at Gabby's enthusiasm. "She's a busy person, though, so don't count on it."

Gabby nodded as they pulled under the giant portico. Once they stopped, matching uniformed men opened their doors for them and then unloaded their things.

When the twelve-foot-tall carved wooden doors opened, both Dani and Annalisa appeared in the threshold and rushed toward them. What was up with that? Dani said, "Hey, Jake." And Annalisa sent him a finger wave.

Before he could greet them, the ladies each grabbed one of Gabby's arms and pulled her into the house. Dani squealed, "Love your hair, Gabby." And Annalisa said, "It's a pleasure to meet the woman who caught Jake's eye."

*His eye? What the hell?*

He quickly crossed the massive travertine-floored entry. He followed the ladies up the stairs and tugged on Dani's arm. "What's going on?"

Dani let go of Gabby and stopped climbing.

When the others were out of earshot, she said, "I told Mom you wanted to surprise Gabby with a trip to Europe in style—so you could propose. My mother's a sucker for romantic gestures. Unlike you."

"Propose? That wasn't part of the plan."

Dani rolled her eyes. "I had to tell my mom you needed the plane for something big. I couldn't tell her the truth."

He leaned closer, struggling to keep his voice down. "What's going to happen when we come back, and Gabby doesn't have a ring on her finger?"

"You had a huge, messy fight because you're such a pigheaded guy." Dani shrugged. "Mom would totally believe that. Why don't you go supervise the repacking into Mom's trunks while we fix up Gabby?"

"Fix her up with what?" He was still reeling from the proposal lie.

"Clothes. Mom called ahead, and they're going to do the normal thing they do for her at the airport for her privacy. But the paparazzi always seem to find out and will have high-powered lenses. Jeans and sneakers aren't Annalisa's style. We have to upgrade Gabby's look. You could use a shave, by the way. And maybe put on a suit. Mom doesn't travel with cowboy boot–wearing bums." She smiled and headed up the stairs.

His hand flew to his chin. Shaving had been the last thing he'd been thinking about as he and Gabby quickly slipped out of town to avoid being spotted by her goons.

And he wasn't even wearing his boots. "Fine. But I'm not wearing a damn suit."

Dani didn't bother to turn around. She just kept walking away. "It was worth a try. For Gabby's sake."

"For Gabby's sake?"

"Uh-huh. One look at you in that black suit and she'd be yours forever. It's still hanging in the guesthouse where you stripped out of it like it was on fire the last time you wore it to one of Mom's parties."

"Because it's uncomfortable." He shook his head and started out for the garage. He had an electric razor in his bag. If he hurried, he could beat Annalisa's staff before they put his and Gabby's bags inside the designer trunks to complete the charade for the press. Along with Gabby's heavy tool bag. They'd leave the guns home, but he'd still have his backup knife. Hopefully, he wouldn't have to use it and have any explaining to do to his boss.

Maybe he'd grab the suit. Just in case he needed it in London. They were probably fancier there than he was used to.

~

Gabby blinked at her reflection in the lighted mirror. How was it possible she was sitting in the same makeup chair Annalisa Botelli used? Getting glammed by a handsome man with caramel-colored skin called Almondo. All while sipping champagne.

Having Annalisa fuss over her made Gabby miss her mom. And Dani made her wish she had a sister. Who knew hitting Jake would lead to her having a spa day with two women who treated her as friends?

Dani tilted her head as she studied Gabby's makeup. "Yeah. I think that looks great. Mom? What do you think?"

Annalisa, who'd just been digging in her gargantuan closet for clothes for Gabby to keep—that alone was enough to make Gabby want to giggle—leaned close to inspect the makeup artist's work. "Almondo, you have outdone yourself. You look lovely, Gabby."

Almondo smiled. "Some of my best work, if I do say so myself."

Gabby had to agree. She'd never looked so pretty. But still not as pretty as Annalisa. No one looked that good.

Annalisa, a younger version of Sophia Loren, had an impossibly sexy body. Women half her age would be proud to have one like it. And she'd just said Gabby was lovely. Gabby had the urge to pinch herself to be sure it wasn't a dream. "Th-thank you" was all her starstruck brain could think to utter.

Dani laughed. "Gabby, I promise you, my mom puts her diamond-and-emerald-studded earrings in one at a time just like everyone else. No need to be intimidated."

"No need at all." Annalisa held out a hand to help Gabby out of the chair. "Now let's go try on some of the things I picked out for you. And then you can tell me all about you and Jake."

"Me and Jake?" She cut her eyes toward Dani. What was she supposed to say?

Dani nodded. "You know, Gabby. How you guys have been spending so much time together. And how you convinced him to take a whole month away from work because he needed to relax for a change. He'd hardly ever taken a full weekend off for me, so he's obviously enamored with you."

"Enamored?" Gabby's cheeks heated. Annalisa knew Jake far better than Gabby did. But she knew *some* things about him. "I think Jake finally figured out he needed some time off on his own. To reflect and learn to like his own company. He has so many off-limit topics he needs to face before he'll be truly happy." His suspension wasn't her story to tell.

Dani quickly said, "Jake discussed the touching issues the first night he met her, Mom."

Gabby added, "And later, his claustrophobia, as well as the pain of his brother never coming home."

Annalisa's brows arched. "Really? He's told you all that? It took Dani years to learn about Jake's skeletons. I think that says a lot. And I think we need to pick out a few extra outfits for you to wear in London. Have to be prepared for anything, right?"

Gabby was still focused on all of Jake's skeletons. But she managed a smile anyway. "This is so generous of you, Annalisa. Thank you."

"It's nothing." She waved a hand. "You taking these gives me room to buy new. Let's try this first."

Gabby stood with her arms out like a paper doll as Dani and Annalisa draped clothes on her to see if it matched her coloring. She should be checking out the rows and rows of designer handbags and shoes because she'd never see a collection so great again, but her concern for Jake filled her mind. He really did need someone he could talk to about his past. She had her aunt, who understood what it was like to change her identity, hide, and have secrets her whole life, having been married to her mobster uncle until he was killed.

That's what Jake needed. Someone with a messed-up past like hers who could understand his pain and anger. Maybe then he'd be able to have that family he said he wanted.

Jake's most pressing problem loomed at the airport, though. "Dani, what'd be the best thing to help Jake get through the long flight tonight?"

Annalisa chuckled as she packed the fourth outfit away in a leather satchel that lay open on the center island. "I find having sex with an attractive man the best way to make any flight go faster, Gabby."

"Stop." Dani swatted her mother's arm. "She doesn't want to hear about your mile-high-club adventures, *Mother*."

Gabby asked, "Do either of you have some over-the-counter sleeping pills Jake can take?" Because Jake was an incredibly handsome man who might tempt her to try sex on a plane for the first time. He'd be a lot less appealing and unable to flirt his way into her pants if he was incapacitated.

Annalisa nodded. "I'll go get the pills. He probably won't take them, but you can try. I still say sex would be the better answer."

After Annalisa had left the closet, Dani whispered, "Sorry about that. I told my mom you guys were a serious couple looking for a nice vacation so she'd lend you her plane. How's it going with you and Jake?" Dani laid a pair of black stilettos at Gabby's feet.

Gabby slipped into a luxurious, silky dark-blue dress, stepped into the buttery-soft shoes, and then turned for Dani to zip her up. "He just told me he was a cop, so you can imagine how well I took that."

"Yeah. I figured." Dani swept Gabby's long hair over her shoulder and then pulled up the zipper. "But you guys need to get past that part. Be a team when you get to London, okay?" Dani laid her hands on Gabby's shoulders and gave a quick squeeze. "You'll be staying in my mother's house in Mayfair. There'll be security during your stay, so you'll be safe there, but be careful, okay? My dreams showed the people who want that statue are dangerous."

Gabby studied her reflection in the mirror. She wore a designer dress, had beautifully styled hair, and makeup covered up her freckles. She almost didn't recognize herself. "Do you know who those people are?"

"No. I only got bits and pieces." Dani huffed out a breath. "I know Jake can come off as bossy, but there's no one I'd trust more with my life than him. And for the record, he flirts and teases a lot, but he's the most loyal person I've ever met. He'd never betray you, Gabby."

"He'd arrest my father in a heartbeat." Something she'd best not forget. She'd never forgive herself if her relationship with Jake caused her father to be arrested.

Dani nodded. "He would. Because he wouldn't see it as a betrayal to *you*. He believes in the oath he took when he became a police officer. But that doesn't mean Jake is incapable of bending a few rules. Just be sure you keep your father as far away from Jake as you can."

"That's the plan. We have to get past my bodyguards first, though. They're probably waiting for me at the airport."

"Good luck." Dani gave Gabby a hug. "I'll look forward to hearing all about it when you get back."

"Thanks."

Annalisa returned with the bottle of pills and handed them over. "Here you go." Then she tied a scarf over Gabby's head and slipped a pair of oversize Chanel sunglasses onto her face. "When you get out of the limo, throw your shoulders back and glide across that tarmac like you mean it. Enjoy your adventures in London, Gabby."

When Annalisa drew her into a tight hug, Gabby smiled. How had these wonderful, generous ladies come into her life? She hated that she'd probably never see them again if her plans to disappear worked out as she'd hoped. Every time she watched a movie Annalisa starred in, Gabby would always have a warm memory, at least.

~

As they approached the private tarmac, Jake closed his eyes and drew a deep breath. He needed to focus on getting Gabby onto the plane and past the guards, not on the long flight ahead. The dark tinted windows in the limo would get them close, but those last few feet were the kicker. Even though it was dark outside.

He turned to Gabby. "Your bodyguards know your mannerisms, so just—"

"I've got this, Jake. Annalisa told me what to do. She also gave me some sleeping pills for you to take once we get underway."

Ignoring the pill comment, he said, "When we stop, wait for me to come around and open your door. Grab my arm and head straight for the steps. I'm going to assume that's your father's plane right there, because there's Sal loading a bag."

Gabby whispered, "Dammit," under her breath as she scanned the tarmac. Then she said, "Our pilot still has to file a flight plan even though it's Annalisa, right?"

"Yep." He pulled out his field glasses and spotted the paparazzi right where Dani said they'd be. "Annalisa is going to France. To visit an ailing friend. Dani put the word out on social media in case your goons are smart enough to check on this plane. We'll get ourselves to London from there without filing another flight plan. And avoid the London airport where your guards will be waiting for you. Sal is only yards away." He glanced at her. "You look beautiful tonight, Gabby, but you're taller and not as curvy as Annalisa in the hips. A fan, and especially a male one, might notice that up close."

Gabby's eyes grew wide. "What are we going to do?"

"We're going to hope your protection squad is still monitoring the credit card I took from your wallet." He grabbed his phone and texted his friend. Telling her to put their plan in place.

The driver called out, "I'll unload the luggage, while you guys sit tight."

After the front door had slammed shut, Gabby said, "You stole my credit card?" She shook her head and crossed her arms. "You could've just asked, Jake. Don't keep me in the dark like I can't handle the truth. You're as bad as my father. I should just ditch you once we get to London."

He tucked his phone away. "I sent you a text while I was loading up our luggage. You were too busy being primped apparently to look at your phone. We needed a plan B."

"Oh." Gabby reached for her phone. "Wait. What's this new app?"

"It's a tracker. In case we get separated. It's all explained in the text. Along with how you should be more discreet when you type in your phone's password." When her lips thinned with annoyance, he reached out and laid a hand on her leg. "And please don't ditch me in London. I'll be scared all alone."

"Funny." Gabby swatted his hand away and then crossed her arms again. "Maybe I'll send you a text explaining how I secretly drugged you with sleeping pills tonight. You could read it after we land."

"Touché." He smiled as he peered through the glasses. "There's Louie coming down the steps of your dad's plane. He's probably in a hurry because you just got charged for a flight to Dallas that connects to London. You'll be heading toward security any minute now." He noted the call numbers on her father's Gulfstream, then typed them into his phone.

She watched him as he typed in the information. "Don't bother. I'm telling my dad you know that belongs to him now." Gabby put Annalisa's sunglasses on. "The ticket was a good idea."

"We're not out of the woods yet." He gave her a soft shoulder bump. "I'll come around and open your door. Put your phone against your right ear, and let's roll."

He tugged down his baseball cap and jogged to the other side of the limo, keeping his face lowered. It was dark, but there'd be security footage her guards might watch later, so he'd left his cowboy boots at home. His white T-shirt, black sweats, and tennis shoes were as nondescript as it got.

When he opened Gabby's door, her hand was the first to emerge, and her fingers dangled in front of his chest. He stifled his grin as he helped her out. Her normally chipped nails were light pink with white tips now. One long, sexy leg and then the next slinked out of the limo. She beamed a bright smile and said, "Thank you, Blondie."

He tucked her arm through his as she added an enticing sway to her hips and strutted on her high heels to the steps. He held a hand out, indicating she should go first, and then he followed her up the steps. *"Blondie?"*

She whispered, "That's for all the times you called me 'Red.'"

He followed close behind as they climbed. "It's how I restrained myself from calling you *babe*." He moved his mouth near her ear. "Are we good after the credit card thing? I don't want you to think I'm not a team player. I'd never keep you in the dark on purpose."

She nodded so he wouldn't push any further.

Once inside the plane, Cindy, one of Annalisa's two usual flight attendants, greeted them. "Welcome aboard. Nice to see you again,

Jake. If you'll choose your seats, we'll be on our way shortly. Champagne to start, Ms. Knight?"

"That'd be lovely. Thanks." Gabby smiled as she slipped into one of the big captain's chairs, looking as calm as he wished he felt. Just stepping through the cabin door always sent waves of tension through his body. He reminded himself to take deep breaths.

"The usual for you, Jake?" The smile Cindy sent him was filled with invitation. "And maybe a relaxing shoulder massage later?"

"Just the beer, thanks. How long until we're cleared for takeoff?"

"The captain said they needed some additional paperwork, so another fifteen or twenty minutes probably. Be right back with those drinks."

As Cindy disappeared into the galley, Jake glanced around the familiar cabin with its big leather seats, couches, and dining table for six. Annalisa had added a work desk in the rear by the bedroom that hadn't been there before. Maybe he'd use the new computer on that desk to pass the time, get lost in a war game or something.

After wiping the sweat from his upper lip, he grabbed their awaiting carry-on luggage and stowed it in a side bin. He sat in one of the large swivel chairs beside Gabby and peered out the window. "All that pomp and circumstance helped get you on the plane. It won't take long for your guards to think they missed you before you got through security, though. They'll probably be back soon. Then try to beat you to London. Be waiting at the airport there for you. I wish I could've bought us more time."

Gabby's calm expression turned pinched as she glanced out the window. "I'll buy us some more time. Hand me your knife, Jake."

"What are you thinking?" He pulled out the knife strapped to his leg but stopped short of handing it over.

"I'm not going to be a team player, that's for sure." Gabby stood and grabbed her backpack from the bin. "Especially when my teammate is a cop who'd arrest me for slashing tires on a plane. But technically, it's my family's plane, so no harm, no foul. Be right back."

He jumped up, followed her to the bedroom, then closed the door behind them. "I can't let you do that. There are security cameras out there. Tampering with an aircraft is a federal offense."

"Unzip me, please. Quick." She turned her back to him. "You forget something, Jake. Bad guys don't report crimes. They'll know I did it to slow them down."

The silky material slithered down her body and left him breathless. And wanting to touch. Badly. It made it hard to think with her standing in front of him in just her bra, skimpy red panties, and heels. He was going to be thinking about that the whole flight. "I thought you wanted to discuss things together first."

She slipped the sweater she'd been wearing earlier over her head. Then she turned around and danced out of the shoes. The sight of her in just a sweater and tiny panties was going to be etched on his brain forever.

She said, "You know this makes sense." Gabby ruined the view when she pulled up her jeans, then sat on the bed to tie her sneakers. Then she ran to the sink, rinsed off all her makeup, and wiped her face with a towel. "Let me have your hat, please."

Her idea *was* a good one, dammit. It could slow the men down for hours if they had to have replacement parts flown in. A smaller airport might not have the right tires for Luca's plane. Or they might rent another plane, but chances were they'd fix Luca's.

"Okay. Be quick about it, though."

He handed the cap over, and she punched it inside out so the emblem on the front wouldn't show. Next, she stuffed all her hair up under it. The dark-blue hoodie she pulled out completed the outfit. With the loose jacket, it was hard to tell if she was male or female.

She was better at sneaking around than he'd given her credit for. "Head down at all times, Gabby. Away from cameras."

She smiled and held out her hand. "I bet this is just killing your cop's heart, isn't it? Knife, please."

She *was* killing him, but not in the way she thought. The bold version of Gabby made him want to lock the door, throw her on the bed, and show her how much he wanted her.

He handed her the knife and whispered, "Don't make me have to visit you in jail."

"Awww. You'd visit a lowly criminal like me?" She laid a hand over her heart. "Not hate me for my crimes?"

She wasn't anything like his scum parents, but there was no time for that debate. "Only for the conjugal part. Now go."

She tucked the sheathed knife into her jacket pocket. "Be right back." She opened the bedroom door and started to leave but stopped and turned around. "I'm still undecided about the conjugal part." Then she turned and jogged down the aisle.

He hoped to God she'd decide quickly. He couldn't take much more.

# Chapter Eleven

Gabby slipped down Annalisa's plane's steps into the night and walked toward her father's aircraft. She didn't have much time, but she didn't want to draw any unwanted attention to herself by running, which was her first instinct.

She needed to do enough damage so the sensors wouldn't let them go anywhere. She didn't want to cause anyone harm, just delay them a bit. If her father would've listened to her request to call off her guards, she wouldn't have to do what she was about to do. Or so she kept telling herself. She needed to stay focused on the greater goal. Saving international treasures.

Watching her feet the whole time, she slipped under the wing of her father's plane. The side farthest from the cameras that were perched on the nearby hangar. She pulled the knife from her pocket, debating how many tires she'd damage. She didn't want to make her dad furious, just mildly annoyed.

Holding the knife in her fist, she jabbed the point through the tough rubber. Luckily, Jake's knife was super sharp. But she had to stab the rubber multiple times before it started to shred.

She had to hurry. Couldn't get caught.

Her heart still pounded with fear as she went to work on the fourth tire, stabbing and ripping it with all her might. The adrenaline pumping overtime through her veins and the lack of oxygen to her lungs forced her to stop for a moment to catch her breath. Should she pierce the front landing gear, too? She glanced in that direction and spotted suit-clad legs and a pair of loafers standing just in front of the wing.

All the air whooshed from her lungs. Had the man seen her?

A familiar deep voice softly whispered, "I knew that wasn't Annalisa."

She needed to run. Make a break for it.

Tucking the knife into her jacket's pocket, she slowly crawled away from the tires and out from under the wing.

Just as she stood to run, her father said, "I don't know whether I should be proud of you or lock you up forever. Get your ass on my plane right now!"

She stopped in her tracks, then spun and faced him as a new round of panic hit. Only the wing separated them in the dark. Soft moonlight illuminated his frowning face.

Her father was risking his freedom by standing in the open. Because of her.

She walked slowly backward. "If I don't get on that plane behind me in two minutes, a cop is going to be out here asking questions. Please. Go back inside. I'll be fine. Jake will keep me safe."

"Jake, the *cop*? Whose last name you haven't shared with me?" Her father's jaw clenched.

She stopped her retreat at the vile tone of his words. "He's a good guy. I honestly like him."

"*Like* him? He's a man, Gabby. He knows just what a nice girl wants to hear. He'll pretend to fall in love with someone like you, get what he wants, and leave." He crossed his big arms.

*Ouch.*

"Because no one would ever legitimately want to fall in love with someone like *me*, right?"

He shook his head. "You're a beautiful woman. I didn't mean it that way. But you haven't had much experience. He's going to break your heart, and then I'm going to . . ." He stopped himself. "Let me take you home before you get hurt. It can't end well with this person. You know that. How could it?"

"It'll end well when I have the statues back. I'm not looking for anything more than that from Jake." She took a few steps closer. "He's kind, didn't turn me in for nearly killing him when he could have, and has been a perfect gentleman. Let me have the chance to gain that experience you think I lack. Please?"

*Don't make me go back. Please let me do this one thing for myself.*

She sucked in a deep breath and held it as she waited for the ax to fall.

"You are as stubborn as your mother. Too sweet and trusting for your own good, like her." His eyes narrowed. "We'll be watching you. And your cop, too. If you're in trouble, you know what to do to alert us. We'll take care of the cameras out here. Hurry back to *Jake*." He turned to leave.

She called out, "Do you know where Dean is staying in London?"

"I'll e-mail what I know. And ditch the plane tomorrow. See you over there." He disappeared around the front of the plane.

She let out the breath she'd been holding. He actually let her go? He could've dragged her inside if he'd really wanted to—he was a huge, muscular man who stayed in shape—although he'd never laid a hand on her before. What made him change his mind?

Was he waiting for her to find the artifacts? Then demand she hand them over? Like the second thief in the movies? One thing was certain. Her father wasn't going to let her get too far out of his sight.

Dammit. She couldn't let her feelings for him cloud her vision. She had to plan for the worst and hope for the best.

Seeing her father again evoked feelings of love for him, as opposed to her overwhelming need to escape the bubble he'd created for her to live in. She appreciated how much he tried to protect her but hated the bubble.

She jogged back to Annalisa's plane and up the steps. Once inside she yanked off her cap, shook out her hair, and flopped beside Jake in the main cabin, suddenly exhausted. "Done. Let's get the hell out of here."

She wished she could tell Jake to change the flight plan back to London, because it made no difference now. Her father knew exactly where she was going. Mostly, she wanted to ask what Jake thought about her father letting her go. It could make for an important development in their strategy. Jake was good at working things out and having plan Bs. She needed to work on her own skills in that department.

Now *she* was the one withholding the truth from Jake. She had no choice. Jake would arrest her dad if he knew he was thirty yards away.

He'd kept his identity from her until he knew what her motives were. Maybe she'd let her irritation with that go since she was no better by keeping her father's location hidden. She'd forgive him. Hopefully, he'd do the same when he found out her secret.

After slipping the knife out of her pocket, she discreetly passed it back to Jake. He'd been sitting in the leather chair next to hers, studying her closely with those all-seeing cop eyes of his. "Thanks for the borrow."

He accepted the knife and then handed her a glass of champagne. "You okay? Your freckles are even pale."

Before she could answer, the woman who'd flirted with Jake earlier, Cindy, finally closed the front hatch. Then another pretty, blonde flight attendant appeared from the galley, whose name tag read "Monica." The woman held out the usual gear for the lecture about safety no one ever listened to and began her spiel as Gabby downed her whole glass of champagne. She'd never needed a drink so badly.

Her father's words spun around in her head so fast that she slowed them down so she could analyze their meaning. He'd be watching Jake, too. Was she endangering Jake's life by dragging him into her problem?

Or was her dad being a typical father worried about a man hurting his daughter? Her dad was wrong about that. Jake wouldn't hurt her.

Light pressure at her waist made her look down. Jake buckled up her seat belt for her and then took the empty glass from her hand. "They're just tires, Gabby. It's not like you killed anyone."

She met his gaze, and her stomach sank. Jake's safety suddenly meant as much to her as her dad's freedom. She'd never want to have to choose between him and her father. Jake's well-being had to come first because he hadn't chosen the life her father had. Jake was protecting her when he didn't have to. She'd do anything to guarantee Jake's safety. And that was a bit of a surprise.

Sure, she'd been attracted to Jake pretty much from hello, but was she developing real feelings for him?

Feelings for a man she could never have?

After the seat belt sign had gone off, Jake jumped up and into the aisle of the main cabin. He paced back and forth to stave off his anxiety at being trapped in a tin can hurtling through space. He glanced Gabby's way again.

She chewed on her thumbnail and frowned.

Where had the fierce woman ready to slash any tires that crossed her path disappeared to? Maybe her conscience was still bothering her. She had an unusual gentleness about her for someone who'd been forced to live with thugs most of her adult life. He admired that. And while her tongue could be a little sharp, that contrast between naughty and nice was what he liked the most about her.

Forcing his unease aside and focusing on Gabby instead of himself, he sat beside her again. He didn't like to see her upset. Maybe if he teased her a little, she'd stop worrying. "Hey. I need a distraction. Want to play some cards? Or watch a movie? Maybe we could check out the thread count on the sheets?"

She stopped chewing her thumbnail, then looked up and blinked at him. Like he'd disturbed some complex situation she'd been pondering. After a moment she said, "If you're just looking for a distraction, I'm certain Cindy would be happy to join you in counting threads. She flirts as much as you do."

He grinned at the tiny spark of fire in her eyes. The bold Gabby was back.

"I'm more attracted to bad-girl tire slashers like you."

When she smiled, all was right again.

She said, "You're just a riot when you're all tense, aren't you?"

He shrugged. "I'm fine."

"Really? Let's see just how relaxed you are. Cindy gave me a good idea." She unbuckled herself and then grabbed his hand and pulled him to the couch farther back in the cabin. She sat down and then pointed to the carpeted floor. "Sit. And take off your shoes."

Touching was going to be involved, but if anyone was going to do it, he was glad it was Gabby. He untied his shoes and tugged off his socks. "For a treat, I can roll over, too." He sat with his back to the couch, between her knees. "Or all sorts of other fun things from down here."

"Behave." She tugged on a lock of his hair. "Okay if I touch your neck and shoulders?"

*Yep. Touching. Hooray.*

"I'm all yours." When her warm hands landed on his tight shoulders, he tried not to cringe.

While she kneaded, she whispered, "I've been thinking about how you kept that you were a cop from me, and I get it now. You were just doing your job, and I'm sorry I got angry with you, Jake. You've been nothing but kind to me, and I appreciate that."

Music to his ears. "It's not just kindness, Gabby. I like being with you. And I'm hoping to be more than just your friend. If that's something you'd like, too."

Digging her fingers into his neck muscles, she said, "I've been thinking about that, too. You have definite boyfriend potential despite that smart mouth."

He leaned his head back onto her lap. "I bet you can think of a good way to shut me up."

She smiled and slipped her soft hands under his chin, tilting his face sideways, and laid her sweet lips on his. She nibbled on his bottom lip, then went for the top, driving him nuts. When her tongue joined the party, he nearly sighed. He'd wanted to feel her mouth on his since their last kiss. Her skills belied her lack of experience with men. No one had kissed him better.

When she slowly leaned away, he slipped his hand around the back of her neck and stopped her. Running his thumb over her bottom lip, he whispered, "I love the way you kiss me, Gabby."

Her dimples appeared again. "You're not so bad yourself."

She started rubbing his shoulders again while he analyzed her comment. *Not so bad? Maybe I'll have to step up my game next time.*

After a few more minutes of deep-tissue torture, she'd taken him somewhere between extreme pleasure and pure pain. But the hurt was all worth it when the muscles finally relaxed under her strong hands. She was pretty damn good at giving massages. Not that he'd ever had one before.

Her warm breath tickled his ear again when she whispered, "Picture a lovely beach in your head. We're lying in the warm sand, watching the waves roll onto the shore. Can you smell the salty ocean in the breeze? Hear the birds calling?"

"Nope. Because your bikini looks just like the bra and panties you're wearing. It's very distracting. You're a beautiful woman, Gabby." He untied her shoes.

"You're just saying that to get me into bed. Try harder. Visualize."

Her hands were magical. Long fingers that turned his muscles into putty. With her so close, touching him like that, he couldn't think about anything *other* than having Gabby in bed. "When you see what you want, it's hard to unsee it." He pulled off her shoes and socks.

Cindy appeared. "How about a snack before bedtime? We have ice-cream sundae makings in the galley, Jake. I remembered how much you like those. Or another beer maybe?" Her eyes landed on Gabby's hands still busy on his shoulders. "I see you got that massage already."

Couldn't she see that he and Gabby were together? Well, he hoped they'd be. He still wanted the rest of the month with her if he could get it.

He pulled out his phone. It was almost ten o'clock. "I'd love a sundae before we turn in." He glanced over his shoulder. "Want to share some ice cream with me, Gabby? Or do you want your own?"

Gabby gave his shoulder an extra hard squeeze. "Two spoons would be great. Thanks, Cindy."

After she had left, Gabby whispered, "I still haven't decided if I want to sleep with you, Jake. But you like plan Bs, so good thing Cindy's here. She seems willing and able to accommodate you." She started in on his neck with her thumbs again, and he nearly groaned.

"It's been all *you* in my head since you bashed me with that pan. Maybe cavewomen had it right. Bonk the one you want on the head and make him yours."

Gabby laughed. "Or too scared if he leaves her for a pretty flight attendant he'll get clobbered again?"

If he told Gabby how centered and content he felt with her around, it'd probably scare her away. Something about being with Gabby made him forget how tired and cynical he'd become lately.

Maybe his LT had been right to put him on leave.

But they'd agreed it'd be her decision if they slept together, and he'd respect that. She wasn't likely to stick around. Just like all the other women who he'd cared about, so he'd take whatever time he could have with her. "Cindy's not my type, by the way."

Gabby asked, "What's your type?"

"I like my women sweet, sassy, and sincere. Like you."

"My father pointed out that whatever happens between us can't end well."

"Because *he* doesn't want it to. Did his e-mail also tell you to ditch me and disappear as soon as you find those statues?" He needed to find a way to help get Gabby out from under her father's thumb. She deserved a normal life.

"I was joking about ditching you in London. So serious all of a sudden." Her hands stopped performing their magic. "I think you should take those sleeping pills now."

"I'd rather *you* helped me sleep." He stood and sat beside her on the couch. Taking her soft hand in his, he said, "I wasn't only talking about sex. You've already made this trip easier for me."

"Annalisa thought sleeping with you was better than the pills, too. Maybe we *should* try that."

*Yes! Thank you, Annalisa.*

She laid her hand on his cheek. "But if I have to disappear in London, it wouldn't be because of y—"

Monica appeared this time. "Here you go. One sundae, two spoons. Need anything else? Want me to go turn down the bed in the master?"

"Nope. We're good, thanks. Night." After Monica left, he grabbed Gabby's hand and tugged her toward the bedroom. "I have all I need right here."

Gabby yelped in surprise, then dug her feet in. "Wait a second. I want the ice cream, too." She grabbed the sundae and the spoons.

His heartbeat revved up to overdrive. If he had only a short time with her, he'd make every minute count.

~

After Jake had shut the bedroom door behind them, Gabby found it hard to draw a deep breath. She wanted to make love to Jake, but her father's words kept spinning around in her head.

*It can't end well with this person.*

Jake pulled her toward the bed with eager enthusiasm. But when they got to the edge, he turned to her and said, "Are we really eating that sundae first?"

She nodded. "I need to . . . um." What? She wasn't sure what she wanted other than to know he wasn't just bored on a flight and using her to pass the time. Especially because she was developing feelings for him.

"You're in charge, Gabby. So, let's eat the sundae." He scooped up a spoonful. "Open."

She complied and let the cool, chocolate, nutty, creamy delight slide down her throat.

He took off his T-shirt. "How about we lose an article of clothing with every bite? Your turn to feed me."

Leave it to Jake to make a fun sex game out of eating a sundae. One she was eager to play.

She scooped up a bite, and then Jake slowly sucked the ice cream into his mouth. He laid his hand over hers and held the spoon in place as he licked it clean. Then he kissed her—long, slow, and deep—sending a swirl of desire low in her belly. When he leaned away, he whispered, "Your top please, ma'am."

She handed him the parfait glass. As slowly as he'd licked the spoon, she crossed her arms and grabbed the hem of her sweater, lifting it over her head.

"Mmmmm." Jake's gaze raked over her exposed skin. The desire in his eyes sent a quick spark of thrill up her spine. "You're so beautiful, Gabby."

She took in his hard chest, scarred but strong, with defined muscles. Her hand reached out, of its own accord. She ran her fingers over a puckered scar on his side, making him flinch slightly. "Gunshot wound?"

"Yeah. I'm pretty beat up." He filled up the spoon again. "But your skin is so smooth and soft and perfect. I can't wait to touch it. And taste it."

She accepted the bite he held out, and then the sundae so that Jake could slip out of his sweats. She'd never wanted to be with any man as much as she wanted to be with Jake. But she should be practical about their situation.

"This is just physical relief for us, right? Or maybe like that syndrome where two people thrown together in a tense situation bond quickly? Then when it's over, they go their separate ways?" But they'd have to go their separate ways anyway, so what did she want him to say? Not the words all women want to hear just to get them in bed, like her dad said. She wanted real words from Jake.

"Could be, I guess. But I'm hoping when we're done with the statues that you'll come back to the cabin with me, Gabby. Your jeans now, please."

"Why?" She slipped out of her pants.

He laid the sundae on the nightstand and pulled her close. "You promised to help me learn to be alone, remember? And because you'd never judge me for my past. You're still saying yes to sex, right?" He kissed her, slowly, thoroughly, not like a man only looking for a good time. His hands moved gently, up and down her body, exploring each curve with such tenderness it drove her crazy with desire.

When his lips left hers, she stared into his eyes. The sincerity in them made it easier for her to breathe again. He wasn't using her like her dad thought.

She whispered, "Yes, I want to have sex with you, Jake. And you're the only one still judging yourself for your past. But I need to tell you something before we do this."

"What?" His hands snaked around her back and unfastened her bra.

"Well, it's something . . ." It was hard to concentrate when he pushed her panties aside and parted her, rubbing his finger in a circle on the place that ached most for his touch.

God, she wanted him. "I can't tell you some things I found out earlier today until after we land. To protect my father. Okay?"

His mouth moved to her chest, his lips teasing and laving, making her back arch. She closed her eyes and reveled in all the delicious sensations brewing low in her belly. He must not have heard her. Or maybe he didn't care?

Jake abruptly stopped, whipped the covers on the bed back, and then lifted her onto it like she was five foot two and 110 pounds, not the six-foot-tall woman she was. He yanked his boxers off and then crawled on top of her.

"I can live with that." After his heavy body had settled on top of hers, pinning her to the mattress, he lifted her arms above her head and clasped her wrists in one of his hands. "Do we need a safe word?"

"What?" Alarm skidded up her spine. "I don't do that—"

"I was kidding." He laughed. "God, you're so adorable." He released her hands and then leaned down and nibbled on her neck.

"See?" She poked him in the ribs. "You can't be serious more than nineteen minutes in a row."

"Good thing my time starts right now." His mouth moved to her collarbone, nipping and teasing until she shivered. Then his lips moved lower, and she hoped he'd do—

Yes. That. Her breasts were so heavy with need. His lips and tongue teased and aroused until she nearly cried out, but then he'd back off and lay gentle kisses on her sensitive skin, before he'd start all over again. Driving her nuts, but in such a good way. Her hands fisted in the sheets to avoid running her palms over his scarred back or through his thick hair.

When his rough hand covered a breast, and he gently kneaded, she writhed underneath his heavy weight.

She whispered, "Can I touch you? Please?"

His mouth moved lower, to her belly, and he mumbled, "You're in charge, Gabby."

In charge of what? Lying underneath him and letting him please her beyond reason? Not that she had any complaints so far.

But he kept heading south, farther out of her reach. He hooked his arms under her knees, lifting them up.

Gently, he nudged her knees aside, exposing her fully to him. Rather than dive right in as she'd hoped, he softly kissed her inner thighs, taking his time to get to the good stuff. Jeez. At this rate, nineteen minutes of serious Jake might not be enough. She wanted to tell him to hurry and put her out of her misery, when something dawned on her. Was going downtown his way of avoiding her touch?

When he finally hit the bull's-eye, her hips bucked, and all thoughts about touching Jake were replaced with the intense focus of the methodical, lovely torture of his tongue. Then he curled his thick fingers inside her and made her whimper for mercy. His steamy breath along with the flicks of his tongue drove the warm simmer in her belly into a hot roar.

His fingers began to move slowly in and out in long strokes while his tongue stoked the fire inside.

She was almost there. The pressure inside maddening, the primitive need for release overwhelming. He laid a hand on her stomach to hold her jerking hips in place before his tongue and busy fingers intensified their assault, taking her to a whole new level. She wasn't sure she could've stood all the sensations building between her legs another minute. On the brink, she'd wanted to beg him to make it stop. Or start. She hadn't been sure. "Jake."

When he lifted his head, then crawled beside her body, the storm inside her lessened a fraction but still raged on. Her chest heaved with all the pent-up desire inside. Desire to find elusive release.

As she lay on her back panting, Jake fumbled for a condom from his sweats. Her eyes tracked the motion of his hands rolling the ribbed latex down his length. The idea that a fancy condom could give her more pleasure than Jake already had seemed impossible.

Then he gently rolled her over and grabbed a pillow to place under her hips. He knelt behind and nudged her legs aside with his knee. He pressed himself inside her, going slowly at first, allowing her to adjust to him, before his rhythmic strokes began.

She absorbed all the fantastic sensations swirling inside, but she was sad that he'd probably picked this position so she wouldn't touch him again. Not that it didn't feel incredible. Her body thrummed and pulsed around his.

She had a choice. She could close her eyes and enjoy the steady buildup of desire again, or she could be in charge. Like he said she was.

She wanted to kiss him. Wanted to run her hands all over him. Feel every scar, every dip and valley his lean muscles formed on his chest. And she would. The next time they made love. If there was a next time. For now, she'd let him please her in a way that pleased him.

As Jake increased the pace and intensity, she placed her hands against the soft headboard to steady herself as her body clenched his in time with him, faster and faster, until he groaned, "Gabby."

The absolute need in his voice only added to the insane power built up inside her, like a rough ocean thrashing her back and forth, teasing, tempting her to let go and let the powerful rush of the waves overcome her.

When she couldn't take another second, she gave in, let all the sensations waiting to burst wash over her, and let herself go.

Jake followed right behind, moaning with each of his last thrusts, finally stilling inside her.

He didn't collapse on top of her like other men did but gently pulled away and then crawled beside her on the bed. He laid his head next to hers on her pillow and whispered, "That was amazing, Gabby."

She nodded, as she slowly reached out and ran her fingers through his hair. "Except I wanted to touch this. And you."

One eye squinted for a moment, as if he'd bitten into a lemon. He whispered, "Sorry. It takes time for me to . . ." He leaned closer and kissed her. Gently at first and then more urgently, slipping his hand along her face and softly caressing her cheek with his thumb.

While his tongue danced in harmony with hers, she carefully scooted closer and ran her hand up and down his back, his muscles quivering under her light touch, but he didn't shy away. Her palm gently explored the rough, hard, and occasional smooth parts. Even with all the scars, Jake's back was incredibly sexy, all tight muscles and damp skin.

When they finally had to stop their kiss for lack of air, he said, "That's why you can't ditch me. I need more time. To be able to make love to you the way you'd like me to."

Her heart melted into a big puddle of goo in her chest. "This time was pretty amazing. But that's something worth sticking around for." As her fingers gently caressed the back of his neck, her desire to disappear from her father's enemies warred with wanting to be with Jake. If even for that month in the cabin. She'd do anything to be able to have at least that, before she had to go back to her normal life full of secrets and hiding.

Jake rolled out of bed and headed toward the bathroom. "But when we run out of these fancy condoms, you have to buy the next round."

She glanced at the clock beside the bed, then rolled onto her back and smiled. "You're slipping, Jake. You just went a whole thirty minutes without joking."

He returned and slid under the covers. "Bet I could go even longer this time."

"Prove it."

"Done." While he kissed her, she couldn't have cared less about their bet. His mouth and lips did magical things to her, took her to new heights she'd never felt before. He slowly leaned away. "You want to be in charge of the touching this time?"

"I do." She straddled him and then placed both hands on his chest. "I promise this won't hurt a bit, Jake."

He cringed, then nodded. "What's the record for being serious?"

"Thirty-one long minutes. And I plan to use every bit of it to enjoy your incredible body for my own pleasure."

"I'll probably live. Let's do it."

Smiling, she leaned closer and kissed his full, soft lips. She'd taken his mind off his claustrophobia. And fallen a little bit more in love in the process.

# Chapter Twelve

Gabby blinked her eyes open, orienting herself. She was on Annalisa's plane, still in bed, naked. With Jake.

She smiled and rolled over. She'd finally spent the whole night with a man she'd had sex with, and she looked forward to the morning-after routine she'd only read about in books or seen in movies.

But the bed was empty. Jake was nowhere to be found. Figured. Her one and only opportunity to experience morning sex was not to be had. But the night before made up for that. The first time had been great, all about her, but then Jake let her make love to *him*. When she'd touched him at first, he'd fisted his hands in the sheets. But after a few minutes, he'd smiled and relaxed a little, so that had been progress. And a whole lot of fun to see how much pleasure she'd given *him*. Her new goal would be to get him to agree to both of them touching at the same time, not just one or the other. That is, if they ever got the chance to make love again. Who knew what the days ahead would bring?

She threw the covers back and headed for the shower. Annalisa's plane was the nicest she'd ever been on. And her bathroom, if still a tad small, didn't skimp on luxury. She looked forward to using the salon hair products she'd seen earlier in the shower.

She checked the time, amazed she'd slept so long, and then opened a shade to see where they were. Still over the ocean with the lowering sun shining off the waves below. Beautiful. But she needed to hurry and get ready. They'd be landing in a little over an hour.

When she stepped out of the bedroom, dressed in jeans and sneakers, Jake was at the desk in the main cabin, studying the computer screen intently. He looked so handsome, dressed in his button-down shirt and jeans, but weirdly she missed his cowboy boots.

Still so happy about the night they'd shared, she wanted to wrap her arms around his shoulders and give him a hug but didn't want to push his boundaries. She'd done plenty of that the night before. "Good morning."

He looked up from the computer and grinned. "Hey. 'Bout time you woke up. Ready for breakfast? I'm starving." Without waiting for her answer, he called out. "We're ready to eat now."

Monica appeared. "Be right out."

When the attendant disappeared into the galley, Jake stood, slowly lifted his hands, and then laid them on her shoulders. "Last night was fantastic, Gabby." He gently squeezed.

"Best night ever." She'd have preferred the hug, but if that was the best Jake could do, she'd take it. Dani had warned her that he wasn't good at expressing himself physically. He'd probably snuck out of bed so she wouldn't roll over and accidentally cuddle with him. "You didn't have to wait to eat."

"A little credit here, please. I patiently worked on my waiting-for-women skills the whole time you slept and then primped."

"My hero." She never primped. It'd taken her all of twenty minutes, and her hair was still damp, although it smelled lovely. Like flowers and exotic spices.

She headed for the bin where her backpack was stowed and sat. "I need to check my e-mail. Hopefully, everyone got back to me while we've been in the air."

"Yeah. We need a plan." Jake sat in a big club chair across from her and stared out the window, his knee jiggling up and down.

She laid a hand on his leg to still it. "We're almost there. You're doing great."

He took her hand and weaved his fingers through hers, probably because it was bugging him to have it on his knee, and then laid a soft kiss on her knuckles. "Being with you helps."

That made her heart soar. "You're a pretty good time, too." She'd miss him terribly after their month in the cabin was up. But one problem at a time. She needed to focus on the task at hand.

She shook off her sadness and powered her phone on, then quickly logged in to her e-mail account. Her father had left a message. But not the information about Dean, as promised.

> Tires slowed us down, but on the way now. Drive from Paris to give me time to catch up, please. I'll fill you in on Dean after you tell me where you're staying in London.

She wasn't sure she should tell him. "Jake. Remember the stuff I couldn't tell you last night about my father?"

He whipped his attention from the window to her. "Yeah."

Cindy appeared with their breakfast. "Would you like it here or at the dining table?"

"Here, please." He lifted their tables from the sides of the big leather chairs for her to set everything out. "Thanks."

Gabby waited until they were alone and then said, "I ran into my father last night at the airport. He wanted to take me home, but when I resisted, he let me go. I can't figure out why he's allowing us to chase Dean when he thinks it's so dangerous for me to be involved. He's going to be in London later and asked if we'd drive, so he can catch up. He said he's going to be nearby and watching us."

Jake dropped his fork filled with cheese omelet onto the china plate with a clatter. "He was *thirty* yards away?" He stood and paced the cabin back and forth, muttering something about criminals needing to be behind bars.

She waited for him to have his moment and then said, "It doesn't add up. Right?"

Jake leaned down, put his hands on the sides of her chair, and opened his mouth to speak, but then stopped. He closed his eyes for a moment, as if reeling his temper in, then sat beside her again. "No, it doesn't make sense your father would let you go."

Jake shook his head, picked up his fork, and stuffed his mouth full of eggs. Evidently, that was all he was going to say on the subject, so she took a bite of her eggs and checked her phone.

"Oh. Will left me a voice mail." She hit the speaker and laid the phone on her tray.

"Gabby, so glad you called. Dean's in trouble. I'm in London trying to decipher a crazy map to find a statue and trade it for his life. I need your help. Please call me as soon as you can!"

Jake's right brow spiked as he dug into his hash browns. When he began calmly buttering his toast, she wanted to scream.

"So? What do you think?"

He added some jam. "Heard from your friend from London? Charlie, wasn't it?"

"Let me look." She hadn't checked her regular e-mail. She'd been avoiding it, but now that her father knew her plans, it wouldn't matter. She called up her account and scrolled through the junk until she found what she was looking for.

For time's sake, she read the e-mail out loud.

> Gabs, the love of my life! Too long since we've had a chance for a chat. Or had a fun sleepover. What the hell are you doing mixed up in this steaming pile of shite? Everyone is after those statues. Especially some blue bloods, second or third cousins to the

queen. They claim both statues belong to them. Some gift from the king of Spain in the day. They thought they'd lost them during the war. Call me the minute you hit town. Can't wait to catch up, gorgeous!

Both of Jake's brows lifted as he finished his toast. "Fun sleepover?"

"Seriously? After the barrage of new information, that's what you comment on first?" Jeez. She and Charlie were just friends. "My dad said he'd send what he knows about Dean but asked where we're staying first. What do we do?"

"The love of his life?" Jake frowned as he finished off his eggs.

"Focus, please." She shook her head and dug into her eggs and hash browns, nearly groaning with pleasure. She'd been starving, too, but hadn't realized it.

Jake wiped his mouth on his linen napkin and then set it down. "Don't want to drive to London. Paparazzi know it's Annalisa's plane landing and will follow us. We need someone else to book us a ride. Would your boyfriend send a chopper for us? That is, if I'd be invited, too?"

The scowl on his face made her smile. Jake was jealous. She shouldn't love that so much, but she was only human. "I can ask. Or we could always tell him you're my butler or something."

"*Your butler?*" Jake stood and stalked down the aisle to the bedroom. The door closed firmly behind him.

Pissy Jake was new. But she couldn't blame him. One of the most wanted men in America had been yards away. The cop in him had to be struggling with that. Charlie's e-mail hadn't helped.

She'd give Jake a few minutes to get ready and then talk to him. In the meantime, she finished her breakfast and then sent an e-mail to Charlie, asking for the chopper. She wanted to call Will back but didn't want to do that without talking to Jake first. She stood to find him just as Cindy announced they were starting their descent into France and should be on the ground in forty minutes.

She slowly stepped inside the bedroom and, when she didn't see Jake, headed for the open bathroom door. Jake stood in nothing but a towel, shaving. The view was incredibly sexy, so she leaned against the frame to watch. "Charlie's not my boyfriend. I haven't seen him in years. We're e-mail buddies."

"Good." He glanced her way. "Have a seat. Here's what I think we should do."

Seemed his jealous moment was over.

The only seat was the toilet lid, so she squeezed behind Jake, squelching the urge to give his nice butt a pat—she didn't want him to flinch and cut himself—and sat. "Shoot."

For Jake, being in a chopper was about as fun as being buried alive. Thankfully, it was almost over. The airport lights were in sight. He reminded himself to breathe. And to be nice to the Charlie guy who was picking them up. "When are we meeting Will?"

Gabby, annoyingly calm, smiled as she stared out the window at the English countryside below. "He'll meet us at Annalisa's home in Mayfair after we get back from dinner. Charlie suggested going to our favorite place to eat whenever we were in town on university breaks."

*Our favorite place?* "Maybe we should just go to the house. Keep a low profile? I'm sure Annalisa's chef will whip something up for us."

She tore her face away from the view she'd been admiring and blinked at him. "No one knows we're coming or who we are . . . yet. I think we'll be fine, don't you? Besides, it's a really fun place. I think you'll like it."

He decidedly would not like Gabby beaming those big brown eyes at another man. But they had to eat, and Gabby seemed excited, so he'd go along with the plan. "Fine. But no messing around. We eat and then we're out. Got it?"

"It's called 'messing about' here. And I'm going to ignore that bossy tone and hope it improves. Looks like we're here."

The chopper took a final spin and then landed on the tarmac. Thank God. He wiped the sweat from his upper lip and willed the big guy approaching the chopper to hurry and open the door so he could breathe again.

When the door finally opened, Gabby let out a yelp. "Charlie!" Her body flew into arms that could be mistaken for tree trunks covered by leather. The guy was rich according to Gabby, so he probably didn't have anything else to do other than going to the gym.

Charlie, smiling as if he'd just won the lottery, said, "You look amazing, Gabs. And I love your new hair."

While the two of them admired each other, Jake picked up Gabby's two-ton backpack, grabbed his gear, and hopped out of the coffin they'd spent the last eighty-two minutes in. He scanned the private airport, checking for unwanted company, but the place was deserted. Just a few hangars stood open, and a bunch of tied-down small planes lined up like soldiers waiting for their orders. All very tidy and neat. Sort of like Gabby and her English habits.

After the hugs and kisses—on the mouth, no less—Gabby finally turned and smiled. With her arms still filled with the bodybuilder, she said, "Jake, I'd like you to meet Charles Weathersby the Third. He knows *almost* as much as I do about archaeology."

*Great. Should make for scintillating conversation.* He stuck out his hand. "Nice to meet you, Chuck."

He laughed. "No one has called me that since this one here." He gave Gabby another squeeze. "Must be an American thing, right?"

"Yeah. Must be. Maybe we should get going?"

"Right! I'll just pop your bags into the boot, and then we're off. Load up, you two."

Jake opened the back door of a black Range Rover and stepped aside to let Gabby in first, but she'd already climbed into the front seat. So he'd sit in the back and admire the backs of their brown heads, which oddly matched the fine leather.

The car smelled brand-new. He usually loved the smell of new leather. Today, not so much.

After Chuckie III had joined them, he and Gabby started reminiscing in archaeology speak, so Jake tuned out their chatter and concentrated on their plans as he watched to see if they'd been followed.

Gabby's father should be in town soon and knew where they'd be staying because Gabby had told him. He had his own agenda, or he'd have locked her up and thrown away the key again. And the people who had Dean might be following Will, so they needed to stay alert. Well, *he* did anyway. Gabby was too busy laughing and squeezing her buddy's forearm with each new story Charlie told, in his quiet, sophisticated British accent, of how their classmates had turned out.

Gabby used to run with a fancy crowd. Did she find Jake too . . . basic? Just a blue-collar cop, whose arm she avoided touching when she laughed because he'd flinch every time she did?

Maybe sleeping with her had been a mistake. It had made him want to be with her even more. The "spend *every day*" kind of be with her. A dangerous desire when the chances of her ditching her father and being with him were slim. Her first allegiance would always be with her father, the *criminal*.

He glanced over his shoulder again, and a familiar blue car was still behind them. "Hey, Charlie? Do you see that blue sedan behind us?"

Charlie's eyes narrowed in the rearview mirror. "I've had company ever since I inquired about your statues, Gabby. Whatever have you dragged me into?" Charlie smiled at her, not seeming the least bit concerned.

Which concerned Jake.

Charlie reached out and took Gabby's hand. "Darling, would it be a terrible disappointment if we had a change of plans?"

Before Gabby could answer, Charlie swerved a hard left and floored it. He still held Gabby's hand in his as their tires screamed around the corner. They sped down a road so narrow Jake hoped no one decided to get out of their car at that moment or they'd be dead.

He kept watch behind as Charlie continued to drive like a man who wasn't riding in his first rodeo. He turned around and called out from the back, "What is it you do, Charlie?"

Chuckie's eyes met Jake's in the mirror. "Art dealer. And you?"

"Jake is a cowboy," Gabby answered for him. "Bet you never met one of those before."

Charlie's eyes were back on Jake's reflection again. "No. I can't say as I have. Is that a real thing still?"

Gabby turned and widened her eyes in a plea to play along. She was going to have some serious explaining to do later. He answered, "Ranching is popular where I come from. Cattle, horses, the whole works."

"Ah. I see." He returned his gaze to the road ahead, not sounding the least bit convinced.

Charlie didn't look like a fancy art dealer. Not with those muscles. And his driving skills could challenge Jake's. "I think we lost them. Why don't we go to Annalisa's house, and you can tell me all about selling art over dinner, Chuck?"

Gabby frowned at him but gave Charlie the address. "A guy named Will, my boss's brother, is going to meet us there. He loves archaeology, and I thought you might want to help us solve something of a riddle. You were always quite good at that at university, remember?"

Quite good at that? Gabby's English accent was back. She was nervous about something. Something she was hiding from him.

As they pulled up to the garages at the rear of Annalisa's house, two guards he recognized from home lifted their chins in greeting as they checked their IDs. He gave them a heads-up that Will was coming later, too, and asked them to keep an eye out. Then they were led inside, and their bags were whisked away upstairs.

A woman dressed in stern black directed them to a living room so fancy it could make the cover of a magazine. She promised to return with refreshments. Who knew what that would entail, but probably not a beer. Charlie and Gabby were still connected at the hip like Siamese twins, with their arms around each other.

A suspicious bulge at Charlie's lower back caught his attention. A gun? Why would Gabby's friend be carrying a concealed weapon? In a country with strict gun laws? He didn't want to wait for an explanation. Gabby could be in danger.

Jake lunged forward, grabbed Charlie's gun, and pressed it firmly into his kidney while he twisted the art dealer's free arm up his back. "Gabby, step away. Charlie and I need to have a little chat."

Gabby turned around. "Jake. Stop. He's going to help us."

He marched Charlie toward the couch and shoved him. "Sit. And start talking. Why does a law-abiding English art dealer carry a gun?"

Charlie righted himself and then brushed the wrinkles from his suit pants. "He's either stronger than he looks or very well trained for a cowboy, isn't he, Gabby?" He chuckled and met Jake's stare. "I'm afraid Gabby hasn't been on the up-and-up with either of us, mate. But I pose neither you nor Gabby any harm."

Jake glanced at Gabby, who was chewing a thumbnail. She turned to Charlie and said, "Jake *was* a cowboy, but now he's a detective." Then she turned his way. "Charlie deals in artifacts, has a store to prove it, but not all of what he does is necessarily something I'd like to share with my boyfriend the cop. I should have told you both the truth, but I was afraid neither of you would help me if you knew what the other did. And I *really* need you both."

Jake ran a hand down his face and sucked in a deep breath for patience. Another criminal he wasn't supposed to bust. It was getting tedious. But at least she'd called him "my boyfriend the cop" in front of the crooked art dealer, so that was something. What the hell had he gotten himself into? "Gabby, look—"

"Please, Jake?"

When she smiled at him, dimples blazing, he handed the gun back to Charlie and then headed for the kitchen. "I'm going to see about dinner."

Charlie called out. "No dinner for me. I have to take care of something. Be back in a few hours."

Good. Then he had Gabby all to himself. "You two work out any details I shouldn't know about, please. And when you get back, we'll talk about finding those damned statues. Legally!"

He turned down a long hallway, and after passing a study filled with more books than a person could read in a lifetime, he found the kitchen. A man actually dressed like a chef, with the tall hat and everything, bowed his head slightly. "Mr. Morris, I presume. Annalisa asked me to prepare anything you wish. But she told me you enjoy steaks, baked potatoes, and, of course, chocolate cheesecake for dessert. If you'd like to go dress for dinner, I'll be happy to serve it within the hour."

Dress for dinner? Jake looked down at his sweats and tennis shoes. Maybe he *should* get cleaned up. If he was going to compete with Charlie for Gabby, he'd better wear the suit he'd brought. "That sounds great. Thanks."

~

After Charlie left, promising to be back soon, Gabby wandered around the big house, finally locating the dining room. Jake stood at the end of the table, his phone in hand, scrolling through messages. He looked so handsome in a dark suit, gray striped tie, and white starched shirt; she'd be willing to skip dinner and make a meal out of him upstairs. "Don't you look *debonair*? I'd better go change."

Jake's head whipped up and he smiled. "No need." He pulled out a chair at the head of the table for her. "You look gorgeous no matter what you wear."

"Thank you." She sat in the chair, and he helped her scoot it closer.

Then he sat in the chair beside her. "Dinner will be ready soon. Want some wine?" He held up a bottle of red. "I asked them for the best Annalisa had."

She laid her napkin across her jean-clad lap, feeling totally underdressed in the fancy dining room that sat twenty. "Isn't that kind of rude?"

He shook his head and poured. "She'll expect us to use it. She thinks I'm going to propose to you tonight."

*Propose?*

She opened her mouth, but words wouldn't come out.

He laid the bottle down and picked up his glass. "I see you're as surprised by that as I was when Dani told me the ruse. She told her mom that so we could use the plane. But why not enjoy it while we can? Cheers?"

After her heart rate had slowed a bit, she tapped her glass against his. *"Saluti."* She took a deep drink and nearly moaned at the rich and fruity elixir that danced on her tongue. "Wow. That's incredible."

"It is." Jake took her free hand. "And so are you. Have I told you how beautiful you are, Gabby?"

Many times. Jake was acting a little weird. "You're looking pretty nice yourself. I love the suit. But you didn't have to go to all that trouble for me."

"No trouble." He lifted her hand and nibbled on her fingers. "I'd do just about anything for you, Gabby."

"If I didn't know better, I'd think you really were going to propose to me." She withdrew her hand. "What did you do with the real Jake?"

He leaned closer. "The real Jake has many sides. This is my James Bond look. The blond guy, not the original one."

She laughed. "The smart-mouthed cowboy version is kinda fun, too."

Their food appeared before them, so she leaned back and thanked their server. After he was gone, she picked up her knife and cut into a tender piece of steak. "This looks amazing."

Jake frowned as he chewed.

"What? You don't like yours?" She took a bite. The meat was juicy, cooked just right.

"No. The steak is awesome." He went in for another bite.

When he silently started in on his baked potato, she laid a hand over his. "Then what's wrong, James Bond?"

He didn't smile at her use of the nickname. "I figured you were used to fancier guys, growing up in boarding schools and all. So, I wore the suit to show you I can be one, too. Sometimes. Like your pal, Charlie."

Was he still worried about her feelings for Charlie? It made her smile. "I'm not used to *any* particular type of guy, seeing as it's hard to date when you live in a prison. But you look so hot in that suit that I might have said yes if you'd actually proposed."

Jake grinned as he cut himself another bite. "If I *had* proposed, how many kids would you like to have?"

She pondered while she ate. "Two. Maybe three. But where would we live with these imaginary children? We live thousands of miles apart."

"Wouldn't matter." Jake's eyes sparkled with amusement as he took another drink of wine. After he had put his glass down, he reached out and took her hand. "As long as we're all together."

James Bond Jake was making her heart go mushy. "You realize if you married me, you'd have to let me drive the Bond sports car, right? The one that can fly and go underwater."

"Nope. Can't do it." He laid his fork down and leaned closer. "The car only responds to James." He ran his fingers over her left hand and entwined them with hers. "But I'd buy you a decoder engagement ring instead."

"Oh well, then. That'd almost make up for it." Still holding his hand, she said, "But you'd need to throw in a bathroom like yours, too."

"Deal." He kissed the back of her hand. "Come home with me after this is over, and we'll find your favorite shower setting."

"I'd like that very much, Jake." She laid a soft kiss on his lips. "Thank you for the best engagement dinner I've ever had." Probably the only one she'd ever have.

He whispered, "It was my best one, too."

If a heart could sigh, hers would have. And then it'd tell her she was officially in love with Jake.

# Chapter Thirteen

After Gabby and Jake's intimate dinner, Will and Charlie had joined them in the dining room. Gabby loved hearing Charlie's stories about their classmates. Even more, she loved feeling like a normal person with friends, like how it'd been in school.

Being in the elaborate dining room, surrounded by fine art and antiques as lovely as she'd ever seen, gave her comfort. It was nice to be back in England, with its unique style and culture cultivated by the passing of time. Not new and American, like home.

She looked around the huge table, and it dawned on her that the only friends she had now were all in front of her. Will, worried sick for his brother, and Jake and Charlie, who were getting along slightly better, but each was still wary of the other.

She'd once wondered if her and Will's friendship could ever grow into a relationship one day, but after meeting Jake, there was no comparison between the two. Will was quiet, kind, and sweet like vanilla ice cream. Jake, on the other hand, was rocky road with hot fudge poured all over the top: exciting and fun. And why was she using ice cream as euphemisms for sex lately? She obviously needed more of both in her life.

But back to business. "Will, what has Dean told you so far?"

Will drained the glass of water in front of him like he hadn't had a drink in days. "Dean saw an opportunity to raise millions for the museum by selling the statues as a pair. He'd had multiple bids, so he sold both statues to the highest bidder."

"He didn't have the authority to do that." Gabby's hands balled into fists. "Did he steal the Father statue from us?"

Will shook his head. "No! The people he's with did, not Dean. When that statue turned up stolen, Dean asked me to run down to New Mexico and dig up the Son statue to keep it safe. But it wasn't there. I sent Dean a picture of the map and letter inside the box I found. He told me to make copies of the paperwork. Then I reburied the copies and the empty box. These are the originals." Will pointed to the paperwork he'd laid on the table. "Dean said we needed your help because you knew the most about the statues and that you grew up here in London. And because we couldn't get in touch with you, I should leave the shard in case you'd decided to look for the Son statue, too. So you'd know to track one of us down. Your phone was just going to voice mail."

She'd deliberately stayed off her regular e-mail, too, so her father wouldn't find her. "That's because I ditched my phone, got a new one, and left for New Mexico after the Father statue was stolen from DC." Assuming her father had taken it. But she couldn't share that part.

Will said, "Two men who Dean had made a deal with for the Son statue showed up at his apartment. They told him they needed him to accompany them to New Mexico to get it. Dean panicked when he realized the men weren't asking. When they found the map in the hole instead of the statue, they gave him thirty-six hours to find it."

Doubt about Dean's motives began to sink in. Seemed like he'd send his brother to the police if it were all about raising funds for the museum.

"I don't understand how this statue thing ever ended up in New Mexico." Jake frowned at the faded, weathered paper in front of him. "It makes no sense."

"This is the stuff Gabby and I loved while at university." Charlie leaned forward as if telling a juicy secret. "During World War Two, many of England's treasures and important papers were scattered over the countryside, hidden in the larger estates, or shipped overseas. To protect them from the fires the bombing raids on London had caused. In 1942, we asked your State Department to hang on to many great pieces of art by Goya, Rembrandt, Botticelli, among others. They sent it all down to some place in the Carolinas. What was it again, Gabby?"

She took a sip of tea, then said, "The Biltmore House in North Carolina. There, a curator originally from New Mexico was checking the manifest and noted that both the statues, formally separated and owned by cousins, had ended up together again. Knowing the legend of the curse that supposedly caused the fall of the Incas and World War One, he took the Son statue back to his Native lands, had it blessed by an elder, and then buried it there for safekeeping until after the war."

Will asked, "Did the curator tell the owner what he'd done?"

"He tried by sending a letter, but he never heard back before he passed away. After the war had ended, the Father statue was sent back to England with the rest of the art, but no one claimed it, so it was sold on the open market. Seems both cousins who owned them were killed during the war. And no one in their family wanted them because they were convinced they really were cursed. That's how the Father statue ended up in our museum in DC. And just recently, someone found that letter the curator sent, and so the fun began."

Jake asked, "So why move the Son statue back to England? And leave a note where it's buried?"

"I can answer that." Will cleared his throat. "From what Dean deciphered from the Native writing, bad things had happened to the tribe ever since the statue had been buried there. The elders insisted it be returned to their deceased owner's lands and buried again. So the bad spirits would leave them alone and finally rest where they belonged. But Dean couldn't make any sense of the partial map of London that was in the box. He couldn't make out any of the street names or find a landmark to orient a search."

"Spirits and curses?" Jake grunted. "All I know is Dean's in trouble. Do you know where he is? And have you gone to the police here?"

Will shook his head. "Dean told me not to. He said they'd kill him if I did. And I don't know where he is. We're communicating by text."

Jake turned to Charlie. "Who could pull off a heist in a heavily guarded museum in DC?"

"Not too many. Even then, I'd venture Dean helped them." Charlie's right brow arched. "No offense, Will. That's probably why he doesn't want the cops involved."

"Yep. My take, too. Why don't you guys work on this map while Gabby and I have a little chat?" Jake stood and headed for the stairs.

Jake wasn't a happy camper. Therefore, she probably wasn't going to be one, either. She slowly stood and followed behind Jake upstairs. When she caught up, he stood with a bedroom door open, waiting for her.

"After you." He held out a hand.

She passed by him and forced a smile. "Everything okay?"

"Nope." He shut the door behind them. "I need you to e-mail your father and find out if he knows who we're dealing with. And then I'm going to call the local police and tell them what's going on. After that, we're going home and staying out of this."

"But, we're so close. Charlie—"

"If my gut's right, and it's rarely wrong, Dean is working with these people and using you and his brother to abscond with a fortune. There are too many holes in Will's story. Think about it, Gabby. If Dean was under duress, there's no way they'd be letting him talk to his brother like that. And why lead the others on a wild-goose chase around New Mexico unless he was trying to give Will time to find the statue and then give his partners the slip? Once that Son statue is found, chances are Dean's dead anyway."

Gabby's stomach started to ache. "So you think Dean planned to sell them and disappear forever? But when he couldn't figure out what the clues meant for the Son statue, he asked Will to find me? Dean knew I cared about saving the statues for the public enough that I'd help him. Dammit!" She hated that Dean had manipulated her. He did that all the time at work, too. Preyed on her inability to say no to her boss. Made her do his dirty work.

Jake pulled her close and ran a comforting hand up and down her back. "Don't beat yourself up, Gabby. The good in you is what makes you so special."

She wrapped her arms around Jake's waist. Her heart did a happy dance because he thought she was special. But in her head, she berated herself for being so gullible. Dean couldn't have known who her father was, though, and now her former boss was going to wish he'd never helped steal the Father statue. She asked, "Would you guess Dean has the Father statue here with him? Maybe to sell the pair?" Jake hadn't let go of her, so she snuggled closer.

"Good chance of that. And I think your boy toy knows more than he's letting on, too."

She smiled. "He does know more. You cut me off before I could tell you. The people following him are the police. He was just playing with them earlier."

Jake's hand stopped rubbing her back. "Gabby, please don't tell me we're harboring a wanted criminal. At this rate, I'm never getting my badge back."

"He's not a wanted criminal . . . yet." She gave his waist a squeeze. "After I'd asked him to see if there was any buzz on the statues, the cops—who monitor the online traffic Charlie allows them to monitor—approached him to help them find it. Charlie said winning a few brownie points with the police by retrieving an artifact that rightfully belongs in England couldn't hurt. Cops are outside watching the house right now. So no need to call them. And did I forget to mention that Charlie is gay?"

Jake leaned back and blinked at her. "How did I miss that?"

"Probably because you were so busy being jealous of him. Which I thought was pretty cute."

"I was protecting you."

"Right. Lucky for you, you're the only boy toy I want to play with."

"Good." He laid a quick kiss on her lips. "Now that the police are involved, I feel better about all of this. E-mail your dad. Let's get that Son statue back for England and try to keep Dean alive."

"Okay. Have I thanked you for helping me, Jake? I couldn't have done this without you. Wouldn't want to have done it without you."

"Happy to help. But I have ulterior motives. I'm looking forward to after all of this is over. When we can spend the rest of my time off together." His smile was so sweet it melted her heart.

"Then let's get this over with so we can get started with that." She crossed the room and found her laptop. After she had sent her dad an e-mail, she and Jake headed downstairs.

She smiled every time she walked into the massive dining room. It had beautiful portraits on the light-blue silk-covered walls and lovely old vases on the sideboards. It was like eating in a museum, her favorite place on earth, and made her feel right at home.

Jake leaned down and whispered, "I hate how all those people's eyes in the pictures seem to watch while I eat. It gives me the creeps."

To each their own.

Will and Charlie had their heads bent over the map. She laid a hand on Charlie's shoulder and gave it a squeeze. "What are we thinking?"

Charlie shook his head. "The lack of detail on this map is unusual. And I only have this ruler when I could really use a proper scale."

"I have one. Be right back." As she passed by Jake, she held out her hand. "You owe me ten bucks. I told you on the way to Annalisa's we'd need something from my backpack. I think you'll be paying me off again before we're through."

Jake scowled as he dug out his wallet and tugged out a twenty. "Here. There's an extra ten so I don't have to hear about the next one.

I'm going to talk to the cops outside. See what they know. Be back in a few."

Jake walked out the front door while she ran upstairs to get the scale and her laptop. Maybe her father had answered. When she returned to the dining room, she sat beside Charlie and studied the London map. It was odd how things were outlined—no details were filled in—but it was clearly a partial section of a specific part of the city. She'd never seen another like it. And the bottom edge was ragged like it'd been torn, and there was no printed scale. On the top, the heading read "Special Emergency Edition," and a memory struck. "Charlie. Could this be an ARP?"

Will glanced up with a wrinkled brow. "What's that?"

"A map used for Air Raid Precautions planning during the war." Charlie's handsome face lit up with a smile. "Yes, that's why the scale isn't making any sense. The maps were rushed and never available to the public. Gabby, do you recall the scale? You're the genius with sums and numbers."

She closed her eyes and conjured up what she'd learned so many years earlier. "I think this should be one to twenty-five thousand."

Charlie laid the scale down and used his phone to do some quick math. "Yes. That makes more sense. Now, if only we can figure out where this piece of the city is." He went back to studying the vaguely outlined landmarks.

After Will had gone to the wet bar in search of a stiff drink, Charlie whispered, "This map is worth a fortune. They were never released to the public, and there are only so many. If it goes missing, can we call it payment for services rendered?"

"I'll pretend I never heard that. And don't even think about taking anything in here. Annalisa was nice to let us use her lovely home."

"I had my eye on that vase over there, but this map might be all it takes to stifle my desire to nick it."

"Stop." Gabby smacked his arm. "Jake won't hesitate to turn you over to those cops outside."

"Duly noted. But I can see why you're smitten. Jake's rather dishy, isn't he?" Charlie smiled as he studied the faded ink.

"Yes." Her heart did a little backflip. "But we're just having a fling. We live on opposite sides of the country. He has his life, and I have mine."

"Anyone told *him* it's just a fling, then? Because it's a wonder you two don't just burst into flames there's so much sexy tension when you look at each other."

"Part of that is because he can be bossy. And he knows how to push my buttons. It annoys me sometimes." She propped her chin in her hand. "But there's something I can't put my finger on that makes me happy when I'm with him. He's so different from anyone I've ever met. I think I'm falling in love with him."

"You've already taken the fall, love. And look here. I finally found a street name that I can make out. I think I just figured out where our little gold friend is buried."

Gabby leaned closer, thrumming with excitement. "Where?"

"In a graveyard that's been around forever, of course. Logical, coming from a burial site in the states. In Paddington, no less. Lots of war casualties buried there. Spooky and delicious at night, I'd wager."

"But where in the cemetery? The whole place is marked with an *X.*" Gabby picked up the note left with the statue and studied it again. It'd been addressed to the man who'd last owned it. "Wait. Lots of war casualties are buried there? Both cousins who'd owned the pair of statues died in the war. What do you bet he's buried with this man?" She pointed to the name on the envelope.

Charlie lips spread into a slow grin. "Yes. That'd make sense. We should go tomorrow and check things out, then later dig it up when it's dark. Don't want to go through all that red tape required for a permit."

Charlie stood and took a picture of the map. "For my catalog. The one the cops don't know about."

Will said from behind them, "I need to tell you guys something."

Gabby turned around, and all the air whooshed from her lungs. He had a gun in his hand. Had she been wrong about Will? Was he working with Dean after all? "What are you doing?"

Charlie glanced over his shoulder. "His brother's dirty work. Seems they were in on it together, Gabby."

"No, we're not." Will lifted both hands as if in surrender. "Dean warned me that Gabby would try to turn the statue over to a museum. He wanted me to take it from you to save him. I just can't do it, though. Now that you know where the Son statue is buried and Dean has the Father, I want to go home." He lowered his hands from above his head and stuck the gun out toward them. "Here, take this, please. You might need it."

Jake walked in, and his face hardened. In a lighting fast move, he disarmed Will and then held him in a headlock. "Gabby, come take the gun, please."

Will whimpered, "I was just trying to give it to Gabby."

"He's telling the truth, Jake. You can let him go." She took the gun and checked the safety.

Jake slowly released him. "How did you get a gun? And what were you thinking?"

Will rolled his shoulders. "After I told Dean I was meeting you, he told me to get on a bus. Some guy sat beside me, handed me a bag, and then got off. I wasn't going to shoot anyone, Jake. I never even put the bullets in. Dean told me to get the Son statue." He handed her the bullets. "I just wanted to help my brother, but when guns came into play, I drew the line."

Charlie hissed, "Dean's been using you. By adding a gun to the mix, you could've gone to jail for a long time."

Will winced. "I know. I didn't know what else to do. He's my brother."

"A brother who betrayed you. You best get on a plane and go home. We'll take things from here." Charlie turned to Jake. "Okay with you?"

Jake met his gaze. "We need to haul his ass outside and hand him over to the cops. Let him tell them what he knows about Dean."

Will's eyes widened. "No cops. Please. I have my practice back home to think of. I haven't done anything wrong." He turned pleading eyes to her. "Please, Gabby. You know I'd never hurt you. I didn't know what else to do. But I'm worried sick for Dean."

Will was a rich doctor, in over his head, too, who loved his unlovable brother. She had no more sympathy for Dean after she'd learned he was going to sell the statues. He was responsible for his own fate, but it wasn't fair of Dean to take his brother down with him. "We could just send him home. Get him out of harm's way, right, Jake?"

His jaw tightened. "I vote for the cops outside. What if he's still working with his brother, Gabby? Let the police sort that out."

Will turned to her again. "I didn't realize I was doing Dean's dirty work. And I'd never hurt you. You know that, right?"

"Yeah." She huffed out a breath. "Give me your phone. And the password."

Will slowly dug it from his pocket and handed it over. "It's eight, zero, zero, zero."

She tried the password. It worked, so she stuck the phone in her back pocket. "Don't contact Dean. And go straight home. You've already done more for your brother than he deserves."

"He's all the family I have left. I know he's flawed, but—"

"I understand loving a flawed person, but Dean didn't hesitate to put both of our lives in danger. A brother who *loved you* would never do that."

Will opened his mouth to protest but then slowly closed it. His shoulders slumped like he'd just taken on a massive burden. Or perhaps in relief. He wasn't cut out for espionage any more than she was. "You're right. But someone followed me here. I don't know if they'll let me get to the airport alive."

Charlie said, "They'll never know you left. I'll sneak you out in my car. Let's go."

Will laid a kiss on her cheek. "Please keep Dean alive if you can."

She nodded as Charlie took Will's arm and hauled him toward the garage. Charlie said, "I'll see you two in a bit." Then they disappeared through the garage door.

Jake sighed as he laid his forehead against hers. "That might have been a big mistake, Gabby. But seeing a gun pointed at you . . . my heart nearly stopped."

Jake's concern warmed her soul. "Thank you for letting him go." She slowly slid her arms around his shoulders.

Jake didn't flinch or even hesitate. Instead, he wrapped her up and lifted her against his chest. "Add one more thing I'm ignoring. How many is that since I've met you?"

"More than I should ask of you." She kissed his cheek. "You're officially my favorite cop, if that helps."

He grinned. "And you're my favorite trespasser, assailant, and airplane tire murderer."

"You probably say that to all the girls." She kissed him, taking her time, savoring him, until he grew impatient and took over. He upped the intensity, and made her insides turn to mush all over again.

Just when she was considering hauling him upstairs with her, he leaned away and said, "You've made getting bashed over the head worth the pain, Gabby." Then he kissed her again.

Her heart just fell another few feet in love.

# Chapter Fourteen

Jake ended their kiss but still held Gabby tight, reluctant to put her down, at least until his system settled. That split second when he thought Gabby was being threatened with a gun made it clear how much he'd grown to care for her.

She said, "As much as I'm enjoying this, I need to tell you something. First, Will just told me that Dean has the Father statue. And we think we know where the Son statue is. Now might be a good time to get it while everyone is chasing after Charlie. It's in a cemetery in Paddington. Not too far. We could take the Tube."

"Now?" He leaned away so he could see her face. "We still don't know who's out there following us. Why not just tell the police what you've learned and let them dig it up?"

She shook her head. "Then Dean becomes useless, and they might kill him. I don't like the guy, but I promised Will I'd try to keep him alive. I have Will's phone, so maybe we could use that somehow."

He wanted to keep her safe. To hand over the damn artifact and go home. Maybe she could ask her father to get it. And keep Dean safe at the same time. "Have you heard back from your dad?"

"I haven't had a chance to look." She wiggled out of his embrace and headed to the table for her laptop.

He sat beside her as she flipped the lid open and logged in to her e-mail account. He noted her keystrokes and memorized them. Maybe he'd have to send his own message to Moretti. Because the one thing they both had in common was the desire to keep his daughter safe.

"There's a really long message from him." Gabby read the screen for a few minutes before her face paled. "Oh my God. No wonder he let me come over here." She closed her eyes and laid her forehead against the heels of her propped up hands. "This is such a mess. And Dad'll kill him, Jake. I can't let that happen."

"Kill who?" He laid a hand on her back to soothe her. "What's going on?"

She slowly turned her head. "Remember how my father had originally sent someone to buy the statues from Dean? Part of the deal was that the cops wouldn't be looking at Dean for the museum theft. Dean told him that he'd set me up to take the fall and not to worry. He can prove he wasn't even in DC when the theft happened. Later, Dean told him he'd gotten a better offer for the statues. Maybe Dean thought by throwing out the man's name, Rafael Garza, it'd make my father's man back away gracefully."

Jake's stomach dropped. Garza was the head of the most powerful organized-crime family in the world. Things just got a hundred times worse. "Another reason for us to pack up and go home, Gabby. We know you're innocent. Let Charlie get the statue."

She blew out a long breath. "It gets worse. One of the men with Dean is Rafael's son, Pablo. The man who killed my mother and brother. Eye for an eye, my father said."

Jake stood to pace. "Your father let you come over here to flush out Pablo? To kill him?"

"No." She slowly shook her head. "That's just a side benefit. My dad's really here to capture Dean alive. Make him confess so I don't take the fall. Garza's men have Dean locked down tight. My father is just waiting for his chance to grab Dean, and then he said I have to go home, too. He won't risk my life anymore."

"But he needed you to stay involved to keep tabs on Dean. Because Dean is still communicating with you through Will."

"Right." The defeat on Gabby's expression just made Jake more determined.

He officially hated that bastard Dean. But wanted him alive now, too. "Did the police interview you before you left DC?"

"Yes, the next morning after the theft." She groaned and laid her head on her folded arms. "I told them how everything worked there, the procedures we take when we work on artifacts, who has access and who doesn't, and even where I thought the holes were in the system so that someone could steal something. Worse, I don't have an alibi, Jake. I went home that night of the theft, watched some TV, and went to bed. This makes me sick."

He crossed the room, sat by her again, then took her hand. "You have guards who know you were at home all night. They can testify."

Tears filled her eyes. "They can't testify. Not with fake credentials that might not hold up to that kind of scrutiny. These guys are loyal to my father because he helped them stay out of jail. I'm screwed if Dean did a good enough job framing me."

He wiped a tear away that had tracked down her cheek. "We'll just have to stay a step ahead of Dean. By getting both statues back while keeping that jackass alive." How, he wasn't sure. But he'd figure it out.

"Thank you." Gabby forced a small smile as she slowly rose from her chair. "But I can't let my father kill Pablo. As far as I know, my father hasn't committed a crime since my mom died. Breaking that streak and killing Pablo Garza won't bring back my family. And it could land my father in jail. Revenge isn't worth my father's freedom. I need to talk to my dad. Be right back."

After she had gone upstairs, he took out his phone and made a note of her e-mail log-in.

He glanced at the computer beside him, sorely tempted to e-mail and ask Gabby's father to intervene for her own safety. Insist she leave and let him sort things out in ways they couldn't legally do. But maybe he'd wait and see how their phone call went first. Maybe her father had told her the whole story so she'd go home and be safe. Back to her life as a prisoner in DC.

He hated that idea about as much as he hated the danger she was in of possibly going to jail for something she didn't do. Could he trust that justice would prevail? The system wasn't perfect. He wasn't willing to let Gabby be a victim of that imperfection if he could help it.

Going home wasn't the answer anymore. Staying and helping the British police retrieve the statues was the best way to ensure Gabby was cleared. A confession from Dean wouldn't hurt, either.

Maybe they could use Dean's greed against him. He sent Gabby a text.

Ask your dad if he knows how much Garza said he'd pay Dean for the statues.

He stood and paced the thickly carpeted hallway and then the living room, waving people away who kept asking if he needed anything, as a plan formed in his head. The cops outside had said they'd agreed to give Charlie some leeway in exchange for finding the Son statue for them. It'd be easier for Charlie to hand it over to them, in exchange for dropping an outstanding misdemeanor charge against him, than chase it down themselves.

Maybe there was a way to use Will's phone, and Charlie, to save Dean after all. He'd run his plan by the cops outside so they could all work together.

If anyone would've asked him a week ago if he'd ever dream of conspiring with a mobster and an art thief to save a woman he'd met only days before, he would have called them crazy. Maybe it'd been fortuitous timing that he'd been temporarily relieved of his badge. What he was planning might entail coloring outside a few lines.

~

Gabby hung up from a forty-five-minute call with her father and then dropped onto the side of the bed. She'd let her dad have it for keeping her in the dark for so long. He'd apologized but still wanted his revenge on Garza. Hopefully, he wouldn't get the chance to take it.

Her father had reminded her he was nearby if she needed him. If she found herself in trouble, all she had to do was text the word she'd known since she'd been old enough to speak. But she wasn't foolish enough to think her father wouldn't have people following her around London.

She went downstairs and found Charlie and Jake deep in conversation in the living room. Jake sat on the couch, while Charlie, dressed in dark clothing now, sat across from him, sipping a drink. It was after midnight, but she was still on New Mexico time, wired with adrenaline.

She sat next to Jake on the soft, satiny fabric. It surprised her when he reached out and took her hand. Then, while he and Charlie talked about art auctions, he ran his thumb back and forth in a comforting pattern. She could use a little comfort. God knows she didn't get much from her stubborn and upset father.

Will's phone dinged in her back pocket, so she dug it out with her free hand. "It's a text from Dean. He's asking if we've made any progress with the map." She glanced Jake's way. "Will must not have told him we think we know where the statue is. Let's hope he's really on a plane home and won't give us away."

"Taken care of." Charlie took a long drink. "I personally placed him on my plane. With Wi-Fi turned off. We have a few hours before he'll get a chance to check in. He said I could have the map he found, by the way."

Gabby suppressed a grin. That probably wasn't true and said just for Jake's sake, but they had bigger problems to tackle. "What should I write back?"

"We were just discussing that." Jake squeezed her hand. "Did your father know how much Dean was promised for both statues?"

"Yeah. Ten million."

Charlie laughed. "Those statues together would fetch far more than that in the private sector. And Dean's 'friends' obviously know that, too. Your plan might just work, Jake."

"What plan?" Her temper heated again at being left out of the loop.

Jake gave her a shoulder bump. "The one we were just trying to figure out. Tell Dean we're making progress but are about to give up for the night. And there might be a way to make some more money for the museum. The art dealer with us is willing to include the shards in his private auction tomorrow and split the proceeds fifty-fifty. Can he slip away with his shard and meet you somewhere? Gabby has hers and is on board if your museum gets the profits."

Gabby typed it in and hit "Send." "You're using the shard as a code word for the statues, right? In case Garza's men are reading the texts?"

"Yes. Dean will know we're really talking about the Father statue. He might see this plan as a way to circumvent his captors." Charlie finished off his drink, and someone instantly appeared with a fresh one. After he had waved the man away, the server made a silent retreat. "Actually, Jake, I'm not sure Gabs should know the entire plan. She's a horrific liar."

That was kind of true, but she didn't want to be left out of the plan that directly affected her life. Before she could think of a retort, Jake said, "I'm still not sure I want to use Gabby as bait to lure Dean out of the shadows."

*Bait?*

"Wait. What are we thinking?" The phone dinged again, and she read the screen. "Dean says how much?"

Charlie smiled. "Seems Dean is a greedy man or just a wanker. Tell him twenty million. Maybe more. But both shards have to be together or no deal."

She typed it in, then said, "What's next?"

Jake answered, "We're assuming Dean and his friends are nearby and hoping to hear from Will when we head out to get the Son statue. So they can take it after we find it."

That made some sense. Before she could reply, Will's phone chimed again. She read the screen. "Tell Gabby I'll meet her with the shard tomorrow. Where and when?"

Jake's jaw clenched. "Dean has either told his buddies it'd be a good idea to grab Gabby because she's the most likely to find the statue, or he's going to give his friends the slip. I wish I knew which it was. There's only one way to find out, unfortunately. And I don't like it."

"Here, Gabby. Type this in. The police asked that we meet here." Charlie handed over a piece of paper with the location and time. "I'll just go find something else to do for the next few awkward moments between you two."

She turned to Jake. "Why is it going to get awkward?"

Jake pointed to the phone. "First, type that in, please. And then say Will's bunking with us tonight to keep an eye on things."

She typed it all in. "Done. So, what's the plan?"

"After weighing the danger to you, and because I don't want you to get shot at, Charlie will do the actual digging up of the statue tonight, and then—"

"Nope." She crossed her arms. "I'm doing the digging. I didn't come all this way—"

"I know you want to be the one to find that damned thing." Jake laid his hands on her shoulders. "But I can't let you get hurt. If all goes well tonight, and Charlie finds the statue, we'll grab Dean and the Father statue at the meeting point tomorrow. And then we'll be done with all of this."

Anger at Jake for giving Charlie the chance to find the statue instead of her warred with her gratitude that he wanted to protect her. "What about the part where I'm bait?"

"Still working on the details. I'm going to coordinate with the cops, make sure you're safe, or we find another way. I'm worried about you meeting Dean, though, and want to discuss some options with you in the morning. But let's see if we can find the Son statue first. Then we'll talk about the next step."

She hated not being the one to find that damned statue, but she didn't particularly want to be shot at, either. "Should I tell my dad the plan?"

"Yes. Everything. Tell him to be around for backup. Especially if guns come out, remind him Dean has to be safe."

"He'll keep Dean safe. For me. But you have to promise you won't turn him in to the cops, Jake."

He nodded. "I promise. Just for tomorrow. After that, all bets are off."

"Deal." She went to the dining room and found her laptop. After she had written to her father, she returned to the living room, where Jake stood staring into the dying embers in the fireplace.

She hated that Charlie was about to risk his life for her. Moving behind Jake, she wrapped him up in a hug. "Maybe I could help Charlie from a distance. I'm an expert shot."

He laid his hands over hers. "You already admitted you'd never shoot anyone."

"That was before. I could if I thought you or Charlie were in danger. Please let me help."

He took a hand and led her toward the stairs. "You can help right now. Charlie just slipped out the back. On foot. He's going to dig up our little friend and then hand it over to the police. *If* that map was right. Meanwhile, you and I are going upstairs to go to bed. We'll be sure to draw the curtains closed so everyone out there watching us will see we're still here."

She stopped in her tracks and tugged his hand. "You sent Charlie out there alone?"

"He insisted he knew how to steal a statue. I don't want to know why. Let's try to get some rest. Tomorrow is going to be a big day."

Jake was right. Charlie could take care of himself. She followed Jake into the bedroom, and then they made a big production of closing the curtains together. After they had been drawn, she slid to the side of the bed to take off her shoes. "You realize you just sent a thief to get something worth a small fortune, don't you?"

Jake stripped down to his boxers and pulled the covers back. "I think the map he stole—vital evidence for this case I might add—will keep his thieving hands satisfied for the moment, don't you?" He patted the sheets beside him.

"I'm pleading the fifth." She stripped and then joined him, hoping to take his mind off Charlie and focus on her. "Speaking of being satisfied, you could help a girl out."

"That so?" He drew her against him. "You need a hot cup of tea or something?"

"No. But maybe those lovely big hands of yours all over my body could do the trick." She snuggled closer.

"Your snotty British accent is back." He ran his hand lightly up and down her bare back. Giving her comfort and the shivers at the same time. "Are you scared about tomorrow?"

"I'm a bit worried." She was more scared of falling even more in love with him. She switched to her most American voice. "How about a little distraction, cowboy?"

His lips slowly tilted. "Have I mentioned how much the snotty Brit voice turns me on?"

"Really?" With her best exaggerated English accent, she said, "So shall we try making love together this time? Instead of at opposite ends of one another?"

"Mmmmm. Very hot." He rolled on top of her, trapping her under his delicious body weight. "Anything you'd like. You're the boss, Gabby."

She snorted. "Hardly. *You're* the bossy one. Not me." And she hated that she liked it in bed. Outside the bedroom, not so much.

He kissed her neck, and then her collarbone. "Feel free to make suggestions as we go." His hand covered her breast and lightly squeezed. It made her back arch for more.

"Carry on. You're doing just fine, thank you." She ran her hands over his scarred back, through his thick hair, and then took his face in her hands and kissed him. Hard. When he stayed on top of her and kissed her back, she sighed. Progress. At last. They were going to make love together this time.

He went back to caressing her neck with kisses, so she closed her eyes and let the sweet sensations sweep her away to that new place Jake took her. Then she indulged in a silly fantasy that she could be with him like this forever. Even though it'd be impossible—her father was a criminal, and Jake was a cop—she'd pretend and enjoy him while she could.

# Chapter Fifteen

Jake paced the lavish master bedroom, with its deep carpet and antique four-poster, where matronly, heavyset Detective Inspector Edwards, the head of the operation, prepped Gabby for the meeting with Dean. She'd run Gabby's wires under her first layer of clothes and tested her equipment while giving her basic instructions. Luckily it was cold outside, so all the layers would hide the electronics.

Charlie had texted earlier that he had turned the Son statue over to the police. It'd be returned to its rightful owners. So half the problem had been solved. Hopefully, Dean would show up with the Father statue as planned. Then the police would arrest him and Garza's men, and the Father statue could go back to DC where it belonged.

He'd promised Gabby he wouldn't mention her father's presence to the detective, as much as it went against his grain. But Moretti hadn't done anything except look out for his daughter so far, so he'd concede there. If Gabby's father killed Garza's son, Pablo, then things with Gabby would get a whole lot more complicated.

The policewoman left to retrieve glasses with a built-in camera, so Jake adjusted Gabby's Kevlar vest and then checked her audio one last time himself. He couldn't let anything go wrong. The British police had all been accommodating and professional, but he still had a bad feeling about the meeting between Gabby and Dean.

He asked, "Vest feel okay?"

Gabby nodded. "It's bulky. But not too bad."

"Good." Something wasn't right, but he couldn't put his finger on it. Or, maybe it was because he'd never used someone he cared about as bait.

The detective might be back any second, so he grabbed the gun he'd taken from Will and stuffed it into her backpack. "Let's keep this on the down low. How are your self-defense skills?" Weapons weren't all she might need. Especially if Dean tried to kidnap Gabby. At least she had some height on the guy.

She glanced up at him. "I have a black belt in karate. But I've never had to use it other than on sparring partners."

One more surprising fact about her.

He grabbed her by the shoulders and twisted her in front of him, his forearm across her chest, a tight grip on her right upper arm, leaving his "weapon" hand free. He poked a finger against her forehead. The most common hold a gunman taking a hostage assumed. "How would you get out of this?"

In the blink of an eye, her hand slapped his away from her head at the same time that her foot wrapped around his leg and tugged, upsetting his balance. With both hands on his forearm, she sent him flying over her shoulder. He landed with a thump on his back. Before he could roll over, she stepped on his wrist with the heavy boots they'd dressed her in, to secure his "weapon." And then she dropped her knee to his chest, making the air whoosh from his lungs, to hold him in place. It made him damn proud.

She leaned down and laid a quick kiss on his lips. "Feel better now?"

"No. That hurt. Maybe if you'd kiss me again, I'd feel better."

Gabby's dimples flashed as she moved her sharp knee off his chest and then obliged him. Her kisses always held a blend of sweetness and heat he'd come to crave. And when they'd made love earlier, something new had pulled at his gut and heart simultaneously. His usual need to be in charge of the touching when in bed was easy to set aside with her. Instead, he'd wanted to please her and, in doing so, had been sated, too. And relaxed enough to hold her afterward. Something he'd rarely done even while married. How was he ever going to let Gabby go once they got back home?

She slowly ended their kiss, then jumped up and held out a hand to help him. He stood and wrapped her in a hug. "Do what you have to do to defend yourself, okay? Even if that means shooting someone. Promise?"

She moved her mouth near his ear, her warm breath sending a whole new spike of desire straight to his gut. "I'll try. But I'm glad to know the cops, you, and my father are going to be nearby. My own personal army. Which reminds me . . ." She took her cell from her back pocket and typed "Benji" into a text box but didn't hit "Send." "I need to have this ready just in case."

It had to be a code word between her and her father.

He handed over her forty-pound backpack. "Here's everything you own."

"Very funny." She took the bag and smirked. "A girl needs her stuff."

She might need the gun inside. He hoped she'd be brave enough to shoot someone if she had to.

The detective inspector returned and made the final adjustments to Gabby's glasses. She said, "All set. Jake, you can send Dean the text now. Just about ready to go."

He grabbed Will's phone from his pocket while Gabby finished getting dressed with layers of clothes to hide the wires and vest. She needed a jacket to cover up the shape the vest would make. Especially since Gabby mentioned Dean made a habit of studying her chest. Which pissed him off even more. Using more force than was necessary, he typed:

Think we know where to find the Son statue. I'll let you know. Still meeting with Gabby at 10:00 at the park?

After a few moments, a reply came.

Yes. 10. Then we'll find it together. Where is it?

Jake ran a few of the responses he'd discussed with the cops earlier through his head.

They sent the art dealer to get it at some church while Gabby meets you. I'll stay here and then let you know if they find it.

Jake studied the screen, holding his breath, hoping Dean wouldn't ask Will to accompany Gabby to the park, or the jig might be up. Finally, the phone chimed.

Do as we talked about as soon as you see the statue. And say your good-byes to Gabby, bro. She'll be all mine after she sees how I rescued her precious statues. Not that you ever had a real chance with her.

Jake blinked at the screen. What the hell did that mean? "Gabby, have you and Dean ever dated?"

"No!" Gabby made a gagging sound, and the detective chuckled.

"Did he ever ask you out?"

Gabby stood in front of the mirror, studying her new badass reflection—a leather jacket, jeans, and biker boots equipped with steel toes. "Once. But I told him I'd never date a coworker, much less my boss, so he backed off. Mostly. Except for staring at me all the time when he thought I wasn't looking. Why?"

He tilted the phone's screen so she and the other detective could read it for themselves.

Detective Edwards frowned at the screen. "Sibling rivalry maybe. Shall we go, then?"

"Yep. Let me send this text, and then we're out." Jake wrote back to Dean, relieved he didn't appear to have any plans to harm Gabby.

Gabby's into someone else anyway. I'll check in later.

Dean wrote right back.

Not after today. Let me know if they find the statue.

Will do.

He stuffed the phone in his back pocket and followed behind the two women. Downstairs, the dining room was full of cops waiting to monitor Gabby as well as the officers already in position at the park.

He took Gabby's hand as they silently followed the detective outside to what looked like a cab and slid into the back seat. His heart beat a double-time tattoo while all the ways the meeting could go wrong flashed through his mind. Chances of Dean being alone were slim. It'd be tough to slip away from Garza's men. And Moretti's minions were wild cards.

They'd gone over all the different scenarios they could think of, and Detective Edwards would instruct Gabby with the tiny mic in her ear, but still. He turned to her and forced a smile. "Not too late to back out."

She shook her head. "I need for Dean to confess what he did to frame me while everyone is listening. Just in case Garza's men decide to off the rat after they get what they want."

He smiled. Gone was the timid woman who'd never hurt a fly, replaced by the brave version. He hoped she could stay tough. "Remember, if he has the statue—"

"I know. We've been all through this, Jake." She gave his forearm a squeeze.

Detective Edwards called out. "I'll drop you here, Gabby. That couple over there will keep an eye on you while you make your way across the park to the meeting point, then they'll move on. Just follow the path. All the people round the fountain are undercover cops, so please don't make eye contact unless you need help. We'll be on the other side, in the van, watching and listening. Good luck."

"Thanks. See you in a few." Gabby leaned in to Jake for a quick kiss, then laid her fingers over his lips to prevent him from saying anything. "I'll be fine, Jake."

She got out and headed for the fountain in Hyde Park they'd chosen near the street. His mood was as gray as the day, with heavy clouds of doubt looming above. He hoped to God it wasn't a mistake to send her out there.

He kept an eye on her and the couple who followed a short distance behind as long as he could. Finally, he lost sight of them as the car made its way around the corner to join the surveillance team.

The way Gabby had deliberately straightened her shoulders had sent a pang to his heart. She was probably scared to death.

DI Edwards said, "Gabby, please cough once if you can hear me." After a moment, Edwards whispered, "Perfect. And the glasses are sending video. All good to go, Gabby." The cop met Jake's gaze in the mirror. "She's in good hands. We'll keep her safe."

"Counting on that." He hoped the detective was right.

◇

Gabby walked steadily to the meeting place. Growing up, she'd been to many events in the same park, but all those times had been happy ones, with festivals and concerts.

She followed the path that cut through the grass and trees on either side, reminding herself to breathe. The cold seeping into her lungs should have made her shiver, but instead, her nerves kept the blood flowing at a stellar pace, heating her veins.

The police had picked the park because not too many civilians were bound to linger in February's cold, wet air in the remote section of greenery.

She'd studied the area on Google Earth until her eyes bled earlier that morning. Now, as she approached the meeting site, her heart rate tripled from its already accelerated pace, making her head feel light.

*Deep breaths. Deep breaths. I can do this.*

There were a few benches set in a circle around the silent fountain that depicted a woman hunting with a bow and arrow. The foliage surrounding the fountain would have been dense in the summer but now was stark and lifeless.

The benches were occupied by two couples and a single woman, and then Dean. He had a smile on his face and stood as she approached.

"Hi, Gabby. I almost didn't recognize you with the glasses and new hair. Great to see you."

Great to see her? Why was he acting like they were old friends happy to see each other? "Dean. You've been a busy man." She quickly sat on the bench and laid her bag at her feet. Dean had a bag with him, too, and she hoped he'd brought the Father statue. Maybe they could end things quickly.

A soft voice in her ear whispered, "Ask to see the statue as soon as you can."

Dean sat beside her and cleared his throat. "Yeah. I've been busy planning our new life." He reached into his coat pocket and sent a spike of fear up her spine. Was he reaching for a gun?

He withdrew a British passport. "We both have new identities, Gabby. All we have to do is hand over the pair of statues, and we can start our new lives together."

"What do you mean?" His words hit her as hard as if he'd slapped her. But staying in character, she said, "I thought we were going to sell them and then give the money to the museum."

He shook his head as he opened the passport. It had her picture on it and a new name. "You don't understand, Gabby. This is your ticket out."

He wasn't making sense. "My ticket out from what?"

"We'll go to Peru and participate in digs as you've always said you wanted to do. You don't have any family, and I only have Will, so what's stopping us from living our dream? Together. You know we were made for each other."

*Oh, hell no.*

The detective's voice said, "Go with it. Tell him you still need the Son statue. Don't upset him."

Don't upset him? The guy was insane. She'd never given him any signals that she was interested in him. But she had a job to do, so she took a second and refocused her emotions. "Well, first we need both statues. Can I see the Father? Did you bring him?"

"He's right here." Dean quickly surveyed the area before he slid his bag into her hand.

She peeked inside and found the Father statue beaming up at her. And the pattern on the tunic was right. Thank God.

Dean's lips tilted into a sick grin. "We'll sell the pair tonight and then head for the airport. I have it all planned out."

Her stomach took a fast dive. "I don't understand why you're doing this, Dean."

He closed the bag and laid it at his feet. "You said you'd never date a coworker, so I found a way we could be together."

She shook her head. "No offense, but I've never thought of you like that. And I love my job in DC."

"You thought I was off-limits, so you just haven't had time to see how great we'd be together. That's all. In time, you'll see things like I do." His jaw clenched. "And you can't ever go back to the museum, Gabby. All the evidence from the statue theft points to you. They must have warrants out for your arrest by now. Don't you see? I did all of this for you. So we could be together. Now let's go get that other statue."

Warrants for her arrest? The guy was beyond crazy.

More like he did it so he could kidnap her. Make her too afraid to go home and be arrested. She'd just risked everything for an artifact.

The detective whispered, "Slowly stand. Tell him to follow you. Lead him close to the couple to your right. Then hit the ground."

*Think straight. Stop freaking out about Dean and his delusions.*

"It sounds like you've been planning this elaborate scheme for a while, huh, Dean?"

Dean's eyes lit up, making him seem even crazier. "For months, Gabby. Getting the passports hadn't been easy, but they're good ones. I hadn't counted on Will finding the map instead of the statue in New Mexico, either, so I had to stall for some time. Originally, I was going to meet you at the dig site, get you out of DC before the cops arrested you, but this way worked out just as well. I knew you trusted Will and would help him read the map if you thought it'd save me. Because you love me as much as I love you, right? We make a great team, don't we?"

Oh God. How hadn't she seen how disturbed he was before? Probably because she spent most of her time at work avoiding him.

"Sure. Um. The other statue's not far. Come with me." She stood and picked up her backpack, ready to take a dive at the earliest opportunity, when Dean's hand snaked out and grabbed her left arm to stop her. Then he slapped a handcuff on her wrist.

She glanced down at their bound hands, and her stomach did a nasty flip. "What are you doing?"

"Sorry, but they made me do this." He slowly unzipped his jacket. "It's insurance my business partners needed. They'll blow us both up if we try to escape with the statues."

Gabby sucked in a sharp breath. Dean wore a bomb strapped to a vest. How had things gone so terribly wrong? And what was she supposed to do now?

"Stay calm. Do as he says, Gabby," Detective Edwards said in her ear.

They hadn't planned on Dean being certifiably crazy. It was getting hard to breathe.

Dean stood way too close and whispered, "The man who wants the statues has the detonator. He's right over there." He pointed to a man who stood fifty yards away, holding something in his hand. The man waved.

She closed her eyes to hold back the panic that engulfed her body, paralyzing her senses, making it hard to hear Dean's words clearly. She had to pull it together. There were people around to help her. *Could* they help her? She opened her eyes, hoping to see where the hell her bodyguards, Sal and Louie, were.

Her eyes still worked, even if her feet felt like they were encased in cement. She finally spotted Sal, probably a hundred yards away. She wanted to signal for help, but if they shot Dean or the other guy, she could be dead, too.

The detective's strained voice commanded, "Everyone hold positions. Let them leave."

She was going to have to save herself. But how? Should she send her father the signal? No, he might not know about the bomb.

Dean's cold, clammy fingers intertwined with hers as he tugged her toward a path. "You want me to carry your backpack, Gabby?"

"No." She shook her head and forced her feet to move forward. "I'm good." And there was a gun in there. She'd have to use it. If she could.

"Okay. Let's hurry and get that statue. I booked us on a flight for Peru tonight. We'll be on our way in hours."

Her stomach did another nasty flip. "I don't want to go to Peru, Dean. You can have the statue, but I don't want to go away forever. I have a life." Tears formed in her eyes as a vision of Jake entered her mind. "I've met—"

"Stop." The detective's raised voice in her ear startled her. "You have to make him think you'll go. Buy us some time, Gabby. You're doing well."

Dean's face crumpled with fury. "You'd rather spend the rest of your life in jail rather than with me?" He wrenched her handcuffed wrist forward. Hard.

She whimpered. She couldn't help it. The metal was too tight. It dug into her skin, as it was. When he pulled, it sent radiating pain up her arm.

Home. She just wanted to go home, where it was safe.

Jake's voice sounded in her ear. "Babe. We're on top of it. Hang tough. I promise everything will be fine."

Hearing Jake's voice choked her up, but his promise gave her the shot of courage she needed. He'd save her. Somewhere deep inside she knew that.

She bit her lip, pulled it together, and nodded her head so Jake could see through her video glasses that she'd heard him.

She said, "No, I don't want to go to jail. It just came as a shock, I guess. Peru will be wonderful. Living there, being part of a dig. That *is* what I've always wanted." She swallowed back the bile rising in her throat and walked beside Dean as they approached a big, white moving van.

Dean's shoulders relaxed a fraction, and he let up on the tension on her wrist. "It's going to be awesome. Let's go get that statue before your friend finds it."

What would they do to her when they found out the statue wasn't there? She glanced over her shoulder. The man working with Dean was a few paces behind, as were Sal and probably a cop or two.

As they approached the truck, Pablo Garza appeared and opened the rear cargo doors. The man who'd killed her mother and brother.

Tears formed in her eyes. Would he kill her, too? Seeing the hate shining in the man's dead eyes made her father's need for revenge clearer now. Garza was pure evil. And was probably in her father's cross hairs. She prayed her father wouldn't shoot him, though. It could get them all blown up.

They were in way over their heads. Garza's crew were professional killers. She and Dean didn't have a chance.

Pablo took her by the elbow, Dean by the scruff of the neck, and roughly shoved them both into the back of the truck. Pablo asked, "Where to, Gabby?" He grabbed the Father statue from Dean's grip.

Jake's voice in her ear said, "Tell him where we found it. We'll move people in place."

She barely squeaked out, "Paddington Cemetery," around the fear that had crept into her throat.

After the doors had slammed closed behind them, she expected to be in complete darkness in the boxy truck, but there was a skylight on the roof. Could they climb out of that? As she and Dean wrestled to sit against the side while shackled together, she said, "Some friend, Dean. Shoving us around. They aren't going to let us go. We have to try to escape."

Dean shook his head and settled in beside her, wiping the blood from a small cut on his face from the rough floor. "He was just in a hurry. Will told us you came here with a cop, so they're pissed. That's all. We just have to hand them over the statues, and then we're good."

They were far from good. They were going to die if she didn't do something.

"Don't you see? We're witnesses, Dean. They can't let us live!"

He shook his head. "Trust me. They just want to make money. Pablo said people like them never get caught by the police. They don't care about people like us."

Dean wasn't only crazy. He was an idiot.

Jake's voice whispered, "Do you have a knife in your backpack? Something we can use to cut wires? Tilt your glasses up and down for yes."

She forced her scattered mind to focus. She didn't have a knife. But she had sharp clippers in her kit. How could she tell him that without blowing her cover? She turned to Dean. "I have my field kit to dig up the statue, but if it's hidden behind some brick or stone around the grave, I only have clippers. Do you have something sharper?"

Dean blinked at her for a moment, then shook his head. "No. But they have everything we need up front in the cab. I gave them a list of materials."

*Good. Maybe I can distract them and buy time by asking them to dig, too.*

Jake said, "You need to hit Dean over the head with your backpack, Gabby. Harder than you hit me that day. Then use your steel-toe boots after that. Knock him out. Then we'll work that bomb. We only have a few minutes."

Her right hand tightened around her backpack. If the bomb was neutralized, they would have a chance. But would it go off if she hit him? Could she kick him in the head? She could kill him.

Jake whispered, "It's your life or his. Do it. For me, Gabby. So we can be together again."

He was right. She might never see Jake again if she didn't do it. Or her father, or her aunt. Or Einstein. Never have the chance to go on a real dig someday, as was always her dream.

She grabbed her bag, closed her eyes, and then swung it across her body with all her might.

"Whaaaa." Dean's head flew back and hit the side of the truck with a sick thud as the backpack fell into his lap. She took their bound hands and laid them against the side of the truck to help her stand, and then she kicked him. He fell to his side, so she kicked him again.

When he lay still, his eyes closed, she quickly dug into her backpack for her gun and then the clippers. She was saving his damn life, too. She needed to remember that.

Jake said, "Good job. Roll him on his back and open up his jacket so we can see the bomb."

Gabby blinked away her tears, but like a robot she did as Jake said. She moved her glasses closer so they could see the wires and what looked like batteries tucked into the little pockets.

The van rounded a corner fast, throwing them both against the side of the truck. After the vehicle had straightened again, she straddled Dean's legs for stability and searched for the damn clippers in her backpack. Jake was right. She did have too much crap in there.

Another cop's voice filled her ear. "Okay, Gabby. Listen and please do exactly as I say." Had to be a bomb expert.

She blinked away her tears and tried to concentrate on the voice in her ear, moving wires gently with her fingers for him to see through her glasses. God, what if she tugged the wrong one? They'd all be blown to bits.

She had to stop thinking about that and concentrate on the words in her ear. After moving her head slowly so the camera got a view of the entire bomb, the voice asked her to move a red wire gently aside so he could see underneath. It revealed a rat's nest of different colored wires below that. How would anyone know which one to cut?

"Okay, Gabby, could you move to the one on top of the battery on the right? The blue one, please? Just give it a little nudge aside."

With shaking hands, she slowly hooked her index finger around the blue wire and moved it to the left. As she did that, it sprang loose, exposing a bare copper end. "Oh crap!" She closed her eyes and waited for the explosion to hit, as thoughts slammed through her brain about how she wished she'd been nicer to her father the last time they'd talked and how much she'd miss Jake.

The voice said, "Gabby, relax. The bomb's a fake."

She blinked her eyes open and sagged against the side of the truck in relief. "Thank God." She moved off Dean and sat with her back against the side, trying desperately to catch her breath. Then she glanced at Dean, who'd begun stirring, hating the swollen nose and bruises she'd put on his face, even though he was an ass. He deserved it, but she just wasn't cut out for violence. Justified or not.

He slowly sat up. "What the hell has gotten into you, Gabby? I told them you'd come along peacefully. Where's the sweet girl who kept her head down and got her job done every day?" His expression held a level of rage she'd never seen from him. "You're ruining all of my perfect plans! We were supposed to find the statue, hand them both over, and then you and I were going to leave forever!"

When he made a move toward her, with hands cupped as if to choke her, the fury in his gaze showed he'd have no problem snapping her neck.

She pulled the gun from her waistband and pointed it at him. "Back off." Her hands shook with adrenaline, but somehow she managed to point the barrel at him.

Dean's eyes widened, but he let his hands drop. "You'd never shoot me."

"Don't push me." After he had leaned back against the side again, she said, "What do we do now, Detective?"

Dean closed his eyes. "Perfect. You're wired. All you had to do was go along with my plan . . ."

The detective said, "Keep a close eye on him. When they let you out, cooperate. Our shooters will be in place soon, but stall for time if you have the chance."

So the police were going to take Pablo and his helper out. Made sense, since they'd kidnapped them. Maybe her father wouldn't have to kill Pablo after all, and her dad could stay out of jail.

That was a small relief at least. Hopefully, she and Dean would survive long enough for the cops to free them.

# Chapter Sixteen

Jake stared out the window from the back seat of the police car as it sped through the rain toward Paddington Cemetery. That was all they needed. Rain to complicate things even more. Make a clean shot from a distance slightly harder, but not impossible.

He leaned over DI Edwards's shoulder in the front seat. She quietly commanded the placement of her sharpshooters for when they arrived based on an Internet map of the cemetery. Their driver, Steven, expertly weaved in and out of traffic as she worked beside him. She slowly turned her head and met Jake's gaze. A silent "back off" gleamed in her eyes. She was like a kindly mother, and he'd had his doubts about her at first, but she'd handled the situation well so far.

She'd been smart to have him calm Gabby when she'd needed it most, and then to prod her to hit Dean. The detective read people well. She'd sensed Gabby would have a hard time hitting Dean. Even after what he'd done to her. Gabby most likely took after her mother, not her ruthless father, whose men had been nearby all day.

He lifted his hands for peace and leaned back. "ETA?"

Steven said, "Under a minute."

The guy was a constable and didn't carry a gun. Only the special squads did in England. Jake was missing his backup piece but was grateful Gabby had Will's gun. "Everyone in place yet?"

Steven slid his eyes to the rearview mirror. "Let her do her job, mate."

"Yep." Jake huffed out a breath and glanced out the window again. As the cemetery came into sight, so did a black SUV beside them. One he'd seen at the park earlier.

As they passed the SUV, Jake craned his neck. Moretti had made an appearance after all. He sat in the back, dressed in a dark wool coat, while Sal drove.

A part of him wanted to tear his eyes away and ignore Gabby's father's presence, while his other half wanted to alert Detective Edwards and have someone grab him. But keeping Gabby safe was more important at the moment. He'd deal with Moretti later, when they got home.

He finally understood a little better how Gabby could love her father. He'd followed her across an ocean to keep her safe and out of jail while risking his freedom. But how much of Moretti's efforts were to take revenge on Garza?

When their car parked a few blocks away from the cemetery, he called out, "We need people closer. What if Garza spots a shooter? He'll bolt. Or, worse, kill a hostage."

Steven shook his head ever so slightly. "Too dangerous. The shooters aren't in place yet. Better this way for all."

Not for Gabby. Pablo Garza was a seasoned criminal. He'd be ready for an ambush.

One of the sharpshooters in the car behind them got out to move into position, so Jake hopped out of the car and fell in step.

When DI Edwards's voice in his earpiece ordered him back into the vehicle, Jake replied, "Negative. I'll take responsibility for my own safety."

The armed policeman stopped, waiting for her order. Edwards's irritated voice said, "Detective Morris can accompany you, Sergeant."

The man nodded once and started for the cemetery again.

They found a secure spot and hid just inside the gates. When the truck Gabby was in entered a few moments later, he wanted to run, open the back of the truck, and grab Gabby before Garza could get out. Instead, he forced himself to hunker down in the rain and cold and wait for the right moment. The truck pulled into a space near a building and stopped, as if it had business being there. Jake released his knife and held it at the ready. He'd taken out enemy soldiers with only a knife while in the military, and he'd do it again in a heartbeat.

The familiar jolt of adrenaline ran up his spine, just as it always did when he was about to engage a dangerous situation. It was his reminder to stay alert, be ready to react, and stay focused on the objective.

To save Gabby.

~

When the truck stopped, Gabby glanced at Dean, who was holding his face in his hands and moaning about how she was ruining everything by bringing the police.

How had he ever thought his ridiculous plan would work? Fake passports, money—wait.

A fake passport might come in handy later. For the new life she wanted.

She poked Dean in the arm with her gun to gain his attention. "Don't say a word about the gun, understand?" She dug her passport out of the jacket pocket he'd slipped it into at the park. "Or I'll shoot you myself." She tucked the passport away in her jacket pocket and then the gun in her waistband at her lower back. Best to have the element of surprise once they saw Dean's beaten face.

Dean shook his head. "You're not the girl I thought you were at all, Gabby."

"Yeah, well. That girl grew up the day you dragged me into this mess, Dean."

A door swung open, and the man with the fake detonator waggled his curled fingers in a silent "come out" gesture as he glanced behind them. Pablo had his back to them, scanning the area. What if he saw the sharpshooters? What would he do to her and Dean?

Blood pounded in her ears as she and Dean slowly stood and walked across the rough wooden floor toward the open door. What was taking the shooters so long? Why hadn't they taken them out yet?

In her ear, the detective said, "Stay as far away from Garza and his man as you can manage. The shooters are almost in place."

God, it was hard to take a deep breath. She forced her mind to scan the area outside the truck for somewhere to take cover. How would she do that attached to Dean?

They both sat at the back of the truck, feet dangling, ready to hop down together, when Dean suddenly jumped out of the truck, pulling her along with him. They landed in a tangled heap on the gravel. As they both struggled into sitting positions, Dean called out, "She's got a gun!"

*Dammit! The fool was going to get them killed.*

Both Garza and the other man grabbed for their guns inside their coats.

*This is it. I'm going to die.*

Garza took aim at her chest. "Hands up. Where I can see them."

All the air rushed from her lungs, making it impossible to take a deep breath as she slowly lifted her and Dean's hands. Garza switched his aim, pointing his gun at Dean. "I'm done playing games with you."

A muffled shot rang out, and a burst of blood sprayed from Dean's chest. He moaned as his whole body slumped to the ground beside her. Then he closed his eyes and went limp.

Garza said, "You're next, Gabby, if you don't do exactly as I say."

Oh God. She'd never seen anyone shot before. Blood poured steadily from Dean's chest, steaming as it hit the cold air.

She panted for breath as she stared in fear and disbelief at Dean lying motionless beside her. Her whole body violently shook as she opened her mouth to tell Garza she'd do as he said.

A male voice called out, "Police. Drop your weapons!"

A glimmer of hope released the bands tightening around her chest. Would she be saved from a death like Dean's after all?

*Please just get me out alive.*

Garza and the man closest to her turned their guns toward the policeman. A shot sounded, and the detonator man fell in a heap at her feet. His vacant eyes stared lifelessly into hers. He was dead. She should have been relieved, but instead, she struggled against the overwhelming need to pass out.

Garza suddenly made a choking noise, dropped his gun, and then grabbed at his neck where a knife handle stuck out. Jake's knife.

Thank God Jake was there. He would save her.

Then another shot rang out. Blood spurted from Garza's forehead, and he fell flat on his face beside her. She glanced up in time to see the back of her father's head as he hurried across the other side of the cemetery. Her father had shot Pablo. Whether to save her or out of revenge didn't matter. Garza and the other guy couldn't hurt her anymore.

She closed her eyes so she wouldn't have to see that she sat in the middle of three prone bodies. With blood everywhere. With every breath she took, the metallic tang of blood settled at the back of her throat, making her sick to her stomach.

But then footsteps and a familiar voice gave her the strength to open her eyes again.

"Are you all right, Gabby?" Jake knelt at her side.

"Yeah. I think so." A warm wave of relief filled her. It was so good to see him.

His gaze quickly scanned her from head to toe. "Are you sure?"

She lifted her shaking hands and examined the blood. It wasn't hers. "No. I mean yes. I'm okay."

"Good. Stay here. Be right back." Jake kissed her forehead and then took off at a full run, yelling something about holding fire. In the blink of an eye, people she didn't recognize surrounded her. Someone removed her handcuffs, and another cop helped her stand and took the gun from her back. "Let's get you out of here, shall we, Gabby?"

"Yes. Please."

The cop wrapped an arm around her shoulder. "You were very brave, Gabby. Very brave."

She didn't feel brave. She felt like her brain was floating somewhere outside her body. Her thoughts wouldn't line up. And her arms and legs shook violently.

Where was Jake? She needed to find Jake. Why suddenly wouldn't the words she was thinking come out of her mouth?

Then her knees buckled. Another police officer grabbed her other arm, and they rushed her toward the gates of the cemetery. Sirens sounded from everywhere, making it even harder to think. She needed Jake. Where was he?

The cops slowly lowered her, so she sat on the curb as people ran around and shouted out orders. Someone called for medical help inside the cemetery.

Weren't the men dead? It was all happening too fast.

A blanket appeared around her shoulders. Then a paramedic sat beside her and placed an oxygen mask over her face. "Deep breaths, Gabby. All's fine now. You've had a bit of a shock, is all."

A bit of a shock? That was the understatement of the year. But the oxygen was making her brain work again, so she sucked in as much as she could. If only she could stop shaking.

Detective Edwards appeared and sat beside her on the wet curb. "Well done, Gabby."

She pulled the mask away. "Is Jake okay? He ran off. I couldn't find him."

The detective patted Gabby's leg. "He's fine. And Dean's been shot, but alive, so hopefully you'll see justice done there."

*Thank God Jake is okay.*

Finally, she could take a deep breath.

DI Edwards asked, "Are you up to coming to the station now? We need to wrap everything up."

The sooner she and Jake could go home, the better. "Yes. Just a little more air, please."

"Take your time. You might be interested to know that Jake didn't only save you. He helped us catch the man who killed Pablo Garza."

Gabby's stomach clenched. "Jake's knife killed Pablo Garza, right? Because Jake was saving me."

The detective nodded. "Yes, but the gunshot came from someone else. Seems he was interested in those statues, too. Dean opened a can of stink bigger than any of us knew. Jake spotted a known criminal, called Moretti, so we could make the arrest."

Her father had been arrested? Is that what Jake ran off to do? To make sure her father went to jail? The steel bands around her chest came back. But this time they squeezed so hard she saw black dots before her eyes. Her father couldn't go to jail for saving her. He'd done the right thing.

But why had Jake betrayed her? They had a deal. He'd promised her he wouldn't let the police know her father was there.

She'd trusted Jake. More than she'd trusted her father, who was only trying to protect her.

Her hand flew to her chest to rub the stabbing pain Jake had caused. Her father could spend the rest of his life in jail. She'd only felt a similar pain once in her life. When she'd lost her mother and brother. The people she'd loved. Had she lost her father now, too?

Because of her trust in Jake, her father might have lost his freedom. What had she done?

"Gabby, maybe you should have a rest before you go to the station, huh?" She looked up at the sound of the familiar voice. Sal stood before her, anger clenching his jaw, his big hand held out to help her. To take her away. Away from the cops who'd arrested her father and away from England. A chance to disappear. Back to her old life. As a prisoner in her home. The life she'd been dreaming of escaping. But without Jake, what did it matter anymore?

The only thing she knew was that she didn't want Gabby Knight to be a fugitive on top of being a prisoner. That's what she'd be if she let Sal and Louie take her away. Never to be seen again. As was always the plan if the law ever started snooping too deeply into her background. She didn't even care anymore. She was tired of hiding who she really was.

So, she'd risk it. For the sake of returning the statues to their rightful owners, and to see Dean put behind bars forever for what he'd done. If she couldn't have Jake, then maybe she'd have some of the justice he cared about so much more than he did her.

She slowly shook her head and forced a smile. "I need to go to the station first. Clear things up before we leave. Wait for me there?"

Sal's eyes narrowed, as if he didn't trust she wouldn't give him the slip again, but he nodded and took a step back. "I'll follow you. Be waiting out front."

Detective Edwards's brow furrowed as she studied Sal, so Gabby said, "Sal works for me back home. He came as quickly as he could to help when I called yesterday."

The detective didn't seem all the way convinced, so Gabby turned to the paramedic. "Am I good to go?"

He nodded, unwrapped the blood pressure cuff she hadn't even realized had been on her arm, and helped her stand. "You seem recovered. But take it easy for the rest of the day, yeah?"

"Okay." She turned to the detective. "Let's get this over with, please." She didn't know how much longer she could hold it together before she broke down into a useless puddle of tears. She'd do her best to stay composed until she got on her father's plane. Then she'd lock herself in the bedroom and cry for the eight solid hours it'd take to fly home. But after that, no more tears. Ever.

Just like she'd done with her mother and brother, she'd put Jake and all her feelings for him away. For good. It was the only way she'd been able to put the fear for her own life aside as a kid, use the logical part of her brain again, and survive. Both physically and emotionally.

Jake would be dead to her.

# Chapter Seventeen

Jake had never been on the civilian side of the slow inner workings of a police station. He had a newfound respect for those whom he'd made wait while he completed paperwork. If the t's weren't crossed and the i's not dotted just right, criminals got away with their crimes in court.

But it'd been hours. He needed to talk to Gabby. They'd told him she was okay, but he needed to see for himself.

Steven, the bobby who'd driven him to the cemetery, finally returned with a cup of coffee. "Here you go, mate. Just got word you're free to leave. We'll be in touch via e-mail later, no doubt."

Jake took the coffee and drank deeply. He'd been at the station for hours, leaving him tired and hungry. "Have they cleared Gabby, yet?"

Steven shook his head. "Not quite. She had a few minor injuries we need to photograph, and then she'll be set free."

Jake nodded and then paced to a nearby window to sip his coffee while he waited for Gabby. Rain poured from the dark clouds above as people below on the street dashed for a waiting bus. Normal people with normal lives. Something Gabby would never have if she went back home. Her father would never allow it. Might even be worse after what they'd just been through. He wanted so badly for her to have the normal life she craved. And he'd like to remain a part of it.

He worried Gabby wouldn't forgive him for breaking his promise. He hadn't set out to turn her father in. He hadn't said a word to DI

Edwards when Moretti was right next to them while driving to the cemetery. Because his word was all he had to give. He had to explain everything to Gabby. Make her understand that he'd done the best thing for both her and her father by identifying him. If he hadn't, things could've turned out a lot worse.

A phone rang, and then Steven called out, "They're showing Gabby out now."

"Great. Will you tell her I'll wait for her in the lobby?"

"Will do." Steven passed on the message and then stuck out his hand. "You're a fine officer, Jake. Good luck back home."

"Thanks." He shook the bobby's hand, hoping his LT would agree after he learned of Jake's part in arresting Moretti even though he was supposed to be on administrative leave.

Jake picked up his coat and followed Steven to the crowded lobby area where they said their good-byes. Scanning the room, Jake found just what his gut needed. Vending machines. He'd made his way over, his mouth watering at the sight of a bag of M&M's, when a big hand landed on his shoulder. A deep voice growled, "You're a dead man, asshole."

Jake turned to find Sal standing in front of him, with intent to kill in his eyes.

"Yeah? Why's that?" Refusing to be intimidated for doing his job, Jake grabbed his wallet and took out his credit card, thankful the machine accepted it because he had no British pounds.

While Jake punched in his selection of candy for him and Gabby, Sal leaned in close. So close that Jake smelled the coffee on his breath. "You used Gabby. No one hurts her and lives."

"Gabby needed my help. And I needed to do my job." It took all his restraint not to bust into his bag of candy. Instead, he tore off a corner and offered some to Sal.

Sal crossed his massive arms, apparently not interested in sharing, which pleased Jake more than Sal could've known. Jake stuffed Gabby's bag into his pocket and then tilted his bag to his lips, nearly moaning in pleasure as the nutty, chocolate goodness filled his mouth. After he had swallowed, he added, "You've warned me, so leave. I'll take care of getting Gabby home." He found a nearby seat and flopped into it.

Sal shook his big head. "You might not make it home."

Brute Number Two, Louie, appeared and took the chair beside Jake, while Sal stood over them, looming. Seemed things were about to get interesting. Maybe seeing Moretti arrested had made them lose their common sense. Picking a fight in a police station lobby was futile.

Gabby's guards weren't the sharpest swords in the arsenal, so there was no use arguing with them.

Gabby's voice rang out, "Sal? Let's get out of here."

Hearing her voice, seeing that she was okay, sent a wave of relief through him. She could've been killed earlier. But had she really asked Sal to wait? What the heck?

Jake stood and maneuvered around the tree named Sal. "Hi, Gabby. Ready to go?"

Gabby must not have seen him until that moment, because her expression turned from exhaustion to bitter hate. "You can't be serious, Jake. Come on guys."

He reached out and slid a hand around her upper arm to stop her. "Please, Gabby. Give me five minutes to explain."

Dammit. He'd been right to worry about her reaction. She was madder than he'd ever seen her.

She growled. "There is nothing you can say to fix the promise you broke today, Jake." She jerked her arm from his light grasp as her tear-filled gaze met his. Then her brow furrowed as she glanced around the busy lobby. "But I need to ask you one last thing. Not here. Outside." She turned and headed for the double glass exit doors.

He followed behind, sick in the gut he might lose her, trailed closely by Sal and Louie. When they were outside, she grabbed his arm and tugged him down the slick stone steps. She held up a hand toward her guards, indicating they shouldn't follow, then stopped under an awning of the building next door, out of the falling rain. Through gritted teeth, she asked, "Did you tell the police he was my father?"

That was the last thing he expected her to ask. "Of course not." He leaned closer and laid a hand on her shoulder. "I promised you I'd never tell, Gabby. And I won't. Ever."

"I don't trust you anymore." Her shoulders dropped. Then she let out a huff of breath and looked away, as if unable to stand the sight of him. "We can't ever be together long term anyway. Because of my father. So why *not* break your promise to me?"

"No! That's not it at all. I don't want to lose you, Gabby." He shook his head, desperate for the right words to materialize. "I chased after your father—"

"Stop!" She threw her hands up. "Don't you dare try to justify your betrayal. You and my father both had a hand in killing someone today, Jake. Why is it fair they blame my father and not you?"

He'd never felt more lost and alone. He had to find a way to prove he loved her and had only her best interests at heart.

He moved in front of her so she'd look at him. Understand him. "Because I'm a cop. Not someone out for revenge. Big difference, Gabby."

She slowly shook her head. "You both took a shot at Pablo Garza because he threatened someone you supposedly loved. You don't have a badge at the moment, Jake. Today, you and my father were equals. If that's your idea of justice, then you chose well to be loyal to that instead of me. Have a nice life." She turned and walked to where Sal and Louie waited for her. Never looking back.

"Wait, Gabby. I need to tell you the whole story." He started to follow but stopped. She was too angry to listen.

As he stood in the pouring, cold rain, her words raced through his mind. Had he made the wrong choice? He'd never tell the cops that Moretti was her father, he'd promised her that. Maybe it hadn't been right to call out to Moretti by name to make him stop running. But it was the only way to get his attention with all the shouting. The sharpshooters had been closing in and about to stop Moretti with a bullet. Could he have handled it any differently, and with the same outcome? Had Moretti simply thought he'd been saving his daughter's life rather than exacting revenge on Garza? Maybe everything *wasn't* as black and white as he'd made it since his parents' death, like Gabby had pointed out. Had he screwed up big time?

Worse, had he lost Gabby forever?

The commercial plane's tires screeched as Gabby and her guards touched down in DC, a day after all the excitement had blown over. When her mind had cleared a bit, she realized they couldn't have risked flying home on her father's plane. People, particularly Pablo Garza's father, might have made the connection.

As she gathered her things, dreading going home, she focused on the positives. The statues were both on their way back to where they belonged. And Dean would get his due.

When she stood to disembark, dizziness from exhaustion overcame her. She'd had a restless night in the London hotel and had gotten zero sleep on her flight. She didn't care that it was only 6:30 p.m. in DC. She planned to land face-first on her mattress as soon as she got home.

Had it been only a day since her world had fallen apart? It seemed like it had been weeks since she'd said good-bye to Jake. And possibly her father. But as the hours had passed since she'd talked to Jake, and the fist holding her heart had lessened its grip a fraction, she'd developed a whole new worry. Would her father give up his cleaned-up life and have Jake killed now? What would he have to lose if he had to spend the rest of his life behind bars? Thinking of Jake dead and her father in prison because of her sent a new pang of hurt to her heart.

She waited as the passengers in front of her gathered their things from the bins in first class. She'd treated her bodyguards to better seats, too. It was the least she could do after they'd chased her across the ocean and back.

She waited off to the side in the Jetway for Sal and Louie, then the three of them merged into the crowd and made their way to the gate. She'd been grateful for the private-cubicle seat she'd spent the last eight hours occupying. Happy she hadn't been forced to make small talk with a stranger. Get sideways looks as tears streamed uncontrollably down her cheeks.

Having a broken heart sucked.

As soon as they walked into the terminal, two police officers approached them. The taller of the two men said, "Ms. Knight? We're here to escort you to the station. We need to get a statement."

Crap. She was so freaking tired. The last thing she wanted was to talk to more cops. She'd told the story over and over in London. Now she'd have to say it all again. "Okay." She turned to Louie. "Can you go get the car, wherever it is, and then meet me at the station?"

"Sure." Louie shared a glance with Sal and then walked away.

Sal moved closer to her. "I'm staying with you, Gabby."

He still didn't trust her not to ghost on him. It was sorely tempting. "Fine. Let's go."

After three grueling hours at the police station, she and Sal walked out the front doors where Louie waited for them. Along with fifty people, who stuck cameras and microphones in her face. She had to look like death warmed over. But she couldn't care less as she shook her head and said, "No comment" over and over while following in the wake Sal made for her through the crowd.

Because she'd been the prime suspect in the Father statue's theft, her badge picture from work had been plastered all over the news while she'd been gone. Thanks to freakin' Dean, who reportedly was in stable condition back in London and expected to live. Pablo Garza and the other guy hadn't been so lucky.

Gabby threw her bag in the car first, then crawled into the back and laid her head against the seat. Thankfully, when the door slammed shut, the noise level from the press shouting out questions lowered by half. Blissfully fading away completely as Louie pressed forward through the crowd and found open road. He'd be able to quickly shake off the reporters tenacious enough to follow behind.

Familiar landmarks sped past in the dark, barely registering in her jumbled brain foggy with jet lag.

Damn Dean for putting her in the middle of his drama. And Jake for making her fall in love with him, for showing her a glimpse of happiness that'd always be just out of reach. People like her weren't allowed to have normal lives. She'd just forgotten that for a bit.

After hours of pondering Jake's actions as she flew home, she had to conclude that he couldn't have cared for her the way she'd cared for him. Or he'd never have betrayed her like that. They'd had a deal. That Jake would ignore her father's presence just for the day. So her father could be sure she was safe. People don't betray the ones they love like that.

Her phone dinged, but she ignored it. Jake had texted to be sure she'd gotten home safe earlier. She hadn't bothered to reply. What was the point? But she wanted to know what was happening to her father because the police had given her little to no information, so she reached into her purse and snatched up her phone. After she'd unlocked it, a new text from Jake flashed across the display. Without reading it, she swiped it away and called up the Internet. Her father's mug shot filled the screen. Catching the elusive Luca Moretti was big news around the world.

Guilt made it hard to stare into his angry, narrowed eyes. Would she ever talk to him again? Probably not, if his lawyers didn't win at trial. Prison visitors' names were public record. It'd cast suspicion on her if she visited a man who had been trying to steal the thing she tried to save. As the story was being told in the press. They'd made her out to be a hero, but she was far from that. She'd betrayed her father for a man who'd been only using her. Her father had believed her when she'd explained their plan on the phone. She'd said he could trust Jake not to turn him in. God, she was an idiot.

Louie called out, "Hang on. We still have a few stragglers."

She weaved her fingers through the grab handle as she continued to read about her father. His lawyer claimed that after seeing Dean take a bullet, Luca shot to protect the innocent archaeologist. That he was a hero, not a murderer. They planned to extradite him to the United States in the next day or two to stand trial on earlier money-laundering and racketeering charges and now the new one for killing Pablo Garza. Would her father live the rest of his days in jail? All because she'd gotten caught up in Dean's web? Her father would probably never forgive her for exposing him, all so she could chase after a statue.

She closed her eyes as the car's tires squealed around a corner, sending a new stab of annoyance in her ears. Had her father seen the knife Jake had thrown at Pablo? Taken the opportunity to put a satisfying bullet in his enemy's head. Or had her dad really been protecting her? He'd been a fair distance away. He might not have seen the knife.

In any event, she and her father linked together for the world to see was so not good. Would Pablo's father put two and two together? That Luca was protecting his daughter, who was supposedly dead? Would she have to start looking over her shoulder every time she left the house again? Like she'd had to do for those first few years after her mom and brother were killed? The thought drew her even deeper into the dark cloud her life had become. Over stupid statues.

Sal turned and said, "All clear."

"Thank God. I just want to go home." Pull the covers over her head and sleep for days. Or at least for the rest of the night. She had to go back to work, resume her normal routine, not disappear for good as she wanted. Pablo Garza's father could be watching. He'd put a price on her father's head for sure now. She didn't need one on hers, too. But as much as she hated the things her father had done in the past, she didn't want him to go to jail. Except, maybe he'd be safer there. No, if Garza wanted revenge, prison wouldn't stop him. Had her father just traded his life for hers? She could only hope her dad's lawyers could find a way to convince the jury that he'd saved an innocent life by shooting Pablo Garza.

The thought of watching her father stand trial and the grueling weeks to come depressed her. There were going to be more follow-up questions from the police, lawyers to deal with, and questions on the stand. Dean's trial for sure, and possibly her father's. She wanted so badly to speak to her father's lawyers, understand what his charges were, but none of them knew of her existence. Hopefully, her aunt would be able to find out what was happening with her dad.

As they finally drove through the gates surrounding her home, she fingered the passport she'd taken from Dean. It was still in her pocket. She hoped she'd still have the courage to use it as soon as all the legal crap was over.

While the garage door rumbled shut, Gabby left her bags and her bodyguards behind and went straight inside to see her dog. In the living room, Einstein lifted his head from the couch he wasn't supposed to be on, then realized it wasn't her aunt coming in to feed him. He bolted up and ran full tilt to greet her. A little black-and-white tornado.

She leaned down and smiled for the first time in what felt like an eternity, her hands spread to catch him. Einstein jumped into her arms and licked her cheek. There was nothing better than her sweet dog to help lift her dampened spirits. "You're the only man I need. Right, buddy?"

She walked to her bedroom, cuddling her dog, when a memory hit her smack in the heart. The time she'd told Jake that he was good company, like Einstein. If she could ever forgive Jake, she'd probably miss his never-ending teasing and millions of questions. Her short time with him had been the best of her life—until the end.

That part, she'd never forgive him for.

After plopping Einstein into his bed, she fell prone on her mattress, arms and legs spread eagle, too tired to take a shower or even brush her teeth. But then Aunt Suzy came rushing into her room and flopped beside her.

"You're back. And in the one piece. Thank the Lords all of above." Gabby's bitter heart softened a fraction at her Italian aunt's familiar mispronunciations.

Suzy's arms circled Gabby and squeezed hard. "I was so worried, *topolina*."

Her little mouse. Ironic, because Gabby stood over a foot taller than her round aunt. "I'm fine." Gabby forced her eyelids open. "But I can't breathe."

"Sorry, sorry." Her aunt, who was a woman who rarely missed a meal and made sure Gabby didn't, either, moved her arms. Then she laid her salt-and-pepper-haired head on the spare pillow. Aunt Suzy tucked a stray piece of hair behind Gabby's ear. "It's not your fault. Your father a grown man. Responsible for his own self."

Einstein chose that moment to insert himself between them. Tears made Aunt Suzy all blurry. "He was protecting me. If I hadn't . . ."

"Stop! No more. I can see by the eyes you've beaten yourself too much already. What about your handsome cop friend? Huh? The news no tell what happened to him."

She closed her eyes again. "Don't know. Don't care. Dad was right. Jake told me what I wanted to hear, could never be serious about a woman like me."

"Pffft. That's the load of bull dooey. You, *amore*, are a princess. I tell your father you have real feelings for the man. Me, I can know these things. Your papa, he not want to lose his *bambina*, that's all. Sleep now. We talk in the morning."

When Suzy made to leave, Gabby took her hand to stop her. She was angry and upset with Jake, but she was worried for his safety. Her father had to be even angrier at him. "Please tell Dad not to hurt him, *Zietta*. As soon as you can speak to him. Tell him if he loves me, he'll keep Jake safe."

Suzy's brows popped up. "You fall in love with this Jake?"

She shook her head. "I just don't want another death on my hands, that's all."

"Okay, sure." Suzy stood and chuckled as she untied Gabby's shoes and slipped them off. "You say this because you love him. No tell lies to me. Now sleep. I make a big breakfast in the morning, and we get to the bottom of it all, *si*?"

"Yes, in the morning." Gabby was too tired to argue.

"Sweet dreams." Her aunt hit the light switch and closed the door.

Einstein wasn't allowed to sleep with her, but he'd stayed, cuddled at her side. When her pent-up tears over losing her father and Jake began to fall again, Einstein whimpered in sympathy. He always knew when she was sad. "Okay. You can stay. But just for tonight."

His tailed thumped on the mattress. She'd swear the dog understood English better than her aunt sometimes did. He was certainly more loyal than Jake had been.

She wrapped an arm around her bundle of fur and love and pulled him close. "Why can't all men be as perfect as you?" She closed her eyes and let herself succumb to the darkness in her heart and in her head.

# Chapter Eighteen

After sending Gabby another text that would probably go unanswered just like all the rest he'd sent in the last three days, Jake dropped onto his living room couch and stared at the empty bookcase. What was it Gabby had called him? A minimalist?

Or was he just uninterested in his own life? Everyone had told him he worked too much. Needed hobbies, to take vacations, rekindle friendships. Or, maybe he was better off alone?

He closed his eyes and leaned his head back on the couch. The tortured look on Gabby's face outside the police station was tattooed on his eyelids every time he closed them. He hadn't been thinking when he'd run after her father, shouting out his name to make him stop before a bullet could stop him. He'd just reacted. His job was to save lives and protect the public. That's what he'd done. DI Edwards had thanked him profusely afterward for his quick actions. He hadn't thought of anything but putting a stop to the string of people dying in the cemetery. He'd done the right thing, but in the process, he'd hurt the one person he loved.

Dammit.

Gabby must hate him. He'd made her a promise and then broken it. Why did he do this to himself? Ruin everything good in his life. He'd done it to his marriage, and now he'd messed everything up with Gabby, too. It was if his subconscious knew he wasn't good enough for

Gabby, and that she'd figure that out one day and leave him. So his warped mind showed him the best way to screw up the best relationship he'd ever had. Rather than wait to be hurt when she dumped him first.

Why he kept letting his crappy childhood and screwed-up parents dictate his feelings of self-worth was beyond him. But no more. Gabby had been right. She'd told him the best way to move on would be to become a better person than his parents had been. And he was. If his past didn't bother Gabby, then he needed to let it go. Stop letting his deep fear of people he loved leaving him run his life. The department shrinks had told him that was his problem time and time again, and why he pushed people away by hiding behind work and sarcasm.

But did Gabby really believe what she'd said outside the police station in London? That they could never be together because of her father? That a cop with such a strict sense of right and wrong would never be able to share a life with her?

Gabby said her father had given up the life of crime. Until he shot Garza the other day. But maybe what Gabby said was true. Her father might have been simply protecting her, not exacting revenge on an enemy. Who was he to say which killed Garza first? The knife or the bullet. He and Moretti were equally responsible for Garza's death, and yet her father was in jail, and Jake had gotten a pat on the back. There was no way to be sure Moretti even saw the knife before her father fired that shot. He had been yards away and behind Garza. In Moretti's shoes, Jake would've done the exact same thing.

Could he live with having Moretti in his life? The man's past crimes went against every moral fiber in Jake's body. Could he be okay knowing Gabby had daily contact with her father? That he still influenced her life?

But Gabby didn't want that life anymore. And she wasn't anything like her father. She was the most forgiving, bighearted, loving person he'd ever met. She wanted to live a normal life, so she was contemplating disappearing again and starting over. He had to show her how sorry he was for hurting her before she left for good. That he'd do anything to gain her forgiveness.

Anything.

But what could he do?

He couldn't change Moretti, but he could change himself. Being a police officer had been his way to show the world that he wasn't like his parents. That he believed in justice. Maybe it was time to stop trying so hard to prove that and focus on the one person who gave him so much more than self-worth. Gabby made him happy, feel alive for the first time, like a whole person, not a damaged one. So there was only one thing to do. He'd quit his job. Take the barrier between him and Gabby away. That is, if she'd ever forgive him.

No time like the present.

He stood and found his keys on the kitchen counter and then headed out to the garage. As he backed out of his driveway, a million thoughts raced through his mind. What if quitting wasn't enough? What if Gabby still wouldn't take him back? He needed to make a living. But there were other ways to do that.

He'd hated giving up his badge for a month. The thought of giving it up for good made his gut ache. But there was no other way. He had to show Gabby he was willing to give up what mattered most to him, so they could be together.

As he drove to the station he rubbed his chest where he'd had a physical ache that had just grown worse every day since London. He was doing the right thing.

After checking in at the front desk at the station, he was told to wait in Lieutenant Hernandez's office. Jake made his way through the busy squad room and to the coffee bar. He poured himself a cup of courage and then walked the last few yards to his boss's office. He sat in one of the guest chairs in front of Hernandez's desk.

He was ready to do it. To end the career he'd worked so hard for. He sucked in a deep breath as he waited for the ax to fall. His boss's voice mails the past few days had shown how angry he was. He'd heard all about the statues, London, and Moretti's capture and wasn't happy that Jake hadn't returned his calls. Maybe he was going to be fired.

The heavy clomp of shoes behind him made Jake sit up straighter. He smiled at his boss as he circled his desk and slammed his big body into the chair.

"Hey, Lieutenant. How are you?"

"Dammit, Morris. What part didn't you understand about being on administrative leave?" Lieutenant Hernandez's neck muscles bulged. Never a good sign. Probably didn't help that Jake had ignored his LT's calls for four days.

"It wasn't planned. It just happened." He took a long pull from the sludge that passed for coffee at his station.

The LT stood, shoving his chair so hard it hit the credenza behind him. "Don't give me that load of BS. You had a cell phone." Hernandez stomped around his desk and got in Jake's face. "I should fire your ass."

Jake swallowed back the temper rising in his throat. "You can't. Because I'm here to quit."

Hernandez blinked in confusion. "You're what?"

"I'm quitting. You were always on me to get a personal life. Now that I have one, I don't want to lose it because of the job again."

His boss closed his eyes and ran a hand down his face. After a moment of jaw clenching, he said, "You don't mean that. Something's been screwing with your head the last year or so. Even your partner agrees you lost your edge since your divorce."

"My divorce had nothing to do with anything." It'd been Dani's woo-woo dreams that had helped him be the top dog. Close more cases than anyone else. But he was still a good cop. "I just helped catch the most wanted man in America, for God's sake. That doesn't count for anything?" It should have been something to be proud of, but he'd hurt Gabby by doing it, so it didn't feel like an accomplishment. It felt more like a mistake.

His boss growled. "There were better ways to go about that."

"I understand, Lieutenant. But isn't it still our job to put criminals behind bars? To keep the public safe? That's all I was doing."

"Really? That was your only motivation?" Hernandez circled behind his desk again and sat. "You weren't trying to prove me wrong by doing this behind my back? Thought you could show up in my office with Moretti's head on a platter and make everything all better?"

"I saw Gabby needed help, and that became my number one priority. But your doubt in me was unfounded. I understand having to be placed on leave for a shooting, but haven't they figured out by now that I saved the lives of that woman and child?"

Hernandez huffed out a breath. "Yes. But when the job becomes the only focus, when you have nothing but the job to come home to, it messes with a cop's head. Things start to crack and fall apart. Bad decisions are made. I've seen it too many times to count. I didn't want you to quit. Just take a break and get your head on straight."

"My head is in perfect alignment now. Because there's someone more important than the job. Gabby Knight."

The LT's brow furrowed in disbelief. "The statue girl?"

"Yep." He smiled as the weight of the world lifted from his shoulders. It felt right to quit. "She makes me want to be a better version of myself. But she lives in DC. I'm going to see if I can get a job there. Then try however long it takes to make things right between us, because I screwed everything up for this job. I need to show her that she's more important than my being a cop."

Hernandez lifted a hand. "Hold up. Rather than quit over a woman you've known such a short time, take the rest of your leave. See if you can fix things with Gabby. Then, first of next month, we'll talk."

It appeared his boss hadn't been hell-bent on firing him after all. Jake stood and held out a hand. "I appreciate the second chance. But I won't need it."

Hernandez returned the handshake. "As much as I don't want to lose you, I'd like to see you happy, Jake. Your badge has been reinstated. You can have it and your gun. Just in case Moretti decides to retaliate. Can't send you out there with no protection. Take them at least until the end of the month. Then we'll process you out." He opened a desk drawer and drew out Jake's beloved badge and gun. "Good luck."

He'd take all the good luck he could get. But he wouldn't take his things back, even though he'd felt naked without them. "No thanks. I'll be fine. Take care, Lieutenant."

His boss frowned. "You too, Jake. Are you sure about this—"

"Yeah." Jake turned and headed for the door. Hernandez didn't know who Gabby's father was. Giving up police work altogether was the price he'd gladly pay to have Gabby.

He'd miss police work. But he'd be willing to kiss it good-bye for her.

Until he could get Gabby to return his calls or texts, though, he didn't stand much of a chance with her. Would a text telling her he'd quit his job be enough? Was she even reading the texts he'd sent? His new hurdle was to find a way to talk to her.

As he made his way through the beehive of cubicles at the station, waving to his now former coworkers, a thought hit him. Dani said she'd seen things in her dream he hadn't let her reveal. He'd stop by her nearby office and see if she'd like to go to lunch. And help him win Gabby back.

~

Gabby sat on a high stool in front of her workbench at the museum, staring across the quiet lab rather than working on the new pottery shards that had come in the day before. She'd been back for five days, but her jet lag still managed to linger. Or maybe it was depression. Hard to tell.

Reaching into her lab-coat pocket, she grabbed the fake passport she'd carried with her every day since she'd been back in the States. It was her promise to herself, or hope, that her life could get better.

She opened the booklet and stared at the woman with red hair that she'd been only months before. Dean had shot that picture of her at work. They'd just discovered the whereabouts of the buried Son statue, and Dean had asked her to stand in front of the plain background to take her picture for the museum's website. He'd said he planned to write an article and wanted to give her proper credit. Little did she know it'd all been part of his big scheme to steal her away to Peru with him. The thought sent a shudder up her spine. Looking back, she'd seen little cracks in his personality that she'd passed off as eccentricity. She'd never do that again.

She went back to studying her expression on the passport's page. She'd had a big smile, and her eyes crinkled a bit at the corners with excitement over finding the matching artifact to one of their bigger attractions upstairs. Had it really taken so little to make her light up like that? Had she been happy before the statue went missing? Was she so used to the bubble her father had created for her to live in that an ancient artifact could put a twinkle of joy in her eyes?

Pathetic, really. Especially because now she knew what feeling truly happy and free had been like. If only for a few days.

Shaking her head, she put the passport in her pocket and turned her attention to the pottery before her. Using a small brush, she methodically swiped away bits of debris to get to the treasure below.

The intercom on her phone interrupted her musings. "Gabby? There's someone named Suzy here to see you. Want me to escort her back?"

"Yes, please." Why would her aunt show up unexpectedly? She'd never even visited the museum before. Maybe it was news about her father?

She quickly hopped off her stool and washed her hands in the utility sink. Her aunt's voice could be heard long before her arrival. "You looka like you hungry. I gotta the best cookies ever in here. You eat. Tell me how you like."

Gabby smiled. Abe the guard was a tall, skinny man about her aunt's age. Her aunt felt like it was her duty to feed anyone she met. Especially if they were thin.

After Abe left with his cookies, Suzy wrapped Gabby up in a vise-like hug. "Been so long I don't see you I forget what you looka like."

Gabby withheld an eye roll. She'd only missed dinner with her aunt the last two nights. "I'm sorry, *Zietta*. But I wouldn't have made good company anyway."

Suzy released Gabby but held her at arm's length. Her gaze traveled up and down Gabby's body. "You too skinny, and you eyes are sad. You worry your papa is going to start do bad things again? To Jake?"

Gabby didn't know if she could trust the deal her father had made with her. If she stayed away from Jake, her father would spare Jake's life. She wasn't allowed to have any further contact with him. Not that she wanted to see him again. She was still so angry with Jake, but she wanted him alive, so she'd agreed to the deal. She feared her father had nothing to lose, now that he was in jail and his threat might be real. "I'm afraid Jake won't listen. When I texted the terms of the deal to him, he wrote back and said he needed to see me. To apologize. And beg if he had to."

Suzy smiled. "Jake the type to beg, is he?"

"Not at all." Gabby shook her head. "He can actually be kind of arrogant sometimes." And pushy. And flirty. But oddly, that never bothered her. He was just covering emotions when he acted like that.

"Arrogant? Hmmmm." Suzy moved things around on Gabby's desk and started setting out lunch. "So he only think of himself?"

"Well, no. He raised his brother after their parents died. Made sure he turned out honest and hardworking. And he helped me when I needed it most."

"So he might do these things out of duty? Because he a cop?"

Her aunt pulled out fresh-baked bread from her bag. It made Gabby's mouth water. "Maybe. I don't know." Jake was a complicated mess, and it made her want to cry every time she thought about him. It'd been easier to push him out of her mind, rather than analyze the man and his motives.

Her aunt cut off a hunk of bread and laid it on Gabby's plate. "I see on the TV Jake a handsome man, good smile, but he must have a bad heart if you no want to see him anymore?"

"No, that's not it." Gabby sat in her desk chair and dug into the antipasto her aunt had placed in front of her. "Jake isn't a bad person. He's actually a very good person. He just won't allow himself to believe it." She wasn't going to talk about his charming smile. It was sad to think she'd never see it again. "But he broke a promise, and you know I don't abide by that. And not just any promise. Dad's in jail because of it. And me."

Suzy sat in the guest chair and dug into her lunch, too. "Jake hurt you feelings because you think he care for you. Someone care for you, they no lie."

"Exactly!" Gabby took a bite of bread and sighed. "He told me himself he wasn't cut out to be a good boyfriend or husband. Turns out he was right."

Suzy's brow furrowed. "But sometimes we make a promises we no can keep. Like when I tell you uncle I never shoot no one. No matter what happen. He tell me he'd never forgive himself if I arrested because of him."

Gabby laid down her fork. "You shot that guy in self-defense. They broke into your home to kill your husband. You were trying to save my uncle's life."

"Is true." Suzy nodded as she chewed. "You know, you papa told me what happen in the park that day. When he get caught. A lot happen very fast. Maybe you let Jake tell you his side of story. Or, just let him beg a little. Fun to see men beg, no?"

"It won't change anything. Dad was right. He told me nothing could ever come of a relationship with a cop. I mean, we're guarded at home by felons, and we have some sort of lethal weapon in every closet. I don't even know if my car was bought legally."

When Suzy started to reply, Gabby held up her hand. "Don't tell me. I don't want to know." She took another bite and then pushed her plate away. She'd lost her appetite. Again. She hadn't finished a whole meal in a week.

Suzy reached out and squeezed Gabby's hand. "Where my happy Gabby go? I no like to see you like this. You make me worry."

The tears welling in her aunt's eyes made Gabby's water, too. "I'll get over it. I've gotten over worse things before, right?"

Her aunt's smile was filled with sadness. Or maybe pity. "You have more bad things happen than is fair. But maybe this time different? Maybe this time you find way to fix things?"

Gabby closed her eyes to hold back the tears that wanted to drip down her cheeks. The lump that had formed in her throat made it difficult to speak. "Face it, *Zietta*. Dad hates Jake for what he did. Even if I could ever forgive him, Dad will never allow me to be with him. It's why after everything is settled in the courts I have to go away. Forever. It's the only way I'll ever have my own life."

Her aunt whispered, "I know. My heart will miss you every day, *amore*. Until its very last beat."

The idea of her aunt dying without Gabby even knowing because she'd be gone sent a dagger through Gabby's already broken heart. She'd miss her family every day, too, until *her* very last heartbeat.

Maybe by then, she will have gotten over Jake, too.

# Chapter Nineteen

Jake yanked open the doors of Dani's real estate office and stepped inside. Dani's boss, a former Miss Texas who'd had so much work done she looked like a perpetually smiling scary clown, lifted her bloodred-tipped nails and gave them a waggle. "Jake. Nice to see you, sugar. Dani's in the back."

"Thanks." He hurried to Dani's cubicle and leaned over her divider. She was on the phone, so she lifted a finger and then quickly wrapped up the call.

After she disconnected, she fist-bumped the air. "That makes closing number ten! I'm going to be the top producer this month, Jake. Mark my words."

He smiled. Dani's powerful mother had gotten her the job, so Dani had been hell-bent on proving she could be a success on her own. Everyone had their doubts, including him. Seemed she'd figured out how to control her unwanted dreams enough to make a real go at it. He couldn't be happier for her. "Knew you'd get there. How about I—"

"Yes, you can buy me lunch. I'm starving." She grabbed her purse. "And of course, I'll help you with Gabby. That's why you're here, right?" She stood and slipped into her coat. "I had a dream last night that you'd stop by, so I've even had time to think about where I want to go."

That Dani knew what he was thinking before he did sometimes could be incredibly annoying. But he wanted Gabby back, and Dani probably already knew how he was going to do it. Why fight it? "Where are we going?"

She headed for the front door. "This new organic place I've been dying to go to, but Michael says it's too foo-foo for him."

Jake caught up. "If Mr. Suit and Tie won't go, then it's going to be torture for me, right?"

"Absolutely. My advice doesn't come cheap." She waved to her boss and then poked the door open before he could beat her to it. "We'll walk. It's only a few blocks away."

Great. But if it'd get Gabby back, he'd endure a foo-foo lunch. He stuck his hands in his pockets to warm them and matched her stride. "So, do you already know I quit today?"

"No. Good for you." Dani shook her head. "That's only the first step, though. You helped send her father to jail. You're going to have to do a whole lot more than quit a job to convince Gabby to take you back. A whole lot more."

They stopped at the curb to wait for the light to turn. "If I could actually speak to Gabby, I'd tell her what really happened with her father. And hope she'd find a way to eventually forgive me. But I'm trying to prove to her how much I want to be with her by changing my life to make that happen. You would have been ecstatic if I'd quit working so much while we were married."

"You're right." The light changed, so they stepped off the curb together. "But we both know you hadn't met the woman of your dreams yet, so what would it have mattered really?"

As they hopped onto the opposite curb, he said, "Wait a minute. You knew I was going to meet Gabby while we were married?"

She shrugged. "Not until we'd separated, but yes."

"Then why did you tell me I should date Charlene after we got divorced?"

Dani stopped in front of a small café and opened the door. "Because she was interested in you. I'd hoped you'd see how badly you messed that up, before it was time for you to meet Gabby."

He had messed up his relationship with Charlene. By working too much and not paying enough attention to her. He'd been too busy wallowing about his divorce. She hadn't deserved that. "Dammit. So you're telling me getting Gabby back isn't a given? You haven't seen that?"

Dani held up two fingers to the hostess, who nodded and asked them to follow her. Panic filled him as they weaved in and out of the little wooden tables with bunches of wildflowers sticking out of vases even though it was February.

He had to win Gabby back. He'd always love Dani, but he hadn't known he could love anyone as much as he loved Gabby. Like he could finally take complete, deep breaths of air when he was with her.

Dani didn't wait for him to pull her chair out and sat. "I've seen a lot, but not that."

He flopped down in a heap and accepted the laminated menu the hostess held in front of him. "Thank you." After she left, he tossed the menu on the table. "So, what do I have to do? And why does it smell like perfume in here?"

Dani chuckled as she studied her menu. "This is a vegetarian farm-to-table place. The centerpiece is our appetizer. Try it."

What the hell? He shook his head and picked up the menu, hoping they'd have a bean burrito, at least.

Dani chomped on her flowers and tilted her head. "Mmmmm. Lavender and something else. Very nice. You should really try it."

"Negative." He laid the menu down. "You're killing me here, Dani. Please just tell me what I have to do."

When a waitress appeared, Dani placed an order for peach iced tea and the Southwest-greens special for both of them. He didn't care what they put in front of him. He'd probably just get a burger on the way home anyway.

After the waitress had left, Dani took his hand. "Are you ready to open up your life? To really share it with another person? Not just play the role of a husband, but to actually be one?"

"Yes. I'm all in." A year ago, he'd have no idea what she'd meant by that. Now he understood it meant sharing secrets, wants, and needs with a partner. All the things that he never wanted to share because they made him feel weak and vulnerable. Gabby's gentle and kind soul had made it almost natural for him to want to share them with her.

"Good." Dani gave his hand a squeeze before she released it. "The only person Gabby has left in her immediate family is her father, right? And you put him in jail. So that's where you have to start. With her dad."

Jake blinked at her as her meaning slowly sunk in. "What are you suggesting I do with him?"

Their salads and drinks came, so he leaned back as the waitress placed a bowl of green stuff with suspicious balls of something in front of him. "Thanks."

Dani took a bite and moaned. "This is awesome. Try it."

Not interested, he took a slug of the peach iced tea instead. It was like a summer picnic of fun in his mouth. Maybe the salad wouldn't be so bad. He picked up his fork and stabbed at the greens and weird chunks. Delicious spices danced on his tongue as he chewed. It wasn't half-bad. "I don't want to know what the lumps are, right?"

"Nope." Dani laughed. "So back to Luca Moretti. You need to ask for Gabby's hand in marriage. I'm assuming you aren't quitting your job just to date her, right?"

He choked on his salad. Leaning close so the other diners around them wouldn't hear, he said, "Moretti wants to kill me, not give me permission to marry his daughter." And while he hadn't thought that far ahead, the idea of being married to Gabby sat nicely with him.

"I know." Dani happily chewed her lunch. "I didn't say this would be easy. Gabby won't talk to you or respond to texts, right?"

"No. She's iced me out. And I don't know where she lives. She deleted the tracker I put on her phone. They have armed guards where she works, so chances of me being able to talk to her are slim."

"I know where Gabby lives. If you can get Luca's permission to marry her, I think you have a fighting chance."

Easier said than done. How would he ever convince the man he had helped arrest to allow his daughter to marry his captor? Worse, how would he get permission to see Luca in jail? He had no reason to visit him. Only his lawyers would have access at this point.

He asked Dani, "Do you know who Luca's lawyers are?"

She shook her head. "That I don't know. But I saw on the news earlier that his lawyers are holding a press conference later today. To get the public on their side is what the analysts are saying."

"Since when do you follow court cases?" He went back in for more of the delicious tea.

"When they involve people I care about. Go figure out how to get yourself inside Moretti's prison. Then we'll talk."

Piece of cake. Why wouldn't Moretti's lawyers want to talk to the man who had fingered their client?

He'd be lucky if the receptionist didn't hang up on him.

Looked like he was going to have to get on a plane again. But this time, one headed to DC.

～

Jake sat in the plush offices of one of Washington's top lawyers, trying not to fidget with impatience. He'd been granted the last appointment of the day but was warned he'd have only five minutes. He'd been waiting for over an hour to see Moretti's lead lawyer, and the damn suit he wore was making it hot and hard to breathe. He hated wearing suits but wanted Farber to take him seriously.

The receptionist called out, "Mr. Morris? Mr. Farber will see you now. Will you come with me, please?"

Jake jumped out of his chair and followed the older woman dressed in black down a hallway covered with what was probably expensive art. What did he know?

All the spit had dried up in his mouth, making it hard to swallow. He had to make his one chance count.

The receptionist held out a hand toward a conference room. "Mr. Farber will be here shortly. Help yourself to some refreshment if you'd like."

Jake nodded and went straight for the fancy green bottle of water on the side table. He poured himself a glass and then settled in one of the leather chairs around the long conference table. While taking a deep drink, he went over his plan one last time.

"Mr. Morris?" A portly man, about sixty with gray hair, shut the door behind him. "Don't bother to get up." Mr. Farber sat across from Jake and laid a leather portfolio on the table. Then he took out a fat pen and took the top off. "Your phone call intrigued me. As it did Mr. Moretti. However, we aren't willing to compromise the case."

"I assure you this has nothing to do with the case. It's personal. Concerning Benji." He'd remembered Gabby's code word with her father and had used it to get the appointment. He couldn't be sure the lawyer knew of Gabby's existence, though, so he'd have to play his cards close to the vest.

Farber laid his pen down with a thump. "I fail to see what personal connection you could possibly have with Mr. Moretti."

"I don't think I'd be here unless Mr. Moretti were interested in hearing what I have to say."

Farber leaned back in his chair. "I might be able to set you up with a video visitation."

"Nope. What I have to say is for his ears only. It needs to be face-to-face."

Farber's eyes narrowed. "Mr. Moretti has a question. If you answer correctly, I'll arrange for you to accompany me on my scheduled visit with him tomorrow. Only legal counsel has access to him right now."

"I'm aware. What's the question?" Jake tugged at his tight collar. What if he didn't know the answer?

Farber opened his portfolio. "Mr. Moretti would like to know if Benji knows you're asking to meet with my client."

Jake studied Farber's eyes. Puzzlement and curiosity filled them. Farber had no idea why Luca would ask that, and Jake wasn't sure how to answer exactly. Was Luca asking if Gabby knew he'd come to see her father? Like to blackmail him because he knew who Gabby really was?

Or, Gabby could have asked him to pass something on to Moretti for her. That could get him in the door.

Rather than risk the wrong answer, he'd go with his gut. "No. But Benji needs his help. I would've e-mailed Mr. Moretti, but, obviously, he doesn't have access at the moment." He didn't need to know that the help she needed was to be allowed to live her life.

Farber rubbed the back of his neck as he studied his notes. There were four or five lines on his page, but Jake couldn't make out what they said from across the big table.

After a few moments, Farber nodded. "Meet me here at ten tomorrow. You'll have to drive in with me. Check in as one of my staff."

Cool relief swept through him. It'd worked. Next, he hoped he could figure out what to say to convince Luca not to kill him and then let him marry his daughter. "Thank you."

Farber stood, so Jake did as well. The older man said, "Don't bring anything with you. Especially a weapon. And don't be late." Farber headed for the door.

"I won't." He hated to be without a gun but was getting used to it.

Jake waved to the receptionist on his way out and then hit the elevator button to take him to the underground parking garage. While he waited, he pulled out his phone to check for messages. He'd asked Gabby if she'd please meet him for a drink or coffee. No response.

He jammed his phone into the pocket of his suit pants and stepped into the empty elevator. Once inside, he pushed the "G" button and then leaned against the wall and closed his eyes. It'd been a long day. He looked forward to a cold beer and burger at the place beside his hotel he'd seen earlier.

When the doors parted, he stepped out into the concrete structure and headed for his rental car. Heavy footsteps behind him made him glance over his shoulder. Really?

He stopped and turned around as two guys who could be Sal and Louie's cousins approached him. Had to be sent by Moretti to be sure he kept his distance from Gabby, like her text had said. "Look. I'll make this easy for you. I'm going back to my hotel near M Street in case you lose me in the traffic circle. Those things are a bitch." Then he pushed the remote and made his rental beep. "I'm right here, in the silver Chevy. Have a nice evening."

They both nodded and then turned toward their car.

He shook his head before he strapped in and started the engine. He'd probably be safe, at least until Moretti heard what he had to say the next day. After that, who knew?

# Chapter Twenty

Jake showed up at Farber's office fifteen minutes before his appointment. The men tailing him waited in the parking garage below.

The receptionist looked up from her desk. "Hello, Mr. Morris. Come with me, please. We need to get you an employee badge."

He followed the woman down a long hall that held offices on either side. She stopped outside one that had the name "Ashton Reynolds" on the nameplate. She pointed to the man seated at his desk, deep into work. "What do you think? Does he look enough like you?"

Jake leaned his head inside the door. The guy had similar coloring, was about the same age, but skinnier. "Yep. Close enough."

The receptionist walked in and held out a hand toward Ashton. "You drew the short stick. Credentials, please."

He glanced up, gave Jake the once over from head to toe, and then tugged his wallet from his suit pants. He slipped out his driver's license and then unclipped his employee badge from the suit coat hanging on the back of his chair. He handed them over and said, "For the record, I'm not in favor of this plan. And he's taller than me."

The receptionist accepted the IDs. "Farber's orders. Take it up with him. I'm just the messenger." She turned and shoved the plastic-coated paperwork in Jake's direction. "Let's go."

Jake studied Ashton's personal data for a moment, then clipped the badge onto his sports coat jacket. As he followed the woman back to the lobby, he slid Ashton's license into his wallet.

She said, "Have a seat. Mr. Farber will be right out. Memorize Ashton's age, height, and address while you wait. Just in case they ask at the prison."

"Already done." Jake sat on the couch and blew out a long breath. The rest of his life rode on the outcome of his meeting with Luca. He couldn't screw it up. Then he'd have to convince Gabby to take him back.

If only she'd hear him out. She'd made a deal with her father to save his life, but the terms weren't acceptable. Never seeing her again wasn't an option. So he'd negotiate with the devil.

Seemed his strict code of right and wrong, a coping mechanism from his childhood according to the department shrink, wasn't a crutch he needed anymore. But he needed Gabby.

Farber rushed into the lobby, briefcase in hand. "Let's go, Morris."

Jake stood and followed behind the lawyer. He was talking to someone on his phone through an earpiece. Farber continued the conversation as they slid into the back of a black Town Car and headed for the downtown prison where Luca was being held. Jake glanced over his shoulder. Moretti's men were just behind.

As their driver negotiated the traffic, Jake wrestled with his growing anxiety. Tangling with an armed junkie high on meth might be easier than convincing Gabby's father to give his daughter permission to be with a cop.

He'd vowed he'd never again beg for affection like he'd done with his parents. But then he'd met Gabby. He'd do anything to get her back. Even beg and cajole a mobster.

Facing Moretti with confidence, showing no weakness or fear, would be what a man like him would respect. And expect of the man he'd allow his daughter to be with.

As they pulled up to the front of the facility, Jake's heartbeat thudded in his ears. Ignoring his conscience screaming at him for using a fake ID, he followed Farber inside.

Farber said, "I do all the talking. You're my paralegal." He slapped his briefcase into Jake's arms and then went first through the metal detector.

"Got it."

At the main desk, a bored-looking guard said, "Name?"

Farber tossed his license on the desk and then held out a hand for Ashton's ID. The guard glanced at Farber, then Jake, then back at both licenses in his hand.

When a badge, along with the license, slid his way across the desk, he nodded in thanks and quickly clipped on his visitor name tag.

It shouldn't have been that easy, and by the lack of concern on Farber's part, it probably wasn't the first time that had happened.

A guard led them into a small interrogation room. "I'll get the prisoner for you."

Jake pulled out a chair and sat. "I need to talk to Moretti alone."

"Not happening." Farber settled in the plastic chair beside Jake.

Then he'd have to speak in code. That wasn't going to make things any easier.

The familiar rattle of chains preceded Moretti. The door swung open, and the guard guided Gabby's father to a chair across the table before he locked him to it. Moretti's eyes never left Jake's as he lifted his shackled hands toward the guard. "Can we take care of these?"

The guard shook his head. "Got it direct from upstairs. Shackles the whole time, or you can go back to your cell."

Farber said, "We're his legal team. Give us a break, pal."

"Nope." The guard shut the door, but then his face appeared in the observation glass. They weren't letting Moretti out of their sight. Smart.

Gabby's father was a tall, fit man, in his early sixties, with a white mane of hair. Gabby had his eyes. But not the hardness Moretti's carried.

Moretti laid his cuffed hands on the table. "What do you want to say to me, cop?"

Jake cleared the trepidation from his throat and leaned forward. Might as well cut to the chase. "Benji plans to disappear."

Moretti's eyes shifted to Farber. "Go take a phone call in the hallway."

"What?" Farber's forehead crumpled. "We don't know what this guy—"

"Do it." After the door closed behind the lawyer, Moretti shifted his focus back to Jake. "If it weren't for Benji, you'd be dead. I still haven't made up my mind what to do with you, long term. Don't piss me off by lying to me."

Jake held up his palms. "She told me she needs to disappear. For good. She wants a life. I can give her one."

"She's not going anywhere. Especially with you." Moretti's eyes narrowed. "You told her what she wanted to hear. Used her to get to me. Now leave her alone, Morris. Or I will kill you. Am I clear?"

Being told he'd be killed should have scared the crap out of him. Instead, it made him more determined. "She's smarter than you give her credit for. She slipped past your goons once. She'll do it again. Especially if you stay locked up. Next time, she might not be so lucky to meet someone like me. She's an innocent. Easy to take advantage of."

"Yeah. You got what you wanted out of her." Moretti looked away for the first time. "It makes me want to kill you with my bare hands."

He truly cared for his daughter. It was a weakness Jake would keep poking at. "You're right. I helped catch a wanted criminal. Doing my job. But I didn't count on falling in love with her in the process. She's the most incredible person I've ever met. She deserves the life you stole from her." He laid on the parental guilt.

Moretti's eyes snapped back to meet Jake's, glaring with hate. "Garza took that life away. Now his father knows what it's like to lose a child."

"You're going to lose another soon if you don't listen." Jake stood and pushed his chair in. "Go ahead and kill me if that's what you want. If I can't be with her, what do I care?" Jake took a gamble and started walking for the door. It was an interrogation technique that rarely failed, but Gabby's father wasn't a petty criminal.

Jake's fingers had wrapped around the handle when Moretti barked, "Sit down. I'm not done with you, cop!"

*Thank God.*

Jake slowly turned and walked back to his chair but didn't sit. He stood with his arms crossed, waiting for Moretti to speak.

After a full-blown staring match, Moretti finally looked down at his clenched fists. "You don't love her. You've known her less than two weeks."

Jake smiled. Now they were getting somewhere. "I hear it was love at first sight when you met your wife. A guy knows when a guy knows, right?"

"That was different. Don't make me kill you and break her heart all over again. Go back to New Mexico. Stay out of her life."

"What life? You mean the one where she's a prisoner in her own home? Can't go shopping by herself? Can't have friends? Much less find a husband who'd dare to marry her once he found out about you. She'll never have what she wants, what she deserves, if you don't let her. Doesn't her happiness count for anything?"

"Of course it counts!" Moretti slammed his hands on the table. "But her safety has to come first."

Jake glanced at the observation window. Now the guard had been joined by Farber. Jake pulled out the chair next to Gabby's father and sat. "I can give her both. Away from here. Where no one knows her. In New Mexico."

Moretti shook his head. "If Garza realizes who she is, you won't be able to keep her safe. As it is, she's going to have to quit her job. Change her name. Move again. It's all being worked out."

"She can move with me. Take my last name, if she wants. Garza would never believe you'd let her marry a cop. It'd be good cover."

"It's not enough!" Moretti tried to stand, but he was shackled to the table. He defiantly dropped back into his chair. "I can't risk her life."

"I get that. But if you'd asked, instead of assuming you know what's best for her, you'd know she's unhappy. She's got to be scared witless to do it, but she's still going to disappear. Then what kind of risk will she be taking? Isn't it better to know she'll be with someone who'll do everything in his power to keep her safe? Because he loves her. Wants to make her happy. And who wants a family as much as she does?"

Moretti growled as he dropped his head into his hands.

Time to pull out his biggest weapon. "I made a phone call last night. Annalisa Botelli offered to let me build a house for us on her estate. She has better security than the president. And she offered me the job of being in charge of her protection. All I need is your blessing to ask Gabby to marry me."

That got Moretti's attention. He sat up and leaned closer. "She'd have the same protection as Annalisa?"

"Yeah. More if necessary."

Moretti closed his eyes. "Suzy tells me Gabby is madder than hell at what you did. What makes you think she wants anything to do with you?"

Moretti was finally showing signs of cracking. "She asked you not to kill me. That has to count for something. And you and I both know what really happened in that park. If you'll help me talk to her, I think she'll be able to forgive me in time. I'm told I can be very charming, when I put my mind to it."

He slowly opened his eyes. "Charm doesn't work on me." He clenched his jaw. "If you pass muster with Suzy, I might consider your request. I'll tell her to expect you for dinner. *Now* you can leave."

He'd take the deal.

He wanted to ask how Moretti was going to communicate with Suzy but resisted. Better to quit while he was ahead. He stood to leave but stopped and held his hand out. "Thank you. You won't regret it."

"You hurt her, and you won't live long enough to regret it. And I'm not shaking a cop's hand. Get out!"

Jake hightailed it out the door before Moretti changed his mind. Farber stood in the hall next to the guard, red in the face. "What the hell did you do to him in there? He's clearly agitated. Now I've got to go calm him down. Get your own ride back."

"I'd prefer that. See you around, Farber." Jake slipped Ashton's ID into Farber's suit pocket and then smiled all the way to the guard's desk. He returned his visitor badge and said, "Have a nice day."

The guard grunted in return.

Jake pulled his phone out and dialed Dani's number. When she answered, he said, "So where does Aunt Suzy live? I'm invited for dinner."

"You did it?" Her squeal nearly busted his eardrum. "I knew you'd pull it off. Nice work."

He walked down the front steps. "It's not a done deal. I have to get past Aunt Suzy."

"And then convince Gabby to take you back."

"Yeah." He worried it'd be too little too late. And that he'd messed up the best thing that had ever happened to him. "Not sure how to do the convincing part."

"By using your words to express how you feel. Gabby needs to hear how much you love her. And why she should forgive you."

He stopped in his tracks and cringed. "You know I hate talking about that stuff."

"Time to grow a pair, pal. Let me find the address. I wrote it down by my bed."

Jake started walking again toward Moretti's men parked at the curb. The passenger window slowly whirled down, so Jake plastered on a smile and leaned his head inside. "Hey there. Moretti said to give me a lift back to the lawyer's office so I can get my car."

The one guy looked at the other, who shrugged. "Fine. Get in, Morris."

"Thanks." Jake settled in the back of the mobsters' car. Just one more thing he'd never dreamed he do only a few weeks ago.

Dani came back on the line and recited the address in Virginia. Then she added, "Just don't use any of the words you used on me while we were married, and you'll be fine."

"What's that supposed to mean?" He repeated the address twice in his mind to memorize it.

"It means find new words that actually mean something. She won't settle for your go-to line of 'I'm sorry, babe. Won't happen again.'"

He had other lines. A lot of other lines.

But they probably weren't the answer. Time to give up lines and go with the scary, sincere thoughts. "Fine. I'll think of new words. Thanks for the address."

"Yep. Good luck." She disconnected.

He was going to need all the luck he could get. After he got past the daunting roadblock of her father and aunt, maybe it'd prove to Gabby that he'd do anything to have her back. Hopefully, she'd hear the truth in his words when he told her he loved her and how badly he needed her in his life.

# Chapter Twenty-One

Jake rolled down his car window and pressed the call button on the gated entrance to Suzy and Gabby's estate. A male voice answered. "Yeah?"

"Jake Morris. Here to see Suzy." Gabby had told him Suzy had changed her name, too, so he wasn't sure what her last name was.

The gates slowly parted. "It's the one on the left."

"Thanks." Jake put his car into gear and started up the paved drive. There were large trees on both sides of the road and perfectly landscaped hedges. Foliage so thick the homes weren't visible from the main road. At the top of the hill, he encountered a fork in the driveway, so he went left, but he'd have rather gone right to see Gabby. It was just after six, so she might be home from work. But Moretti said he had to get past Suzy first, so that's what he'd do.

Both houses were large two-story brick with white columns in front like much of the architecture in the area. So different from the Pueblo-style stucco home he owned. Sometimes he forgot how wealthy Moretti was. Would it be a huge step down for Gabby to be with him? He'd never considered that aspect. One more potential roadblock to negotiate.

He pulled up under the portico by the front door and then scooped up the plants he'd brought. He'd had a haircut earlier, too. He'd almost bought fancy chocolates for Suzy, but that'd probably cross the line and make him a suck-up.

As he stood before the big front door, he adjusted the tie he hated wearing and then poked the doorbell.

The door swung open, and Sal appeared. "Come in."

"Thanks. Is Gabby home yet?" he asked as he followed Sal into the two-story foyer. The garlic, sausage, and spices filling the air made his mouth water.

"Gabby's still off-limits. Lift your hands." Sal patted him down.

Sal's hand slid up Jake's pant leg, right up into the sensitive goods, and made Jake grunt. Sal smirked as he did the same on the other side. When he was satisfied Jake was unarmed and would feel the lingering effects of the search for some time, Sal turned and walked toward the rear of the home. Jake followed behind.

Sal pushed a swinging door open that led to a ginormous kitchen. "Hey, Suzy? The scumbag is here."

*Nice.*

An older woman wearing a stained white apron over her green dress turned from the commercial stainless-steel stove. She was short and round, and suspicion clouded her brown eyes. "Come in, scumbag who broke my baby's heart."

*Great. Could be a long night.*

He crossed the kitchen and held out the violets he'd bought for her. Gabby had mentioned two things about her aunt. Her thick Italian accent and love of flowers. "Thanks for having me over for dinner."

She wiped her hands on her apron. "You don't know if I poison you tonight or feed you the best lasagna you ever had. Why you bring this instead of cut flowers like normal person?"

Poison? No. She had to be joking. "I brought you a plant because it'll last longer. Remind you every day of the really nice guy you poisoned tonight. One who loves Gabby, by the way."

Aunt Suzy laughed as she took the plant from his hands. "Still optional on the poisoning. Luca said it up to me."

"Then I better be on my best behavior." Thankfully, the stains on her apron were tomato sauce and not fresh blood, or he'd really worry.

Suzy crossed the kitchen and placed the pot beside the forest of other plants near a window. "Lucky for you, I like violets. Tricky to keep alive, though. Like you maybe?" She smiled as she fussed with the leaves. "This is very pretty one, Jake. What the other weird plant for?"

She'd used his name. Maybe he'd scored a point with the plant. The chocolate might have been a good idea after all. "It's a cactus. It'll bloom later. We have them everywhere in New Mexico. I thought Gabby might like it. Will I see her tonight?"

Suzy took the cactus from his hand and laid it by the violet. "Don't know if she want to see *you*. Come help me finish the dinner."

He hated to hear that. But he wasn't giving up.

He followed behind her to the large island filled with veggies, hoping that cooking wasn't part of the test. He'd fail for sure. "Does Gabby know how to cook like this, too?"

Suzy picked up a huge knife. It took everything in him to tamp back the urge to disarm her. "Gabby come here to eat my cooking most nights. But I make her learn. Just in case she find a man."

"She found him. What would you like me to do?" He quickly scanned all the food, searching for rat poison or something, just in case.

"You pour us some wine. Glasses there." She pointed to a glass-front cabinet. "Wine over there. Breathing."

He headed for the cabinet. "I hope *I'm* breathing by the time the night's over."

Suzy laughed. She had the kind of big laugh that made him smile, too. "I'd really like a chance to talk to Gabby. I have some things I need to tell her." *Mostly apologize for.*

Suzy sliced a cucumber with the skills of a professional chef. "You tell her why you arrest her papa? Don't bother. She know why. But what she don't know is how you could do such a thing. Knowing it hurt her so bad."

He'd never meant to hurt her.

He poured out two big glasses of red wine. "Yeah. I have some explaining to do there."

"Yes, you do. You want *bambini* one day?"

He handed Suzy her glass. "Yes. I didn't grow up in a nice family. I'd like the chance to have one of those."

Aunt Suzy clinked her glass against his. *"Saluti."* Then she took a deep drink. "Gabby tell me about you family. She say you were a good big brother. Take care of him. I like that."

Jake took a drink, then laid his glass down. "I was too strict. Worried he'd be bad like my parents. I wish I'd had a little more faith in him sometimes."

Suzy picked up her knife and started chopping again. "We do the best we do. Better to be sure he turn out good. Like Gabby, no?"

"Yes. When I found out who her father was, I couldn't believe she could be so . . . happy. Trusting and kind. I'd like to be more like her in that way."

"Gabby's mama? She make Luca more kind, too. Gabby is much like her mother. Make someone a good mama, too, one day." Suzy threw everything in a bowl and then tossed the salad. "Come, we eat." She pushed the salad bowl into his arms and then turned to the oven. She drew out bread and then cut into a cooling pan of lasagna.

Normally, that delicious smell would make his mouth water. Tonight, it gave him a moment's pause. He plastered on a smile. "Smells wonderful, Suzy. Much too good to be filled with poison."

Chuckling, she led the way, with two full plates, to the nook, not the fancy dining room he'd seen on the way to the kitchen. Probably all part of the joke, like she'd never poison him in the fancy dining room. Too much mess to clean up. Certain poisonings got pretty gross right at the end.

He laid the salad bowl on the table and then pulled her chair out for her.

She said, "Thank you." Then dished out the salad into two bowls. She'd taken hers from the same big bowl, so that was safe to eat.

He unfolded his cloth napkin and laid it across his lap. "This looks fantastic. But we forgot our wine. Let me get them." He jumped up and grabbed their glasses from the center island. "Here you go."

Suzy took the glass and set it down. Then she waited for him to be seated. "It's custom for guest to take first bite of lasagna. Are you willing to take risk?"

Surely, she was kidding. But she'd been married to a gangster at one time. She'd probably know how to poison someone.

No, she was just messing with him. "Gabby's father said I had to get past you to have her. I'd hoped that meant you'd have to give me your blessing, instead of simply surviving the meal."

Suzy tilted her head. "You don't have to eat. You can go. But I don't like no one who don't eat my food when I work all day to make it."

"Okay." He picked up his fork, prepared to dive in, hoping he'd get to see Gabby after dinner. But just in case he wouldn't be allowed, he said, "Tell Gabby I loved her enough to die. If I do. Please." He took a bite.

Suzy drank her wine and watched with a knowing smile on her face.

"This is amazing. Best I've ever had, Suzy. Really." He took another bite of the rich red sauce, spicy sausage, and tender noodles.

Suzy took another drink of her wine. "I like that you like. Nice to see appreciation for good food."

As he went in for another bite, a bundle of black-and-white fur streaked into the kitchen and skidded to a stop by his leg. He laid down his fork. "Hi there. Who's this?"

Gabby answered from behind him. "That's Einstein. Why are you here?"

Hearing her voice, although filled with anger, made his heart leap. He stood and laid his napkin on the table. She was wearing cute sweats and sneakers. He wished he could just scoop her up and take her home. "I wanted to talk to you. And meet your aunt. Poison usually takes about ten to fifteen minutes, so I need to tell you something, Gabby. Fast."

❧

What was her aunt up to now?

Gabby glanced at Suzy, who was trying not to laugh. "You did it again?"

Jake swallowed hard. "She's done this before?"

"She thinks it's a riot to scare people. You're not going to die."

"I was just pulling your pants, Jake." Aunt Suzy chuckled.

"You mean pulling his leg, *Zietta*," Gabby corrected.

"Good to know." Jake grinned in relief. "Because, honestly, this is the best lasagna I've ever tasted."

Jake's smile was making her knees go weak, so she went to the stove to make herself a plate.

Aunt Suzy said, "He eat it with no hesitation. He say you worth it, Gabby." She dug into the heaping plate of food before her, still smiling at her cleverness.

Gabby snuck another peek at Jake. He wore a different suit from the one in London, one that fit his sexy body perfectly. Along with his freshly cut hair, it made him too handsome to look at. Great decision on her part to dress in the rattiest sweats she owned. Not that she was trying to impress him or anything.

She poured herself a big glass of wine and brought the bottle to the table. She'd probably need it.

Einstein, the little traitor, stared up at Jake, drooling in adoration. Jake shoved food into his mouth with one hand and pet her dog's head with the other. Some judge of character her pooch was.

She thought about taking her plate to go, but that Jake was in her aunt's kitchen after their bodyguards had strict orders to keep him away meant something was up. She slipped into a chair across from him. "I thought I'd made it clear you aren't welcome here, Jake."

He nodded. "I know. But I had to talk to your dad today."

Her fork stopped halfway to her mouth. "You talked to my father?" She turned to her aunt. "Did dad really tell you to put poison in his food?"

"No." Aunt Suzy grabbed the tongs and piled a bunch of salad on Gabby's plate. "Luca tell me it make you unhappy if Jake killed. They talk about another way."

"Another way to punish, Jake?" Gabby poked at the salad. Even though Jake being there made her stomach all tight, she ate anyway.

"She meant another way for you to be happy." Jake slipped a piece of bread to Einstein. "I have a plan I'd like to discuss with you. But I needed to convince your dad it was a good idea first."

Her father had talked to Jake. Her dad had to hate Jake for what he did as much as she did. Well, "hate" was too strong a word. For her. Not for her father, though. "Why do you assume I want anything to do with your happiness plans?"

Aunt Suzy threw up her hands. "Who not want to be happy? Hear what the man has to say."

"Fine." Gabby tried to eat but gave up and pushed her plate away. She crossed her arms. "But not until you explain how you can claim to love me and do what you did. We had a deal you wouldn't tell the cops my father was there, Jake. People don't betray the ones they love."

"Your father might be dead if I hadn't, Gabby. The sharpshooters were closing in on him. What they saw was an armed man who'd just put a bullet through Pablo Garza's head. They had orders to stop the shooter by any means. You weren't included in all the communications. I was."

She tried to think back. It had all happened so fast. Jake checked on her, then ran off yelling something. What had he yelled? "What happened next?"

Jake finished his meal and then wiped his mouth with his napkin. "They'd called out for him to stop, but he didn't. So I ran after your dad. Called him by name to get his attention amid all the shouting and confusion. Told him he was surrounded and to lay his weapon down. By that time, the sharpshooters had moved in. Your father saw there was no way out, and he dropped his gun."

Aunt Suzy said, "He could've killed you, too. Stupid to run after him, Jake."

"Probably." He shrugged. "But I didn't want him to be killed. I know I made you a promise, Gabby. But I saw the threat and reacted. It seemed like the best way to save your father in the moment. If things had been different, and I'd had time to think, I would've never broken my promise to you. I hope you can forgive me for it one day."

She laid her elbows on the table and dropped her head into her hands. Would her father have gotten away if Jake hadn't been involved? Or would there have been a bloody gun battle that might have included Sal and Louie, too? She'd never know for sure. "What are you going to say when they ask you in court about what you saw?"

Jake slid his chair around, closer to her, and Einstein moved right with him. The dog wasn't leaving Jake's side after getting table scraps.

"I thought about what you said, Gabby. A lot. How both your father and I were responsible for Pablo Garza's death. I put myself in your father's shoes. And I would've done the same thing he did. You were right. The revenge part isn't for me to judge."

She lifted her head. "So you'll testify he was just protecting the innocent archaeologist, as his lawyers said?"

He smiled and took her hand. "Yes. I'll tell the jury that Luca couldn't have known from that distance if my knife had stopped Garza completely. And that Luca Moretti probably saved your life."

Tears burned her eyes. If Jake said that, it'd weigh heavy in her father's favor at a trial. Had her aunt been right? That sometimes people make promises they intend to keep but can't. Like Suzy had done while trying to protect her husband? She'd been protecting someone she loved, too. Maybe Jake had just gotten caught in the middle of a bad situation, with no right answer, as her aunt had. "I appreciate that, Jake. But you are always going to be a cop, and my dad is always going to be who he is. You and I will never work. Please just go home." It hurt to look at him. She'd missed him so much. Her heart couldn't take another minute. She stood to leave, but his grip tightened on her hand.

"Wait, Gabby. I have a plan." He glanced at Suzy. "Assuming your aunt gives her permission?"

"I'm a sucker for happy ending. You give her one, Jake." Aunt Suzy stood and grabbed the dirty dishes. "Tell her your plan. I find something else to do." She laid the dishes in the sink and then walked out of the kitchen.

Gabby yanked her hand away. "I have my own plan, Jake. One I've thought about a lot. One where I can finally have my own life back. You can't just waltz in here and lay out the rest of my life for me. I already have a father for that." She went to the sink and started rinsing the dishes. Einstein looked back and forth between them, then chose to be with her. Probably because that's where the food was, but still. He needed to get his loyalties straight.

Jake stood and joined her. "*There's* the fiery redhead I fell in love with." He moved behind her, put his hands on her hips, and whispered, "Maybe 'plan' was a bad word. Maybe 'hope' is better. Because I think I've found a way to keep you safe. But I hope you'll allow me to be a part of your future plans no matter what they are. I've missed you, Gabby. Didn't you miss me?"

"Nope," she lied. It was too painful to hear the hopefulness in his voice. There wasn't a good solution where they could ever be together. Jake would never be able to accept her love for her father. He was too much of a cop for that.

Einstein barked and then jumped on Jake's leg. He'd clearly missed Jake's affection.

Jake said, "You didn't miss me at all? Not even a little?"

When Jake nibbled on her neck, she nearly dropped the plate in her hand. "You're too damned bossy to miss."

"I bet you missed this." He moved his mouth to her earlobe and traced it with his tongue. That always drove her nuts.

"A little. Maybe. Can you move, please? You're in my way." She laid the plate in the dishwasher and then slipped Einstein a piece of sausage.

"I've had this ache in my chest since London, Gabby. Right here." He took her hand and laid it over his heart. "Being with you is the only thing that makes it better."

His heart pounded under her palm. Like he was nervous.

It made her anger ebb slightly. "Probably just heartburn. Maybe from all the bootlicking, you've been doing today."

Jake's lips slowly tilted. "I'll do anything to win back your love, Gabby."

She wasn't falling for that smile that always made her stomach do somersaults. "If you wanted something from me, Jake, you needed to ask me first. I'm not going to be told what to do any longer." She was so tired of being treated like a child by her father. She didn't need Jake to treat her that way, too. Besides, she was still trying to figure out if she was mad at Jake for breaking his promise, even though he'd probably done the best thing for her father.

He laid his other hand over her palm, still over his heart. "I tried to ask you first. But you weren't talking to me, remember?"

"Because you'd hurt me, Jake. But I'm not a damsel in distress. You like to save people, but you should really save yourself first. You have more issues than a magazine." She tugged her hand free and started scrubbing dishes again.

He laughed. "I agree. It'll be tough to save someone as messed up as me." Jake plastered his chest to her back and laid his hands on the counter on either side of her. Caging her in. "I was hoping you'd help me, Gabby. You're the only one I'd ever let try."

Why wouldn't he stop saying all the right things to weaken her resolve against him? She needed to be independent. To actually live her life for a change. Not be with someone who'd be as overprotective as her father. Her plan to live in London would work. But she'd be all alone, and she hated that part.

His warm body at her back and his big arms wrapped around her felt nice. Too nice. She needed to stay strong. "My life circumstances would only make your issues worse, Jake."

"You haven't even heard my idea." He slid his hands down her arms, took the plate from her hand, and turned her around. "But first I'd like to kiss you. I missed that, too." He slowly moved his lips toward hers, giving her time to refuse him.

She should turn away. But she'd missed kissing him, too. So she let him lay his soft lips on hers. Didn't resist when his hand slid up her neck, and he tilted her head in that way that always made the kiss deeper, sweeter, more intimate. She closed her eyes and enjoyed all the warm, gooey sensations that swelled low in her belly.

She didn't want to encourage him, but her hands needed to wrap themselves around his big shoulders, and her body moved closer to touch his from head to toe. She'd missed the bossy man's kisses every moment of every day since London. And she'd missed his smart-alecky grin and the way he teased her. She missed pretty much everything about him.

He slowly leaned away, and her brain cells started working again. "You told me yourself. You're not husband or boyfriend material. Kissing me like that isn't going to solve the problem, Jake."

"No, that was just a side benefit." He hugged her tighter. "I've changed since I met you. You made me want to be good enough to be husband material for you, Gabby. And hopefully father material, too."

She stared into his eyes. He wasn't teasing for a change. "I'll repeat what I said earlier. You're a cop, Jake. I'm the daughter of a criminal. I've had to live with a big secret my whole life or be killed. Not the sort you'd like to be the mother of your children. End of story."

Einstein whimpered. As if unhappy with her decision.

He needed to stay out of it.

Jake slowly shook his head. "It's just the beginning of the story, because I'm not a cop anymore. I quit. And if you'd like, you and I can live in the house you'll have complete design control over on Annalisa's estate, while I do my new job as her head of security. We'll all be safe, you, me, and the kids. We have great museums in Albuquerque, one of which I'm sure would love to give a friend of Annalisa's a job."

But he loved being a cop. "You quit your job for me?"

"No." He leaned down and kissed her again. "I quit because I want to actually enjoy life—*with you*, Gabby."

Another good answer. Jake was just full of them all of a sudden.

She chewed her bottom lip as she considered. Did he really love her? Or was it because he didn't want to be alone?

He'd given her a reasonable explanation about her father, and he'd been brave enough to confront a man who clearly hated him. Jake must've said something right for her father to allow Jake in Suzy's kitchen.

She hadn't known Jake long, but her heart knew he was the one. And he'd eaten her aunt's possibly poisoned lasagna without hesitation. If that wasn't love, she didn't know what was. But what about his safety when they weren't at Annalisa's? She couldn't let him be hurt because of her. "What if during the trial Garza figures out who I am? You might be in danger, too."

"I understand Dean's lawyers are claiming mental incompetence. They're talking about copping a plea. There's a good chance you won't have to testify. But if Garza figures it out, then we'll disappear together. I'm sure your father could help us with that."

She leaned back and blinked at him. "What happened to the 'everything's black or white' cop I hit over the head?"

"A smart woman knocked some sense into him, showing him there are more than two colors in the world. And that maybe his way isn't always the only way."

Maybe he *had* really changed. Seen that there wasn't a rule to fit each and every situation. All her residual anger slowly slipped away. "So you're admitting you're bossy and stubborn?" She could probably live with his annoying traits if he'd admit to them.

"Sometimes. Maybe." Jake's face screwed up like he was in pain. "I need to work on that. But you're not being overly cooperative here yourself."

"More like cautious. I'd have *total* design control over the house? Whatever I want? Even a bathroom like the one in your house? You could live with not being in charge for once?"

"Yep." He shrugged. "Within budget. Annalisa doubled my salary, but I'm not wealthy like your father. I don't know what a museum job pays."

She gave him a squeeze. "I'm not worried about money. And I can maybe let you have a say in the garage."

He lifted her chin with his finger. "Just one more reason I love you. So generous."

"I am that. Did my father really give you permission to marry me?"

"No. He said if I can get past Suzy, he'd consider letting you move with me."

Aunt Suzy called out from the hallway, "Suzy say yes! Hurry up and ask. My show coming on in five minutes."

Gabby laughed. "You heard the lady."

"I need to know one more thing before I ask." Jake leaned his forehead against hers and whispered, "Do you think you could ever love me, Gabby? Issues and all?"

"Yes." The uncertainty in his eyes touched her all the way to her soul. "Even when I tried not to these past few days, I couldn't help but love you, Jake." Her heart would always belong to him. No matter what. "But me and my not-so-perfect family are a package deal."

"Understood." He released his hold on her and stepped back. Einstein took that as an invitation to jump into Jake's arms. He caught the dog and said, "Gabby, will you please come to New Mexico with me? Start a new life there. And if after a year or so you can still stand me, will you consider marrying a stubborn, bossy ex-cop like me?" He dug something out of his pocket.

It was a plastic decoder ring. James Bond Jake had remembered their dinner conversation.

He tried her ring finger, but the kid-size ring was too small, so he slipped it onto her pinky. "This is a placeholder until you find the real one you'd like."

Her heart nearly soared out of her chest. She'd almost given up on ever hearing words like that. Having a chance to have a family. Or a normal life with a great guy like Jake. He drove her nuts sometimes but mostly made her the happiest she'd ever been when she was with him.

She'd like her father's blessing but wasn't going to refuse the gift he'd given her to choose to live her life with Jake, rather than insisting she disappear again. She was tired of that life. Ready to start her new one.

Both Einstein and Jake had equally eager expressions on their faces. No way she could refuse that much cuteness. "Yes, on one condition."

Aunt Suzy yelled, "No time for condition. My show starting!"

Jake, still petting his new best friend, asked, "What's the condition?"

"That after this year or so, if you can still stand to be around such a generous, card-carrying Pollyanna like me, maybe you'll consider getting on a plane with me to Peru? I might need help selling a couple of statues. I have the real ones. The others were just fakes."

"What?" Jake's jaw flopped open. "You. No. You have the real statues? *You* stole them?"

"Still want to be with me?" She moved a step closer.

"Yes." He moved a step back. "But only after we find a way to return them. That's why you weren't worried about money?" His voice had raised three decibels.

"No." She gave him a quick kiss. "That's because I have a big fat trust fund from my mom. And I was just kidding about the statues."

His whole body slumped with relief. He lifted Einstein's face level with his. "You didn't think that was funny at all, did you?" He lowered the dog. "He said you just lost your Pollyanna card."

Aunt Suzy called out, "Pretty funny. Had me going for a minute."

"The look on your face, Jake. Priceless." She slipped her arms around his waist and snuggled as close as she could with a dog between them. "You once asked me how I could ever love a criminal. Remember? And yet you still loved me when you thought I was one for all of ten seconds."

He gave her rear end a sharp pat. "Life with you won't be boring, Gabby."

"Never." She smiled as she hugged her two favorite guys.

# A year or so later...

Gabby sat on the edge of her seat, waiting to hear the verdict in her father's trial for shooting Pablo Garza. The outstanding charges for her father's other alleged crime had been dropped. The plaintiff in that case had died the previous year, and the grand jury didn't have enough evidence anymore to bring the case to trial. She didn't want to know how the evidence against her father had disappeared. She chose to believe her father really had cleaned up his act and wasn't guilty. "Don't ask, don't tell" still applied.

Her dad's freedom had hung mostly on Jake's earlier testimony.

Jake took her hand and held it as the judge read the verdict the bailiff had just handed him. The judge's brows arched before he said, "The jury has found the defendant not guilty."

The breath Gabby had been holding whooshed from her lungs as Jake gave her hand a squeeze. The crowd watching buzzed with opinions, mostly in disbelief that Moretti had slipped through the hands of the law again.

Her father stood, shook his lawyer's hand, and then swept his gaze across the gallery. He locked gazes with her for a nanosecond, gave a slight nod, and then turned and gathered his things. People streamed out of the courtroom, mostly reporters hurrying to post the news. When her father walked by behind his lawyer, just a few feet away, he didn't look at her. He wouldn't risk it. But she'd missed him terribly the last year she'd been living in New Mexico.

Jake whispered, "Do you want to go say hi?"

She shook her head. "The press is all around. I can't. What reason would I have to talk to him?" She hadn't seen her father since London. He looked thinner, older, and tired. It still broke her heart that he wouldn't be able to come to her wedding next month. They couldn't give Garza any reasons to make the connection.

Jake tugged on her hand. "Come on. We'll use the press to get what you want, Gabby."

"What are you talking about?" She followed behind as Jake pulled her through the crowds. As usual, he had a plan he'd forgotten to share with her. But she'd gotten used to that and didn't mind nearly as much anymore. It was just Jake. And she wouldn't change a thing about him.

When they hit the courthouse steps, reporters surrounded them, but Jake didn't stop until they were right behind her dad. A reporter asked, "Mr. Morris, how do you feel about the verdict? Was justice served today?"

All eyes, including her father's, were on Jake. "Absolutely. And as many of you know, Ms. Knight and I met during this case and are engaged now. I'd be honored to shake the hand of the man who saved my fiancée's life." Jake held out his hand toward her dad.

Crap! What was Jake doing? Her father would never shake the hand of the man responsible for his arrest.

The lawyer discreetly nudged her father, who narrowed his eyes at Jake but stuck his hand out to return the shake.

Jake closed the gap between them and clasped her dad's hand. Jake smiled and said loudly, "We'd be honored if you'd attend our wedding next month. It would never have happened without you."

The crowd went wild for that. The whirl of cameras was overwhelming. She was careful to keep her face turned away, watching the men shake.

Happy tears stung her eyes. Jake had found the perfect way to justify her father coming to the wedding. She met her father's gaze and smiled. "We'd be honored, Mr. Moretti."

Her dad said, "Thank you. I wouldn't miss it, Ms. Knight." Then he pumped Jake's hand while he slapped him on the shoulder. Hard. "There's nothing better than young love, am I right?"

Jake's left eye winced slightly as if he were in pain, but he quickly recovered. "Nope. Looking forward to seeing you there."

When the reporters moved on to other questions for her father's lawyer, Jake leaned in and whispered, so only the three of them could hear, "Knew you'd shake my hand one day."

Her dad said, "I won't again until I see a grandchild, cop." Then he moved away and down the steps to an awaiting car. Sal opened the door for her dad, then turned and smiled at her. A big genuine smile. She lifted her chin slightly.

He nodded in return. A whole unspoken conversation that he was happy for her. As the car drove off, memories of all the years with her guards filled her mind. She'd been a prisoner in the nicest cell on record.

The jury had just decided that her father had saved her life, but it had really been Jake who'd done that. Not only in London but also on that first day in the cabin. When he cared enough to help someone who'd just bashed his head in.

She smiled and found Jake's hand to tow him down the steps to their rental car. She wanted to go home. Where she belonged now. With Jake.

When they arrived at the car, Jake opened her door for her. "You heard your dad. If I want him to shake my hand at the wedding, you'd better be pregnant. You wanna work on that on the plane ride home?"

Jake still hated to fly, but Annalisa was generous enough to let them use her plane to make it easier for him. "But then what do we tell our kid when she's born eight months after the wedding?"

Jake rounded the car and then slipped beside her. "That we didn't want to wait nine whole months to meet *him*."

Gabby slipped on her sunglasses. "Or, I guess we could say *she* was early."

The corner of Jake's mouth tilted. "Did I mention Dani had another dream?"

"We're having a boy?" Gabby whipped her head in his direction.

Jake winced slightly. "Two actually. At the same time."

*Twins? Wow.*

*Wow.*

*Twins.*

She could barely wrap her head around that.

Just to poke at him a bit for knowing that and not telling her sooner, she said, "We should name one after my dad. He's the one who started all of this."

"Never happening. Not ever." Jake slipped their car onto the freeway to head for the private airport.

"Okay, bossy pants, Sal and Louie it is, then."

He opened his mouth to protest but snapped it shut. He'd been working on his pushiness. "How about we open that discussion again when the time gets closer?"

"How very diplomatic of you, Jake." She picked up his hand that lay on the console and entwined her fingers with his. "I think I'll keep you."

He glanced her way with a raised brow. "You don't have a choice. Cut me loose and I might have to press charges for your earlier crimes."

"Really?" She smiled. "And how long is the statute of limitations?"

"For stealing a man's heart?" He pretended to ponder for a moment. "Ninety-nine years, with no time off for good behavior. You're basically stuck with me forever."

"Ah. But what's to keep you from kicking *me* to the curb?"

He lifted their entwined fingers and kissed the back of her hand. "Love, of course."

"Yes. Always that." Ninety-nine more years with Jake didn't seem long enough. But it was a sentence she could live with.

# Acknowledgments

As always, I'd like to thank everyone at my wonderful publisher, Montlake Romance. Each and every person on the team, from those who acquire, edit, and market to those who give superb author gifts. You all make it such a joy to work with you. And of course, thanks to my critique partners, Sherri, Louise, and Robin, for reading my pages each and every week. A special shout-out for this book goes to Louise, who knows just about everything when it comes to history. And she'll be the first to tell you she's always right! :0)

I also want to thank my agent, Jill Marsal, and my family, who is always there to support me. But, mostly, I want to thank my loyal readers, for you are what makes writing books fun!

# About the Author

Tamra Baumann became hooked on writing the day she picked up her first Nora Roberts novel from her favorite bookstore. Since then, she's dazzled readers with her own lighthearted love stories: *Dealing Double* is the second installment in her Heartbreaker series, which started with the novel *Seeing Double*. She's a Golden Heart winner for Contemporary Series Romance and has also received the Golden Pen Award for Single Title Romance. Born in Monterey, California, Tamra led the nomadic life of a navy brat before putting down permanent roots during college. When she's not attending annual Romance Writers of America meetings, this voracious reader can be found playing tennis, traveling, or scouting reality shows for potential character material. Tamra resides with her real-life characters—her husband, two kids, and their allergy-ridden dog—in the sunny Southwest. Visit her online at www.tamrabaumann.com and on Facebook at www.facebook.com/author.tamra.baumann.